MAGGI CHARLES
Love's Golden Shadow

Silhouette Special Edition
Published by Silhouette Books New York
America's Publisher of Contemporary Romance

Other Silhouette Books by Maggi Charles

Magic Crescendo

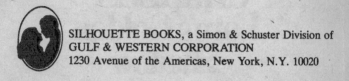

SILHOUETTE BOOKS, a Simon & Schuster Division of
GULF & WESTERN CORPORATION
1230 Avenue of the Americas, New York, N.Y. 10020

Copyright © 1982 by Maggi Charles

Distributed by Pocket Books

All rights reserved, including the right to reproduce
this book or portions thereof in any form whatsoever.
For information address Silhouette Books, 1230
Avenue of the Americas, New York, N.Y. 10020

ISBN: 0-671-53523-4

First Silhouette Books printing May, 1982

10 9 8 7 6 5 4 3 2 1

All of the characters in this book are fictitious. Any resemblance to actual persons, living or dead, is purely coincidental.

SILHOUETTE, SILHOUETTE SPECIAL EDITION
and colophon are trademarks of Simon & Schuster.

America's Publisher of Contemporary Romance

Printed in the U.S.A.

Would She Always Hurt Him Without Meaning To?

"Of course I can *see* you!" he said contemptuously.

Tracy felt her throat thicken. "I'm sorry," she said abjectly.

"Are you always sorry about something?"

"No. I . . . I had a feeling for just a moment, as you were standing in the doorway, that you might be . . . blind."

"I am *not* blind. I can see you and I know that you're blonde and beautiful and have big, hungry eyes. Is that what you want—to be looked at, to be admired? Or do you want more than that?"

Before she could answer, she felt his strong arms move about her, relentless and demanding.

MAGGI CHARLES
is a versatile and prolific author who has written mystery novels and romances, as well as numerous short stories and magazine articles. The mother of two sons, her hobbies are music and language. Ms. Charles lives with her husband, a newspaperman and writer too, in Massachusetts.

Dear Reader:

During the last year, many of you have written to Silhouette telling us what you like best about Silhouette Romances and, more recently, about Silhouette Special Editions. You've also told us what else you'd like to read from Silhouette. With your comments and suggestions in mind, we've developed SILHOUETTE DESIRE.

SILHOUETTE DESIREs will be on sale this June, and each month we'll bring you four new DESIREs written by some of your favorite authors—Stephanie James, Diana Palmer, Rita Clay, Suzanne Simms and many more.

SILHOUETTE DESIREs may not be for everyone, but they are for those readers who want a more sensual, provocative romance. The heroines are slightly older—women who are actively involved in their careers and the world around them. If you want to experience all the excitement, passion and joy of falling in love, then SILHOUETTE DESIRE is for you.

I'd appreciate any thoughts you'd like to share with us on new SILHOUETTE DESIRE, and I invite you to write to us at the address below:

        Karen Solem
        Editor-in-Chief
        Silhouette Books
        P.O. Box 769
        New York, N.Y. 10019

For Jayne—from Maggi,
with love.

Chapter One

*P*eace. As Tracy Graham stood at the ferry rail looking out at the seemingly endless indigo waters of Nantucket Sound, she smiled wryly at the thought that peace of mind, especially, had become so desirable to her.

She doubted that many twenty-six-year-old single women coveted tranquillity as much as she did. But Tracy, over the past few months, had experienced enough emotional pain and mental anguish to last a lifetime, and the effect upon her had been a telling one. During the course of this mini ocean voyage from Woods Hole to Nantucket Island, thirty miles off the Massachusetts coast, she already had come to appreciate the soothing wonder of "getting away from it all."

There was an appealing wistfulness about her as she stood at the boat rail, the salt breeze ruffling her light golden hair which, as usual, had been swept back severely and arranged in a chignon at the nape of her neck. She had lost weight over the summer and now, in September, was a shade too thin, but there was an undeniable grace to her slender figure, and the deep blue pants suit she had chosen for today's trip nearly matched her large, expressive eyes. The past summer had been one in which she had gotten outdoors very little, perferring to immerse herself in work in Florence

Anders' antique shop on Charles Street in Boston, at the foot of Beacon Hill. Now, she was much too pale, the pallor augmented by dark shadows under her lovely eyes made her seem fragile, like an exquisite, porcelain figurine. Delicate figurines, however, shattered easily. Tracy, over those traumatic weeks of summer, had proven that she was made of tougher stuff.

She pressed closer to the boat railing as she spied, on the distant horizon, a thin line of deep lavender haze which, after a moment, she recognized as Nantucket: the wonderful haven—for the next month—that she was looking forward to so much.

Gradually, the haze began to take a more distinct form, and it seemed to Tracy that the island literally was rising from the sea. Entranced, she watched form yield to color, and saw, to her right, a low stretch of beach where people were still sunning on the deep beige sand. They were splashing in the gentle waves, which surprised her, as she had expected the water to be too cold for swimming.

As the boat cleared the stone breakwater guarding the entrance to the harbor, Tracy saw a squat white lighthouse perched on an outcropping of rocks. The ferry blew its long, piercing whistle, sounding like a welcome rather than a warning. Ahead, the cluster of buildings that formed Nantucket Town was a study in shades of gray, the scene dominated by a tall white church steeple, its gilded dome dazzling in the afternoon sunlight.

At Tracy's elbow, a pleasant, low masculine voice said, "It's no wonder they call her the Little Gray Lady, is it?"

Startled, Tracy looked up to see a tall, attractive young man with sandy brown hair, greenish eyes, and a deep, golden tan. He smiled as, perplexed, she asked, "What?"

"Nantucket," he said, nodding toward shore. "They call her the Little Gray Lady and she does look rather prim at first sight, wouldn't you say? At least, that's the way she always appears to me."

"Perhaps," Tracy conceded. "I haven't been to the island in years, and I don't really remember my own first reaction. There *is* a certain sedateness about this initial view, though. I was just thinking that it's a study in grays. The nickname is appropriate."

"Glad you agree," he said easily, and held out his hand. "I'm Gerry Stanhope," he told her.

"Tracy Graham," Tracy responded because there was nothing else she gracefully could do at the moment. His handclasp was firm, and, looking at him more carefully, she noted that his fawn-colored slacks and brown sports shirt were well tailored, obviously expensive. There was an air of assurance to his manner, a casualness that bespoke confidence. Almost inadvertently, because she really didn't want to get to know anyone during the course of this vacation—the whole idea was to have the chance to be alone—she asked, "Do you live on Nantucket?"

"No," he said, "but my aunt does." He didn't elaborate, but gestured instead toward the approaching wharf and added, "If you haven't been here since you were a child, you won't have seen the job they've done renovating the waterfront. Or, maybe I should say, restoring it to the charm of an earlier era. Gas lights, cobblestoned streets—it's delightful."

"I vaguely remember being taken to a play on the waterfront one night," Tracy told him.

"That would be the Straight Wharf Theater," he nodded.

Tracy was looking ahead, watching the men at dockside readying the ropes that would secure the ferry once she was inside her berth. She was very much aware of the fact that Gerry Stanhope was eyeing her closely, and this made her uncomfortable. Questions, she told herself, were almost sure to follow.

"Did you opt for a fall vacation, or do you have relatives here?" he asked.

"A friend of my mother's has a place on the island," she hedged in answer.

"A summer cottage, or a house?"

"A cottage. That's where I stayed with my mother on earlier visits. I don't remember it clearly, though. I was only six or so when I was here. But it seems to me that it was very quaint and pretty and there were a lot of roses growing all around it."

"That's typical, on Nantucket. Will you be here long?"

"About a month," she said, and because she wanted to get away from the subject of a possible meeting while she was on the island she added, "I work for an antique shop in Boston. I have to be back around the first of October."

"Antiques, eh? You'll have to see my aunt's house, then. She lives in one of the old bricks that used to belong to a whaling captain, and she has a real treasure trove of old things."

"Brought back from the seven seas, I suppose?"

"Some of them were," he agreed, and Tracy decided she had better forestall him before he could say anything else.

"Excuse me," she murmured quickly. "I'd like to freshen up before we dock." Without waiting for his answer she slipped away, edging through the crowd of passengers now gathered at the boat rail, then making her way to the rest room. As if to give validity to her excuse, she smoothed her hair and touched her lips with deep pink color. Then she lingered until she could feel the boat thump against the wharf pilings, hoping that when she emerged Gerry Stanhope would have gone on ahead.

She had told him the truth, but not the whole truth. A friend of her mother's did, indeed, have a cottage on the island, and this was where she was going. But her mother had been dead for nearly eight years, now, and the friend, Mrs. Samuel Thorndyke, whom Tracy had always called Aunt Sally, was in Europe at the moment. Tracy had seen her off at Logan Airport in Boston a week earlier. By then, Aunt Sally had persuaded her to take a vacation and to spend it at her cottage on Nantucket. There she could be alone and get the rest she so obviously needed.

Florence Anders, her employer, had been in complete agreement, but then Florence also had been a friend of her mother's. In fact Florence, her mother, and Aunt Sally had gone to school together.

"You've done more than your share over the summer," Florence had pointed out, which was true enough. Tracy had been working in the antique shop for only two months when Florence had taken ill, the illness requiring surgery. Thus, she had found herself in the position of having the main responsibility for the store, and she had acquitted herself well. Fortunately, she had a basically good knowledge of antiques, garnered primarily from her mother, and she always had loved beautiful old things. Also, several years as a legal secretary had given her a grounding in business matters and overall efficiency, and the combination had proven to be quite invaluable.

"If it hadn't been for you, my convalescence would have taken twice as long, Tracy," Florence had continued, "because I couldn't possibly have relaxed as thoroughly as I did with someone else minding the store."

This conversation had taken place several days before Labor Day as they were having supper in the tiny patio area wedged in back of the Charles Street shop, which occupied the first floor corner of a historic old brick house. Florence's apartment was on the second floor. An outer stairway led from it directly into the patio, which was decorated with bright flowers in big bucket tubs and white wrought-iron furniture.

Florence had been back in the store only two days, then, and had been delighted not only at the condition in which she found everything but at the volume of business Tracy had managed to do in her absence.

Now she said, her smile emphasizing the laugh lines in her pleasant, unashamedly middle-aged face, "I might feel I'm not even needed here, except that I've been taking some very good looks at you, my dear, and I'm delighted Sally Thorndyke wants you to use her place on Nantucket. I've never seen anyone who looks like she needs a change of pace more than you do."

"That's not so," Tracy protested stubbornly. "Anyway, I couldn't possibly go away now and leave you. You're just out of the hospital . . ."

"You mean I'm just back from convalescing for a month in Ogunquit," Florence corrected her. "I've been lounging around for so long doing nothing that I'll be getting fat and lazy if I don't go back to work! Whereas you, Tracy, are going to be looking more wraith than human if you don't start putting on a little weight."

Tracy flushed uncomfortably and said, "My losing weight has nothing at all to do with running the shop for you, Florence."

"I realize that," Florence nodded sagely. "It has to do with your father and with Benjamin Devlin," she added, speaking the last name in a tone tinged with acid. Then she saw the expression on Tracy's face and she said, "I know. You don't want to talk about either of them."

"That's right," Tracy agreed. "I don't . . . not yet. Sometime . . ."

"Sometime," Florence said softly. "Darling, I wish I could make you remember that you're young, you're beautiful, you're talented, and hearts *do* mend. Although I know only too well what Ben Devlin has done to yours, damn him."

"Florence . . ."

"All right, all right. Look, Tracy, the job here is yours for as long as you want it, you know that. I'll admit I offered it to you in the beginning in part because, just then, you needed a refuge so desperately. I also suspected you'd be very good at it, though I admit I didn't realize you would excel. You have a feeling for old things, and you also have a way with people. One of these days, I'd like to make you a full partner in my business."

"That isn't necessary, Florence."

"I know it isn't *necessary*, but I think it would be a logical step for both of us. Just now, though, I want you to get away. Give me a few more days to get acclimated to working regular hours, and then *go!* And don't look at me like that, Tracy. I insist upon this!"

Florence had been adamant, and as Tracy boarded the bus from Boston to Woods Hole, and the Nantucket ferry, she was glad her employer hadn't let her wiggle out of this vacation time, as she had been tempted to do.

Florence was right. She did need a rest, time to be alone, time to think things out and try to plan a future course of action. She no longer had any need to feel a sense of responsibility to her father. And Ben Devlin, after three years of the most intense kind of relationship, was completely and forever out of her life.

Still, though she told herself that she was completely free, an inner voice warned that she was not yet ready for another involvement. Not even as casual an involvement as a date with someone like Gerry Stanhope. Because of this, Tracy waited until she was sure the first passengers would have disembarked, and then she slowly made her way down the companionway to the lower deck, joining others still milling toward the gangplank.

Once on the wharf, she paused to claim her luggage. Glancing ahead, she saw Gerry Stanhope being greeted effusively by a silver-haired woman who, she decided, must be the aunt he had mentioned. Tracy watched him move off with the woman toward an adjacent parking lot. Briefly, she felt a twinge of regret despite herself, because she had so easily let him walk away from her. She was not a recluse by nature, and she recognized the fact that it would be fun to have a carefree time with someone like Gerry. But it wasn't the right moment, she told herself again. She was still too intensely aware of her own vulnerability.

She had brought two fairly large but lightweight canvas suitcases with her. Now she redeemed them, then started to look around for a taxi. Even as she did so, a short, chubby man wearing black slacks and a white shirt came toward her and asked, "Cab, miss?"

Tracy nodded. "I want to go to Siasconset," she told him.

"Fairly long trip," he commented. "Want me to see if there's someone else who wants to share the ride?"

She shook her head. "I'd rather you took me by myself, if you don't mind," she told him.

"Glad to," he assured her, picked up her suitcases, and started off.

About to follow him, Tracy glanced back toward the ferry for just an instant, and was immediately galvanized by a pair of eyes fixed upon her, so light and clear that they seemed like quicksilver.

She swallowed hard. The possessor of the gray eyes was unquestionably one of the most attractive men she had ever seen. He was tall. He must, she surmised, stand well over six feet, and he was wearing a pale green knit shirt that fit his broad shoulders snugly, tapering down to a narrow waist cinched by a wide belt with a brass buckle that glinted in the sun. He was not tanned, and so his dark hair seemed almost jet black in comparison to his very light skin. Even from this distance, Tracy could see the cleft in his strongly defined chin. It occurred to her that he would be almost *too* handsome were it not for the rugged masculinity underlying his features. There was nothing soft about this man, nothing soft about him at all! His gaze, in fact, was arrogant; she could think of no other word to describe it. He was looking at her almost scornfully. She expected to see his wide, well-shaped lips curl in contempt, though she couldn't imagine why this should be so.

The man was a total stranger; certainly she had never seen him before in her life. She could think of no reason at all for his staring at her as he was doing, and she resented it. She could feel swift, hot color flushing her cheeks, and she turned away hastily, plunging ahead in the direction the cab driver had taken.

As she settled into the cab, she couldn't resist glancing again toward the dockside, and she saw the dark-haired stranger walking toward the parking lot with a tall, slender woman by his side. The woman had a cloud of black hair that camouflaged her face from Tracy's vantage point. Yet Tracy had no doubt at all that she must be beautiful, and she felt a sharp little pang of something which, she recognized with astonishment, came very close to jealousy.

The couple was passing fairly close to the cab now. They were talking in low tones and Tracy couldn't hear what they were saying, although the window on her side of the cab was open. Then the man laughed, but it was a short laugh, without mirth, and the woman said something to him, her manner almost urgent. As a result, he smiled, and Tracy caught her breath; his smile was devastating.

Only a second later, he looked up directly through the cab window, and as she met those gray eyes again she felt as if she were staring into winter ice. She had never before seen a gaze so cold, and she could only wonder why she evoked this astonishing reaction in someone who didn't even know her.

She was snapped back to reality by the cab driver saying, "Where to in Sconset, miss?"

"Sconset?" she echoed.

"We shorten it, hereabouts," he said. "Siasconset it is, but folks always say Sconset."

"I see. Well, the house is on Scallop Shell Lane, but I don't have a number for it."

"Don't need a number," the driver told her agreeably, and started off.

As they drove along, Tracy decided that she must get a local map so that she could relate one place to another. She knew only that Siasconset was clear across the island, on the ocean side.

They were soon out of Nantucket Town, going along a paved highway that wended its way through undulating moors and a grove of stunted pines that the cab driver pointed out to her with a wave of the hand, saying, "State Forest, they started planting trees out here back about 1912, but we get stiff winds, except right in town. The trees don't get a chance to grow very tall."

He grinned at her in the rearview mirror. "Aren't you going to ask me the question?" he demanded.

Tracy could not help but smile back at him. "What question?" she ventured.

"Well, two questions, I guess you'd say," he told her. "First, folks always ask, 'Do you live here all year?' Then when I tell 'em yes, I'm a native, they get on to the second part, which is, 'What do you do in the winter?' It gets hard to make a polite answer to that one!"

Tracy laughed. "I've spent some summers on Cape Cod now and then," she confessed. "The Cape Codders say the same thing."

"Well," the cab driver agreed, "guess they get asked the same question. We like to think we're kind of different out here on the island, though. Kind of like we live in another world. For such a scrap of land, Nantucket's got a heap of history. Whole island's only forty-nine square miles, and a lot of that's still in moors and beaches. Back aways, though, matter of fact it's getting close to two centuries back, this island was the whaling capital of the world. The whalers went out from here for two, three years at a time on their voyages. Brought back the oil that lighted the whole country's lamps. Then, later, New Bedford got into the whaling act. They passed us by in the early eighteen hundreds, but it wasn't until oil was discovered in Pennsylvania late in the century that whaling started to decline. Then Edison discovered that incandescent lamp of his and there wasn't much use for oil lamps any longer except as curiosities."

The man shrugged. "Tourists are our big business today," he admitted. "Folks still come here into October, best time of year it is, too. There's nothing like a Nantucket Indian Summer. You going to be around long?"

"Through September," Tracy told him.

"You should try to stay a mite longer," he said. "October brings warm sunny days and the bluest skies you've ever seen. There's a chill to the nights but you put a couple of extra blankets on the bed and I guarantee you'll sleep like a baby."

She laughed. "I have a job to get back to," she told him.

"What place are you going to on Scallop Shell Lane?"

"Mrs. Thorndyke's."

He nodded. "In Europe, ain't she?" he asked, conversationally. "Nice woman, Mrs. Thorndyke."

"Yes, she is. I've known her all my life."

They were coming to a crest in the road and the cab driver said, "This here is called Bean Hill. Look out, there ahead. That's Siasconset Village, and"—he waved to a towering red and white lighthouse on the left—"that's Sankaty Head Light, one of the brightest lights on the whole East Coast, and just about the first the passenger ships used to see back in the days when there were passenger ships in the transatlantic trade. Only time I ever left the island for very long was when I went to work for the United States Line. I made about forty crossings before I came back here and settled down for good. Those ships were the queens of the sea; there'll never be anything else like them, more's the pity."

They were passing through Siasconset Village proper, and the cab driver said, "See the flagpole outside the post office there? It's rigged like a ship's mast, you'll notice. That road there leads down to the shore, and they got a sign posted at the end that reads 'To

Spain, To Portugal, 3,000 miles.' This here is the old village. Some of these cottages used to be fishermen's shacks and they're pretty small. Today, most of them are owned by summer people."

"They're delightful," Tracy said, looking out at the small, gray-shingled dwelling places all but jostling each other. Most of them were surrounded by fences covered with roses which, even now, bloomed in red, pink, and white profusion.

"Scallop Shell Lane's up toward Sankaty Head," the cab driver informed her. "Dirt road, from this point on, and people like Mrs. Thorndyke hope it'll stay that way. You get to the point where progress becomes a pain, know what I mean?"

"Yes," Tracy said. "Yes, I do. It would be a shame to spoil any of this."

It was rough road and the cab jounced along it so that her words came in little gasps. Then the driver pulled up in front of a low, gray-shingled cottage on the right, and Tracy saw with delight that it, too, had a fence out in front separating a small grass plot from the road. The fence was covered with deep pink rambler roses.

"This is *it*?" Tracy asked, enchanted. "I was here years ago when I was a child, but I don't remember it clearly. It's absolutely delightful!"

"Pretty place," the cab driver agreed laconically. Briefly, he hesitated, then he added, "May be a mite lonely for you, though. All the houses are summer places along this road and most of the folks have gone back to the mainland by now."

"I don't mind in the least being alone," she assured him.

"Spoken like an islander," he commended her.

As she waited, he took her suitcases out of the car trunk, then asked in an almost fatherly tone, "You got the key?"

"Yes."

He frowned. "Nearest place to get supplies is at the store back in the village," he told her. "It would be a fair walk to haul groceries from there for anyone as slight as you are."

She laughed. "I'm stronger than I look," she said, "and anyway Mrs. Thorndyke has left her car here, and she said I'm to use it."

The cab driver gestured toward a shed that jutted out from the left side of the house. "It'll be in there," he said. "Some of the folks along here have converted sheds like that into garages. Done a pretty good job, too; doesn't spoil the looks of the places."

He waited until she opened the door, then hoisted her suitcases inside for her. As she paid him, he handed her a business card and said, "Mike's Taxi Service, and remember I'm as close as your telephone. You need anything, just call me."

"I'll do that," she promised him.

Tracy stood in the doorway until the cab had driven off, feeling a pleasant glow because the man had been so genuinely friendly. Accustomed to city living, she found this very warming. As she glanced up and down this lane, where the houses were spaced much wider apart than they had been in Siasconset Village, it was good to know that she knew someone whom she could call upon in case she did need help for any reason.

As the taxi disappeared from sight, she closed the front door and turned to gaze with delight at the large, low ceiling of the living room that stretched ahead of her, furnished with comfortable chairs and couches covered in bright chintz, and an assortment of pictures and bric-a-brac, all of which enhanced the decor.

Her trained eye recognized authenticity when she saw it. She knew immediately that these were not reproductions but were genuine antiques, many of them Oriental in origin. She had suggested to Gerry Stanhope that some of his aunt's valuables might have been brought back by sea captains, and he had agreed with her. Now she was even more certain that some of Aunt Sally's possessions had found their way to Nantucket aboard ships that once had sailed the seven seas. Very possibly some of them had been whaling ships; traditionally the whalers had brought home gifts from the Orient for the wives, daughters, sisters, or sweethearts who had waited for them patiently during the course of those long, long voyages.

Now Tracy wondered if the whalers had been faithful to the women they left behind, or if each landfall had brought with it temptations too tantalizing to resist?

The mere idea of faithlessness made her wince. It still hurt, hurt deeply, to think of what a fickle thing love could be, and of how completely one's sense of values could be upset by infidelity, one's feelings altered so that there no longer seemed to be such a thing as trust left in the world.

Dark thoughts. She resolutely thrust them aside and paused to finger a cranberry glass basket with careful appreciation before starting out to get acquainted with the rest of the cottage.

Chapter Two

Tracy wandered from the living room into a bedroom that was charmingly furnished in maple, with pristine white dotted swiss curtains at the windows and a matching flounced spread on the four-poster bed.

The bathroom was pink-tiled, with an enclosed glass shower, and the kitchen was equally modern. She tested a light switch and found that Aunt Sally had, indeed, remembered to leave the electricity on. Next she checked the contents of the cupboards and the refrigerator, only to find that both were distressingly bare.

Although she wanted to linger longer in her explorations and, in fact, to extend them with a walk up to the lighthouse, Tracy reminded herself that first she must be practical.

She glanced at her wristwatch and saw that it was nearly four. It seemed likely that at this time of the year a store like the one in the village would close early, since most of the summer people already had left the island. For that matter, there was no guarantee that any of the stores in Nantucket Town would be open late either, which meant that she must go about shopping for some bread and milk and other staples without dallying further.

She smiled, remembering that Aunt Sally Thorndyke had told her she would find the car keys in the Imari vase on the old pine sideboard in the living room. She discovered as she fished carefully inside the vase for the keys, that it was not only an old example of this form of Japanese porcelain but an excellent one. There was a softness to the vibrant blues and reds in the pattern, and a richness to the gold trim that confirmed both the vase's antiquity and its authenticity. The strong colors and the brash gold in most reproductions was a quick giveaway to age and quality.

The makeshift garage door creaked as Tracy opened it, and she found that she had inherited a light blue two-door sedan of a considerably earlier vintage. It looked sturdy, though, and eminently dependable. However, appearances, she soon found to her chagrin, could indeed be misleading! Although she turned the key in the ignition switch with no premonition at all of any impending problem, the car stubbornly refused to start. The engine groaned a couple of times, and that was it!

Tracy felt very much like groaning with it. Although she had been driving ever since she was a teenager, admittedly she was no mechanic. The complicated maze that lurked under a car's hood was foreign territory to her.

She did know that if she kept pressing the accelerator chances were that she would flood the engine, and that would destroy the possibility of getting the car started at all. No, she told herself, better to put her pride in her pocket and seek help.

Help? She remembered the cab driver's concern about her possible loneliness here on Scallop Shell Lane because most of the people who lived in the neighboring cottages were summer residents and had already left.

She also remembered the taxi man saying, as he handed her his card, that if she needed help she had only to call him; she could rely on the fact that he was as near as her telephone. Ruefully she conceded that she would probably be making that call much sooner than she had believed would be necessary.

Clasping her handbag, she climbed out of the car. The entrance to the converted shed was separate from the house, so now she found herself facing the road, and she glanced up and down the length of it. To her delight she glimpsed smoke curling from the squat chimney of a cottage perhaps a hundred feet away.

At that moment, this seemed a twofold blessing. The sun was making its westward safari at a faster rate than she had thought it would, and she felt as if night's shadows were already brushing her. She shivered, realizing that Mike, the cab driver, had been right. There was more than a little chance that when darkness fell it would have seemed decidedly lonely out here, if all the other cottages in the vicinity proved to be unoccupied. Now she knew she had company in at least one of them, and it was a very good feeling.

The car problem would give her the chance to meet her neighbors sooner than she might have otherwise. Since Aunt Sally had been using the car right up until the time she had left the island it didn't seem likely that there was anything major wrong with it. Tracy felt certain that if there were a man in the cottage next door he would be able to help her.

Still clasping her handbag, she started down the lane, wishing briefly that she had thought to change from her slim navy sandals into something a bit sturdier. The sandals, she was finding, collected small pebbles that soon became unwelcome companions. She decided she would have to get some flat, closed shoes if she were going to enjoy walking on such rough terrain.

She paused outside the neighboring cottage, glancing

up appreciatively at the front door, reached by a high, single stone step. It was a beautiful door, painted white with a fluted top centered by a large piece of bull's-eye glass that would have brought a gleam to any antique collector's eye. Tracy raised the heavy brass knocker and let it clang once and then, when there was no response, she raised and lowered it again. She decided that once she got to know the owners of the cottage she would ask them if she could come over and take a color picture of their entrance.

For the moment, though, there didn't seem to be anyone home despite the smoke curling from the chimney. She bit her lip, fighting back a wave of both disappointment and discouragement. This was a bad beginning to her island sojourn because it was following a pattern. Not too many things had gone well for her these past months. She tried to ward off the all too familiar feeling of dejection that threatened to sweep over her, and was about to turn away and chart another course of action when the door was flung open so suddenly that she was startled and nearly lost her balance as she automatically took a step backward.

She looked up, disbelieving, into the hostile face of the tall, dark, gray-eyed stranger who had stared at her so coldly and rudely earlier in the afternoon.

For a moment, it didn't seem that this possibly could be happening, that *he,* of all people, could be her neighbor. But there was no doubt at all that it was the same man. At such a close distance, he was an even more powerful figure than he had seemed before, and it was impossible not to be intensely aware of a very tangible masculinity that would have been intensely attractive under ordinary circumstances. The green knit shirt he was still wearing emphasized his broad shoulders, and outlined the muscular contours of his arms. She again caught the glint of the brass belt buckle at his narrow waist. His dark cord slacks were disturbingly snug, molding firm, well-developed thighs and drawing unavoidable attention to the sheer length of his legs.

He was extraordinarily handsome, and again she found herself thinking that if it were not for a certain ruggedness about him he would be too good-looking. As it was, she found herself staring at the cleft in his chin which, just now, was jutting forward almost angrily, and she had a quick impression of thick dark hair that was tousled, as if he had just been running his fingers through it. Then, reluctantly, she met those gray eyes, and she shrank from the expression in them. His gaze had seemed glacial before, but now his eyes were molten silver, blazing with what could only be described as fury.

"What do you want?" he demanded rudely.

Tracy could feel her indignation flaring, and had it not been for the earlier encounter she would have blurted back something equally rude, but she fought down the words. Since there was no logical reason for her to have the adverse effect on this stranger that she obviously did have, she could only conclude that she must remind him of someone else. Someone he hated! If this were the case it was, of course, too bad. However, there was nothing she could do about it. Perhaps, she told herself, if she got past the first hurdle of establishing communication with him he would become a bit more logical about her and would not be so ready to condemn her for an accidental look-alike.

She said stiffly, "I'm sorry if I disturbed you. I'm staying in the cottage next door."

"Mrs. Thorndyke's cottage?"

"Yes."

Tracy resented the note of suspicion in his voice as he

said, "I hadn't heard there was anyone coming to stay there."

She swallowed hard, fighting the impulse to leave. But despite her anger she was remembering all too vividly that the car wouldn't start, that she had no groceries in the house, and that night, definitely, was coming. She could feel the last golden rays of the sun touching her back.

"Mrs. Thorndyke is an old family friend," she said coldly. "She's in Europe right now, as you probably know if you know her, and she won't be coming back to Nantucket before early next summer. She has loaned me her cottage for the balance of September, but the thing is that she left her car for me to use as well, and I can't get it started. Could you help me with it?"

There was a strange tenseness to the silence that came between them. Tracy felt as if the air itself might snap suddenly and that if it did it would send out piercing, wounding shards, like splintered glass.

She felt herself flinching away from the stranger, but even so she wasn't at all prepared when he said flatly, "No, I couldn't."

The question was inadvertent, because it didn't seem possible that she had heard him rightly. "I beg your pardon?" she asked.

"You heard what I said," he told her roughly. "I won't help you with your car. Now suppose you go find someone else to play mechanic for you! Matter of fact, I'd say your best bet is to phone a garage over in Nantucket Town and see if you can get someone to come out here to your rescue."

With that, he all but slammed the door in her face.

Tracy stood on the high stone stoop, staring disbelievingly at the door's white painted surface. She felt as if her temperature was soaring, and her breath came in little spurts. Despite the miserable things both her

LOVE'S GOLDEN SHADOW

father and Ben Devlin had done to her, she had never really come to hate either of them. In fact, hate was virtually an unknown emotion to her. Knowing its potential for destructiveness, she supposed she had more or less deliberately avoided it, perhaps especially where her father and Ben were concerned.

Now, though, this feeling surging through her was as close to hate as she had ever come in her life. What a *despicable* man this great, hulking brute was! How absolutely incredible to think that he would not so much as deign to get a little grease on his hands in order to help out someone with a problem.

Tracy was trembling so that she staggered as she stepped down from the high step. As she retreated up the road pk har ksj ckppaca sha sas shaking and fuming at the thought of her malevolent neighbor.

Her neighbor! Whereas earlier there had been comfort in the thought of having someone just down the lane from her, now the mere idea filled her with alarm. Who *was* the dark stranger? True, he had known that the cottage she was occupying belonged to Sally Thorndyke, but that probably wouldn't be a very hard thing to ascertain. His roughness, his hostility, she decided now, suggested a person in hiding, although she had to admit that evidently he hadn't been averse to being seen in the wharf area earlier with a beautiful brunette companion.

Nevertheless, that had been at a time when the dock area was bustling with activity, one ferry having just come in with a load of passengers and another getting ready to take off for Woods Hole. Crowds lent camouflage, although it had to be admitted that with his looks it would be almost impossible for the dark stranger to go anywhere unnoticed.

Back in the living room at the cottage, Tracy collapsed into the nearest armchair, literally shaking from her brush with the arrogant, unyielding, and thoroughly despicable man next door.

Why? Why had he behaved as he had? She couldn't fathom an answer, and finally decided that she was wasting valuable time brooding about it. There was no help to be garnered from her neighbor, nor would she take it now if she were offered it. So this made it all the more imperative to get on about the business of finding someone who could get the car going for her.

Still, that question of "Why?" persisted, as did the feeling that the dark-haired stranger was in some sense a man in hiding, and that there had to be a reason—a very good reason—for his behavior. He had so visibly resented having his privacy intruded upon, and while this could be because she reminded him of someone he detested there could also be other reasons. Maybe he simply didn't want anyone to know where he was, or to violate his own stretch of turf.

Well, Tracy told herself, her chin held high, he certainly didn't have to worry about seeing her again!

She drew a deep sigh, then went out to the kitchen where she previously had noticed that there was a wall phone. It took a moment to find the phone book, but simple deduction soon led her to discover it in a top kitchen cabinet drawer. She had to admit that her appallingly bad-mannered neighbor was right. Her best bet unquestionably was to call a garage over in Nantucket Town, and see if someone would come out and solve the car problem for her. Hopefully, they would be able to do this right on the scene. If, however, the car had to be towed in for repairs, she would have to get in touch with Mike first thing in the morning and hire him to take her shopping with his cab. Should this prove to be the case, she would just have to make out with whatever she could find in the kitchen cupboard to eat, since the fridge was quite empty. The cupboard looked pretty bare, too, for that matter, but maybe if she delved deep enough she'd find a can of soup stashed away. As Tracy thought about food, she realized that she had skipped breakfast this morning, and had bought only a cup of coffee on the boat, for excitement over the trip had dulled her appetite. Now, however, her need for food was a real one.

First things first, she reminded herself. She found a garage listed in the yellow pages that offered road service. Then she picked up the phone receiver only to discover, to her complete horror, that the phone was dead!

This was one thing Aunt Sally Thorndyke must have forgotten! She had mentioned that the company automatically disconnected her phone the day after Labor Day each year when she normally left the island. But she had added that she would give them a call to be sure they kept it on this year till October first. Evidently, though, in the final surge of activity geared around her own trip to Europe this was a detail she had overlooked.

As she hung up the receiver, Tracy saw that the shadows stealing across the living room had become mauve, which meant that the last light of day was fading and night with all its strangeness, all its darkness, was about to descend.

She gritted her teeth. It was no time to be proud, no time to think about the miserable way some people behave, nor to try to figure out why the stranger next door should be so horrible.

She needed help, and the only way to get it that she could think of was to phone for it, but she had no idea where the nearest public phone booth might be. Siasconset Village wasn't a long distance away, to be sure. But she was not even certain of the direction, and there would be no sun to guide her now. Further, she realized dismally, she had not thought to bring a flashlight with her, and although a search might reveal one that Aunt Sally had left behind, she didn't want to take time for this just now.

No, there was no sensible way out of asking her truculent neighbor if she might use his telephone!

Chapter Three

In the near darkness, the door seemed forbidding. Tracy stood in front of it for a long moment before she raised the brass knocker. When she finally let it fall she felt as if its clang could surely be heard all around the world!

He did not keep her waiting this time. He flung the door open and, as he loomed before her, she fought down an almost hysterical impulse to turn around and run. The terrible thought even crossed her mind that if she were to do this he might come after her, and perhaps teach her a physical lesson about interrupting someone who so clearly did not want to be interrupted. She shrank with horror from the mere idea of such a thing, imagining that she could feel his angry fingers clutching at her shoulders.

Then, in the background, she heard a voice, and she almost gasped audibly with relief. He had company, there was someone else in his living room; immediately, she thought of the brunette who had been with him on the wharf.

"Well?" he demanded.

"I'm sorry," Tracy said. "Really, I *am* sorry. I had no intention of coming back."

"You again," he said, with a note of resignation in his voice, which, in its way, was surprising. "What do you want this time?"

"To use your phone, if I may," she said. "Aunt Sally—Mrs. Thorndyke, that is—evidently didn't tell the company not to disconnect hers, as they usually do."

"Oh?" It was there again, that tinge of suspicion that was almost like an accusation, and she bristled.

"Look," she said, "I've told you I'm sorry to disturb you and, believe me, I am. I should think you might imagine that you're the last person in the world I want to ask for *anything* just now. But I have a phone that doesn't work, a car that doesn't work, and there is no food in the house. Before I came over here, I looked up and down the lane and there are no lights in any of the other houses . . ."

"They're empty," he said abruptly. "The other people have all left."

This was not at all what she had wished she might hear, even though she had suspected it to be so, and Tracy fought down a chill of apprehension. But before she could say anything further, the man shrugged and stepped back from the doorway.

"I don't know if you can rouse anyone at the phone company at this hour but you can try them," he commented indifferently. "You'll want to call a garage as well, but I can tell you now that I doubt you can get anyone to come out here before tomorrow. As for food, the store in the village is within walking distance —a mile or so, I'd say—but chances are that they're closed already, or they would be by the time you could get there."

Tracy had not seen a car in evidence, but she realized now that even if he had one in a makeshift garage, like Aunt Sally's, he was not about to offer to take her to a store or anywhere else.

He was staring down at her, and he said impatiently, "Come on, will you, and make your phone calls!"

Despite herself, tears stung her eyes, and she walked by him swiftly, hating the fact that he was observing this sign of weakness on her part. But he seemed oblivious to her distress.

He brushed ahead of her, and she saw that there was only one dim light burning in the room, and there was a record spinning on a turntable. So, the voice she'd heard had come from the record player. This, she realized with dismay meant that he did not have a guest with him in the house after all.

As she watched, he carefully removed the record and put it at the top of a stack, and then he said tersely, "You'll find the phone in the kitchen."

Tracy followed his pointing finger, and it seemed to her that his gray eyes bored into her back like twin pieces of steel as she left the room.

She had only one thought, and that was to make her phone calls as swiftly as possible so that she could get back to her own cottage and bolt herself in! Then she became aware of the aroma of something tantalizingly delicious simmering on the stove, and her hunger pangs become so acute that it was all she could do not to succumb to temptation and lift the lid and see what it was.

The kitchen itself was small but well equipped, with bright yellow curtains at the window matched by both the stove and the refrigerator. There was a sunshine quality to the decor that certainly was not at all in keeping with the mood of the cottage's inhabitant!

There was a wall phone here too, and the directory was lying out on a counter. She found the necessary numbers, dialed them, and learned to her chagrin that the stranger had been right. She couldn't arouse anyone at the phone company, and at the garage they told her that the best they could do was to promise service for the next morning.

She was tempted to make a third call to Mike's Taxi Service, but there seemed little point to it. She doubted that even the voluble Mike would be able to open food store doors for her on this island where the tenor of life clearly was geared to suit the year-round residents. Probably there were restaurants open, and the thought of a good meal was a very alluring one. But it would mean having Mike wait for her while she ate, or come back to fetch her later, and just now this seemed like entirely too much trouble. Bed and a good night's rest made a more inviting prospect.

Tracy returned to the living room to find that the rude stranger had built a fire on the wide stone hearth at the far end of the room. The room itself was still dim, with only one light burning, but now there was also the orange light of flames licking the chimney bricks, and as she watched he added yet another log. The firelight's glow etched his profile in sharp relief, and at the sight of him, Tracy couldn't help but catch her breath. He was arrestingly attractive . . . physically, she reminded herself hastily. She could say nothing at all for his personality!

Still, it was impossible not to be intensely aware of him, and equally impossible not to be disturbed by him if only because he was so essentially masculine. There was a sense of latent strength about him, a fluidity to his movements as he poked the log into place, and then stood back, adjusting the fire screen in front of it.

With dusk there had come a chill, and Tracy, without realizing what she was doing, moved over to the fireplace, instinctively holding out her hands to savor the warmth created by the leaping flames. There was a fascination to fire, fascination as intense as the feeling this man by her side was arousing in her. Even as she thought this, she realized that he was standing very close to her, so close they they were almost brushing each other.

She looked up to find his arresting gray eyes staring down at her and he asked, "Cold?"

"Yes, a little," she admitted.

"Do you have a supply of wood for the fireplace next door? It does tend to get cold here, once the sun is gone."

"I didn't notice," she told him. "Probably there is some, I'll check on it in the morning. I was primarily intent on getting the car started so that I could do some marketing."

"Mrs. Thorndyke didn't leave any supplies for you?"

"No. My decision to accept her offer to come out here and use the cottage was made on the spur of the moment. By then, she was on the eve of leaving for Europe, and I imagine she'd arranged her own shopping so that she could use up most of the things she had on hand. It doesn't matter, though. They're coming to fix the car tomorrow, and then I can take care of everything."

She realized, as she said this, that he could very well consider it in the nature of an accusation, for there seemed little doubt to her that he could have solved her car problem, if he had not been so astonishingly selfish. He frowned, and she thought for a moment that he might be going to offer some defense for his actions, but instead he asked, "Why did you decide to come out to Nantucket?"

She was tempted to tell him that it was none of his business, but she compromised with, "Is there any reason why I shouldn't have? As I understand it, this is one of the loveliest times of the year here."

"True, unless we have a hurricane," he agreed. "No, there's no *reason* why you shouldn't have come, I suppose."

"Except," she could not resist saying, "that from your point of view you'd prefer not having any neighbors around, is that right?"

"Yes," he agreed, "that's quite right."

Tracy's deep blue eyes sparked. "I've already told you I'm sorry I bothered you," she said testily. "I didn't *enjoy* coming back here to ask you if I might use your phone, you know. Now I can assure you that when I leave I won't return. You can have your damned solitude! I certainly won't infringe upon it again."

Tears again threatened and she grit her teeth. She was *damned* if she would let him see her cry, and she was only too aware that he was still watching her closely. It was, for that matter, impossible not to meet his gaze, and as she did so it seemed to her that something flickered in those unusual eyes; something that she liked to think was connected with respect.

To her surprise, he said, "I'm sorry. I know I've seemed churlish to you, but I . . ."

"You don't have to explain," she cut in shortly.

"Very well, then, I'd rather not," he retorted. "I was going to tell you, though, that I've a pot of soup on the stove, and it might be a good idea for you to share some of it."

The invitation was proffered stiffly, and Tracy realized full well that he was not giving it willingly. She started to refuse, but he anticipated her intention and said, "There's no reason for you to go hungry. You can eat and run." Was she imagining it, or did just the shadow of a smile flit over his features? "I'm sure you're anxious to settle in next door," he added smoothly.

"Very well," she said, ungraciously.

"We can eat in the kitchen," he told her. "You might go get out a couple of soup bowls and some spoons. There are paper napkins in the door by the sink, and you'll find a loaf of Portuguese bread, and some butter . . ."

"I take it I'm being pressed into service?" It was an icy question.

"Why not?" he countered infuriatingly, then added, "I'll join you directly. I want to put another log on the fire first."

If her handsome neighbor lacked everything else in the world, he certainly had a surplus supply of the power to antagonize. She went out to the kitchen and found the things he had mentioned and quickly set two places at the small kitchen table, and put out bread and butter. Before she had quite finished, he came into the room, going directly to a cabinet over the sink. As she watched, he took out a bottle of whiskey and a glass, and then, as if knowing that she would refuse, asked, "Do you want a drink?"

"No, thank you," she said.

"Ladle out the soup, will you?" he suggested, as he poured himself out a liberal drink, then added a splash of water to it.

She was tempted to tell him to keep his soup, but it smelled too delicious, and the hunger pangs could not be denied. As she carried the steaming bowls across to the table, she noticed that her host was pouring himself a second drink, which he downed nearly as quickly as he had the first one. It seemed to her that there was already something slightly unsteady about his gait as he walked across to the table, the chair clattering as he pulled it out and sat down without waiting for her.

Although she could quibble endlessly with his manners, she could not fault his soup, which at the moment seemed the most ambrosial fare she had ever had. Also, the Portuguese bread was crusty and delicious, and as she ate, Tracy couldn't help but mellow a bit.

"This is very good," she told him.

"The bread? It's made locally; you can get it at the store in the village."

"The bread, yes. But also the soup. I've never had anything quite like it."

"It's a basic Portuguese soup, sort of a variation of the standard Portuguese kale soup. The different taste comes from a smoked sausage, called linguiça, which is used in it."

"Where can you get it?"

"Linguiça? Almost anywhere, in this part of the country. There are many people of Portuguese descent in coastal New England. Fortunately, they've perpetuated their food heritage, because I personally think that the Portuguese cuisine deserves to be much better known than it is."

"If this is an example, I agree," Tracy said. "What I meant to ask, though, is where can you get the soup?"

"I made it," he told her, to her surprise. "I made it yesterday, as a matter of fact. When I fix it I always make quite a quantity because it gets better with age." He took a piece of bread, ignoring the butter, and in a quick change of subject asked, "How long do you intend to stay here?"

"I think I already told you I'm to have the cottage for the balance of September," she said coldly.

"I believe you mentioned it was available to you for the rest of the month," he agreed, "but I didn't know whether you intend to stay that long or not."

"I've already said I won't bother you again," she began hotly.

"Yes, you have," he said, with an infuriating calm. "You never did really answer me, though, when I asked you why you've come out here."

"You don't think that simply having a holiday is enough?"

"I don't feel, somehow, that you've come here simply to have a holiday."

"Then you're wrong," she told him flatly. "I work in an antique shop in Boston and my employer was ill this past summer so I wasn't able to get any time off. When the chance came to take a holiday now, she urged me to do so."

"I see. Will you be alone here?"

"Why?"

"I wondered if perhaps you might have a friend planning to join you."

"As a further intrusion?" she demanded. "I've the idea that what you're really asking is if I have a man coming to join me here, and I can assure you that the answer is no!"

"No men in your life?"

"No longer," she said flatly. "One reason I've come here is to *forget* about men, if you must know, so you can consider yourself quite secure. I want to be alone as much as you do."

She had finished her soup and she noticed that he had stopped eating his. He was toying with a segment of the bread, and she saw that his fingers were exceptionally well formed, long, slender; there seemed something very capable about them. He had averted his head, and there was an almost bleak expression on his face. Was it possible, she wondered, that in actuality he *didn't* want to be alone as much as he had indicated?

This was not a thought to pursue, she told herself hastily. It was enough to be tantalizingly aware of his proximity, but she knew very well that it would be absolutely perilous to be lured into an attempt to try to get to know him better.

She stood and said, "If you've finished, I'll clean the things up before I go."

"Of course." She opened the door wide, and he came past her into the living room, settling the canvas carrier on the floor near the fireplace then going on to place the bag of groceries on the kitchen counter. He seemed sufficiently familiar with the cottage so that she wondered if, perhaps, he did some work for Aunt Sally Thorndyke on occasion.

She was about to ask him about this when he said, "Guess someone will be over to fix up your car before long, but I'll take a look at it if you like. Imagine the problem's that the battery has run down, though. Mrs. Thorndyke takes good care of it. Shouldn't be anything more than that."

"You know Mrs. Thorndyke?"

"Sure. My mother does her laundry," Tim Sousa said easily. "I help out around the place when she needs something. Look, Mr. Medfield mentioned your phone's been turned off. I think he plans to call the company for you but if he doesn't I will. They should be able to get it hooked up again by afternoon. Work starts to slack off, this time of year."

She stared at him, this sudden onslaught of friendliness coming as a kind of shock. Why hadn't her neighbor *told* her last night that he'd call the phone company for her, she wondered. It would have saved her a lot of anxiety. As it was, she would have bitten off her tongue before she would have asked him to do that or any other favor for her.

Tim grinned at her. "Got to get along," he said. "Look, if you need anything my father's in the book, Ed Sousa. He'll give me your message."

"Thank you, Tim."

Tracy felt a sense of loss as she saw him depart. Watching him from the window, she expected that he would get in the pickup truck and drive off. Instead, he went back to the house next door, going around to the rear. She hadn't noticed an outside door in the kitchen the night before, but evidently there was must be one.

Slowly, she took the things out of the grocery bag, finding a container full of the Portuguese soup she had shared with the mysterious stranger the night before, plus a supply of bread, butter, eggs, some canned things, and even a tin partially full of coffee.

These various items had been chosen with care, and Tracy was at once amazed and touched by this evidence of solicitude on her neighbor's part. Briefly, she gave thought to walking over and thanking him personally, then dismissed the idea. Despite this surface display of friendliness, there was no telling what sort of welcome she might get if she were to put the matter to test!

The man from the telephone company arrived to hook up her phone just before noon, and when he had left Tracy reheated some of the soup only to find that, as "Mr. Medfield" had said, it was even better as it aged. She had just finished eating it when the mechanic came and told her that Tim Sousa had been right in his diagnosis: The car battery was run down, and that seemed to be the only problem.

He had brought a spare battery with him, anticipating that this might be the case, but before he left he said, "Fellow next door could have jump-started it for you. You'd have had enough juice, then, to get across to town by yourself."

She felt a swift stab of resentment at this, despite her neighbor's generosity this morning. He could so easily have made her Nantucket arrival considerably more pleasant!

With the car in running order, Tracy found her way to Siasconset Village, which today looked even more quaint and charming to her than it had when she was passing through it in Mike's taxi the previous afternoon. Before grocery shopping in the village store, she took the road Mike had pointed out that led to the shore. She couldn't resist getting out of the car, wriggling off her shoes, then scrambling down a sandy bluff to the water's edge to test its chilly temperature with her toes. Then she indulged in a walk along a wonderfully deserted beach. The deep sapphire ocean stretched all the way from here to Spain or Portugal, if she were to believe the sign posted at the road's edge. She scraped the sand from a couple of clam shells and a twisted piece of driftwood polished by the sea to a beautiful light gray-silver tone that unavoidably reminded her of the dark stranger's eyes. Still, she felt a welcome sense of peace and well-being as she got back into the car again. Despite the rather upsetting beginning, she was thoroughly glad that she had come to Nantucket.

Upon her return to the cottage she separated her own groceries from the replacement items she had bought to take back to her neighbor. She could not, of course, return the Portuguese soup, but she determined that during the week she would make something else that she could offer in its stead. She would also contact Tim Sousa about getting firewood for her own use, as well as to return to the other cottage.

She piled the replacement grocery items in a paper sack, and—not without a fair share of trepidation—was about to start out the front door to make the safari to the cottage next door just as a low-slung red sports car drove up in front of it. Before she even saw the person who got out of the car, Tracy suspected that it would be the same, dark-haired woman who had been with her neighbor down at the wharf yesterday, and she was right.

Further, the brunette clearly was no stranger to the house. She climbed the high stone step as easily as if she lived in the place, and Tracy saw a slim, tanned hand reach up to knock. Then without waiting for an answer, the woman turned the doorknob and went in, obviously assured of her welcome.

It was a bad moment. It was impossible not to wonder if the dark-haired stranger was greeting his visitor by taking her in his arms and meeting her lips in a kiss that, Tracy was sure, would be extremely ardent. She could well imagine that Mr. Medfield could be as passionate as he could be cold and disdainful.

The thought of the brunette in his embrace was close to painful, and Tracy was annoyed at herself. "Ridiculous," she said aloud sharply, as she took the bag of groceries back to the kitchen and put away the perishables. Whatever went on in the cottage next door was absolutely *none* of her business, nor did she wish it to be.

Nevertheless, the idea of those two other people, very possibly together at the moment in the deepest sense of the word, underlined her own sense of solitude.

First, there had been the impasse with her father. Since her mother's death nearly eight years ago, the two of them had been very close. She had realized that one day he might meet a woman whom he would wish to marry, and actually as time passed she had wished that he would. She would have been more than willing to accept a stepmother if he had chosen someone closer to his own age, someone compatible to whom she could relate.

However, early this past summer he had met a woman who was only two or three years older than Tracy herself and he had been captivated by her with a speed Tracy still found hard to believe. Once she had accepted the fact of her father's infatuation, though, she had wanted to like her future stepmother, but it had proved to be impossible. Instant antagonism had flared between the two women and, to make matters worse, her father blamed her for the lack of rapport between Elise and herself, which was not at all fair. It soon became evident that even though the Graham home in Milton just outside Boston, was a spacious one, it would never be big enough for the three of them, and Tracy knew she was the one who must leave. Ironically, this was just the chance she had been waiting for, because of Ben Devlin.

Ben was a junior partner in the Boston law firm where she worked as a secretary, where she had been working, for a matter of fact, for five years. For three of those years, she and Ben had shared a deep relationship. For the past two years, Ben had been urging her to go into an apartment with him, and she had hesitated only because she felt her father still needed her. Now, unexpectedly, it had been proven quite conclusively that he really didn't need her at all!

She still vividly remembered the May morning when her father had come down to breakfast to say that there was something he wanted to talk about before they each went off to their respective jobs. Then he had told her that he had proposed marriage to Elise and she had accepted him, and since neither of them saw any reason to wait they were planning a June wedding.

On her way to work that morning, Tracy made up her mind that the time had come to tell Ben she was ready to live with him. Actually she already *had* lived with him in every way but sharing quarters. Now she wanted a home with him and, ultimately, marriage.

She planned to have lunch with Ben that day, a long and leisurely lunch, during which they could talk and make plans. But it wasn't to work out that way. Ben was not free for lunch, and as the week passed she sensed that he was evading her. Then she began to hear drifts of office gossip, even though the girls with whom she worked tried to be careful not to let it reach her. There was no way, though, to stop this particular grapevine from winding traumatic tentacles around her heart, her pride, everything that she held to be personally important.

Ben, she learned, was seeing the daughter of one of the law firm's senior partners, a girl who had come back from studying music in Europe just a short time before. There was no doubt at all that this would be a far more advantageous match for him than marriage to Tracy ever could be. She realized this, but it still didn't seem possible to her that Ben, of all people, could have changed so quickly. It was not until much later that she realized she had never known him very well. Theirs had been pure physical attraction, a surface togetherness with no depth. Her mind and Ben's, she told herself, had never met and she had learned the hard way how important such a meeting was.

In very short order, Ben's engagement was announced, with a large formal wedding planned for late fall. Tracy was doubly shattered, for in the wake of Ben's announcement she had to attend her own father's wedding, and watching him pledge his troth to Elise had been one of the hardest things she ever had to do.

Finally she knew she had to get out of both her job and the Milton house if she were ever to find peace again. Then fate took a hand, and matters were brought to a head insofar as the house was concerned when her father's accounting firm offered him a promotion that would take him to Chicago. The house was put on the market and went very quickly.

It was then that Florence Anders suggested Tracy

come stay with her in her apartment at the foot of Beacon Hill until she could get her bearings; and, once she had moved in, it was Florence who had offered her the job that would enable her to get out of the law firm and, hopefully, put Ben out of her life forever.

It was impossible for Tracy not to be conscientious about the work she did, so, the last week that she worked for the law firm, she put in long hours so that she might be sure of leaving everything in perfect order for the girl who would follow her.

It was while she was working late one afternoon that she glanced up to find Ben standing by her desk, watching her with an unfathomable expression in his hazel eyes.

He said abruptly, "How can you leave here, Tracy? How can you do this to me?"

As she stared at him in disbelief he reached down and lifted her out of her chair, and in the next instant she was in his arms and he was pressing kisses on her lips while his hands moved over her body with easy familiarity.

Emotions were treacherous, and he knew how to arouse her. But now desire was supplanted by revulsion, and she thrust him away with all the strength she could muster.

Later, she could not remember exactly what she had said to him, only that he had paled beneath the anger of her icy words. Finally he had stalked out of the office, and for the balance of the time she was with the firm he had not bothered her again.

Still, this encounter had made her feel cheapened. Ben, she thought bitterly, had viewed her only as a sex object—what else could she think in the wake of what had happened? And this was a damaging blow to her self-respect.

It was a balm to go to work for Florence, and there was solace in being in beautiful surroundings, handling beautiful things. And so time passed.

But it still hurt. It hurt especially when she saw other people together, not because she herself wanted to be with anyone else, but because the thought of romance only heightened her awareness of the treason that could follow.

Chapter Four

The red sports car was still parked out in front of her neighbor's cottage when Tracy got up the next morning.

She had not slept well. Dreams of both her father and Ben had made her toss fitfully. In the early morning she finally climbed out of bed and went to the kitchen window to stare out at an apricot and bronze eastern sky, gilded to herald the ascending sun.

After a time, she warmed a cup of milk, and when she had drunk it went back to bed again, finally to fall into a restless sleep. She was weary when she awoke which made her annoyed at herself because she blamed it on her own weakness.

She had been overly influenced by both her father and Ben, not only depending on them too much but also giving too much of herself, in varying ways, to both of them. But, she added silently, as she sat at the kitchen table sipping a second cup of coffee, these last weeks had proven conclusively that she was entirely capable of being her own person. There was no reason for her not to command her destiny.

Florence Anders' illness had proven this when Tracy had taken over the management of the Charles Street shop and had done very well. This had given her the confidence she badly needed; now she told herself that she was not going to let it be undermined by an unpredictable, arrogant man who was thoughtful one minute and obnoxious the next.

As she made her bed and straightened the cottage, Tracy reminded herself that it didn't matter a damn to her if a woman had spent the night with her next door neighbor—and a glance through the living room window showed her that the red car was still there. There were more important things to consider. A major reason why she had come to Nantucket, after all, was to give herself the opportunity to think clearly about her own future.

When Florence had first suggested that she should become a partner in the business she had backed away from the idea. It entailed a commitment she wasn't sure she wanted to make. Now, though, as she thought about it, the offer began to seem more and more attractive. She had been studying up on antiques on her own ever since starting to work in the shop, and a future course of action might be to take some courses on varying aspects of this very large field. Boston was a mecca when it came to colleges and universities and there would be no difficulty in finding all sorts of places where she might be able to take night courses dealing with intriguing subjects that would make her all the more valuable to Florence. It was an idea that appealed to her.

Antiques, after all, had not always been antiques; this was something that frequently didn't seem to occur to people, even the people who were buying them. These sometimes priceless objects originally had been made either to be used in a practical sense, or to be admired for their beauty, or both. An antique, whether it was an Imari vase, like the one on Aunt Sally's sideboard, or a lovely piece of Sandwich glass, or an exquisite ancient necklace fashioned from gold, reflected the era in which it had been made, and the history, customs, and traditions of the people who had made it.

There could never be enough time in which to learn all there was to be learned about the things in Florence Anders' shop. There was nothing narrow about this field of endeavor. In fact, the potential versatility could be mind boggling when one began to speculate about it, and as she continued to do so there was nothing contrived about her enthusiasm. For a time she even forgot about the red car parked next door.

Late in the morning she decided to walk up to the lighthouse. It was a vintage day; the cool air a tonic, the sky a deep washed blue ornamented by puffed white clouds.

She walked up the road until she reached a stretch of straggly grass surrounding the giant white sentinel striped midway with a broad band of vivid red. Sankaty Head Light stood at the top of a steep bluff, and Tracy went close to its edge turning once to look at the vista of moors behind her dotted with snug, gray-shingled houses and an occasional pond that reflected the sunlight. But lovely though this sight was, it was the view to the east that entranced her and she found herself feasting visually on the sea. The water, she saw, was not one color but many colors, a rich cobalt in the distance, streaked closer to shore with bands of lapis and, in the shallows, stripes of turquoise merging here and there into a light clear green.

There was a faint scent to the air. Tracy identified the sweet leftover echo of summer as honeysuckle. She breathed deeply. The air was an elixir and she wanted to stretch her hands high over her head and do a sort of ritual dance. But she repressed this desire, because even though she was alone on top of the bluff she felt certain that there must be people in the white frame house attached to the lighthouse. This installation was now under Coast Guard control, as were all lighthouses.

In earlier days, "keeping" a light had been much more of a family affair, a man and his wife setting up housekeeping in the lighthouse quarters and raising their family right on the premises. Tracy remembered stories she'd heard about years of duty in lonely lighthouses, some of them on tiny islands off the New England coast that were far smaller, far more remote, than Nantucket. The "lighthouse service," as it had been known then, was replete with tales of heroism. These people had held their posts in the face of gales, hurricanes, and winter storms. When a woman was going to have a baby the only way to get help was via the water, the trip made usually in a wooden boat that often had to be rowed, with the sea not always offering its benediction for the voyage.

Had people been fashioned of sturdier stuff then? It was easy to think so, but Tracy didn't really believe this. She resented it when she heard someone say that the men and women in her own generation had been made soft by the relative ease of their lives. Put to the test, she felt certain that her contemporaries would come through, just as had other men and women in earlier times. Every now and then, one heard of tales of herosim that proved the point.

Tracy had always wanted to try her hand at painting and, totally fascinated by this locale, she decided that she'd make a trek to Nantucket Town in the next day or two and buy a small set of oils and some canvasboards, then come up here and see what she could do. She'd had a few art lessons in school years before, but essentially she was starting from scratch as far as knowledge was concerned. Still, she knew she had a good sense of color, and to experiment would be fun.

Fun. The word lingered and she turned it over in her mind and examined it. Fun, like a lot of other things, had become too much of a stranger to her. She would have to remedy that!

She wished she had brought a blanket and a picnic lunch, because, just now, she felt she could stay for a long while at the top of the bluff enjoying the beauty, the wonderful air, and a solitude which seemed friendly rather than lonely.

After a while though, she could no longer deny the fact that she was hungry again. But this time she went most of the way back to the cottage via a narrow path that ran close to the edge of the high bluff, then cut back to the road past two or three houses now closed for the season.

The red car, she noticed, was gone. She thought about packing up the groceries again and taking them next door before she fixed her lunch, then decided against it.

Later, she told herself.

Time slipped by faster than she had thought it would. After lunch, she found she was very sleepy and, succumbing to impulse, she curled up on the bed, put the patchwork quilt over her, and took a nap.

It was late afternoon when she awakened, feeling marvelously refreshed . . . even ready, she thought humorously, to greet her next-door neighbor in his den.

Again, she packed up the groceries in a heavy paper bag and had just started out the front door when, glancing to the right, she saw him coming down the road from Sankaty Head Light. She was about to call to him, but she hesitated briefly, and the pause proved to be enough.

As she watched, she saw that he was carrying a heavy wooden walking stick which he placed on the ground ahead of him, now and again, as if for assurance. And, she thought bitterly, obviously he needed assurance! There was something decidedly unsteady about his gait. He was almost lurching.

She remembered the way he had tossed down two whiskeys in quick succession the night she had shared his Portuguese soup, and the conclusion that came now was unavoidable.

So, alcohol was at least a part of his problem.

He passed her cottage without even glancing toward it, turning at the small path that led up to his own front door. Tracy watched him negotiate the front step, stumbling slightly as he did so, and then she heard the door slam shut behind him.

Once again, she went back to the kitchen with the bag of groceries, but this time she also was accompanied by an acute sense of disappointment. She had nothing against social drinking; in fact she enjoyed a drink or two in good company herself. One of her best friends had married an alcoholic, though, and his drinking had ruined their marriage. Ever since, Tracy had hated this kind of excess.

Ruefully, she realized that she would have thought better of the arrogant stranger.

Over the weekend, Tracy used up some of the perishables intended to be replacements for the things her neighbor had loaned her, and so Monday she went to the store again to restock them. At this point she determined that no matter *what* condition the mysterious Mr. Medfield might be in she was going to return the groceries.

She also bought some oil paints, brushes, and a few canvasboards before grocery shopping. After getting home she couldn't resist first going up to Sankaty Head

Light and settling down to try to paint for a while, before making the next-door safari.

To her surprise, she actually executed a facsimile of the lighthouse standing atop its sandy bluff, then matched the sky with her paints and stroked in deeper tones for the sea, which, today, seemed a darker blue than ever.

Her first effort, she thought whimsically, certainly would never win a prize. But doing it had been thoroughly enjoyable and, somehow, very fulfilling.

She stashed the painting in a corner of the living room where it could dry without being disturbed. Then, without pausing to think about it further, she loaded up the groceries and walked across to the next-door cottage with them, firmly lifting the brass door knocker and letting it bang down authoritatively.

When, after a time, she received no response she let it drop again, but still there was no answer. Chances were, she concluded, that the dark stranger really was out this time, very possibly with his brunette *amour*. Tracy had no intention of coming back yet again with the groceries, though, so she placed the bag in the center of the high stone stoop where he couldn't fail to see it upon his return.

As the afternoon waned, she found herself waiting for that return. She moved a chair into a position by the living room window which would give her full vantage point of the lane and the cottage next door. Then she found a mystery novel in a corner bookcase that looked intriguing, and settled down to read it. Neither her eyes nor her mind, though, could stay on the printed page.

Finally, as the daylight began to ebb, she found that she was watching for the towering dark figure with considerable anxiety, and she wondered if, when he did come back to his cottage, he was going to be as unsteady on his feet as he had been the other afternoon. She hoped very much that he wouldn't be and that the other afternoon, perhaps, had been an unusual occasion.

This wasn't to prove the case, though. Finally, he loomed into sight, but this time he was coming up the lane from the direction of the village, rather than down it from the lighthouse. As she watched him, Tracy wondered if, perhaps, there was a bar still open in the village she hadn't noticed. It certainly seemed that he had gotten a supply of liquor someplace as his gait was even unsteadier than it had been the other time.

It was darker than it had been the other afternoon. As she peered through a developing veil of amethyst twilight to see him, she noted that he was using the stout walking stick as he had the other day. But even so, his gait seemed more unsteady than ever.

As he neared the high stone stoop, Tracy found that she was holding her breath. Then, to her horror, she saw that he was paying no attention at all to the bag of groceries she had placed on the threshold. In a terrible moment, his foot seemed to catch at them, and in an instant he lay sprawling across the stone surface.

Tracy didn't even pause to think about what she was about to do. She flew out her own front door, covering the distance between the two cottages in a sprint, thankful that she had bought some flat canvas shoes. Otherwise, she might very well have fallen flat on her face herself.

When she reached the stone stoop she was appalled as she stared down at the long figure lying before her. He had tipped over the bag of groceries as he fell, and they had rolled every which way, some of them still on the stoop, some of them scattered across the coarse grass.

The dark-haired stranger, though, was ominously still, and her pulse pounded in her throat as she stared down at him. It was a moment of total terror, and she never before had felt so helpless. She knew that when someone was injured severely it was not wise to move them immediately. But on the other hand she couldn't simply leave him lying like this while she ran back to her phone to summon help, and she couldn't get into his cottage without literally walking over him.

She bent low, scanning his dark head anxiously. Only the right side of his face was visible, and it seemed to her that his skin had turned chalky white. She could see no blood, even though it seemed that he must have struck his head, probably on the edge of the door frame, this knocking him unconscious . . .

Unconscious. Dear God, she hoped that he was only *unconscious!* Tracy found herself searching desperately for signs that he was breathing. She was rewarded when suddenly he shuddered convulsively, then proceeded to mouth an entire string of extremely pungent swear words.

Relief came over her like a tidal wave. Instinctively she reached out her arms intending to help him, but he shrugged her off as he slowly, carefully, struggled to a sitting position.

She bent closer, expecting to smell a strong odor of whiskey, but she didn't. Instead, she found herself fixed, once again, by those galvanizing gray eyes, and he said hoarsely, "Dear Christ! Not you again!"

"Look," Tracy said. "Please. Let me help you!"

"*Help* me?" he echoed scornfully. "Good God, did you put that bag of stuff right in the middle of the doorstep?"

"Yes," she said, miserable. "I wanted to make sure you'd see it."

"*See* it," he told her scornfully. "It's almost dark, woman, and I wasn't expecting a booby trap."

He was touching his head with carefully probing fingers while she eyed him apprehensively. He said bitterly, "I hit my head on the edge of the door, damn it. It's a wonder I didn't split it wide open."

He spoke almost as if he were talking to himself; in fact, Tracy had the distinct impression that her presence was of very little importance to him at the moment, which didn't surprise her. Still, there was something about his expression, a kind of tautness, that she found alarming.

"Look," she said hastily, "I'll go get the car."

"What car?" he demanded irritably.

"My car," she said. "I'll drive you over to the hospital.

He sat straighter, glaring at her. "The hell you will!" he told her flatly.

"Please," she said, "don't be stubborn about this. "You've got to have someone look at that head, and you should probably have X-rays . . ."

"And you should damned well learn to mind your own business," he retorted. "I have no intention of going to the hospital. I can assure you the last thing in the world I need just now is emergency room care."

Stung, she said, "You do know everything about everything, don't you?"

"Enough," he retorted succinctly. "If you want to be useful, you can help me get to my feet. No . . . on the other hand, I'd better do it by myself. You'd probably only fall down on top of me." He scowled up at her. "Do you have any other hidden ambushes around?"

"No," she said, biting the word. "I'll pick up the groceries once you are inside and, believe me, I've no intention of falling on top of you. You can use that stick you were carrying with one hand, and take my arm with the other . . ."

"If you don't mind," he said curtly, "I'll work out my own procedure."

As she watched, he very slowly and carefully maneuvered his position and after what seemed an eternity said, "All right, give me your arm, if you must."

The clasp of his fingers was firm, and to Tracy it was as if an electric switch had been turned on; she could feel a strangely tantalizing current pulsate through her. She swallowed hard. How could someone be so abominable and at the same time possess such magnetism? This she asked herself as he got to his feet, swaying slightly. Impulsively, she started to reach toward him, stopping herself just in time because she knew very well the kind of rebuff he was likely to offer.

To her surprise, though, he said after a moment, "Give me your arm again, will you? I'm not very steady on my feet. Push the front door open, it isn't locked. Look, I'll lean here against the door frame. Go switch on a couple of lights . . . one in the bedroom, too."

There was an authoritative note to his voice; he spoke like someone not only accustomed to giving orders but to being obeyed instantly. For the first time Tracy wondered what he did when he wasn't secreting himself in a Nantucket Island cottage.

There was no time to dwell on this, though. She moved swiftly through the living room, turning on lights as she went. In the bedroom she found a lamp on a table by the bed that cast a soft glow over a blue and white candlewick spread. She quickly drew back the spread from the pillows and fluffed them out, then sped back to the living room to find her neighbor still propped up against the door, his eyes closed, and his face alarmingly pale.

"If you won't go to the hospital I'm going to get a doctor," she told him, trying to insert a note of authority into her voice that couldn't be disputed.

"Don't bother," he snapped. "I *am* a doctor, if that makes you feel any better. Help me into the bedroom!"

A doctor. A doctor, she thought, who must have considerable prestige in his profession because this man was clearly used to getting his own way! But certainly at some point he had forgotten all about so-called bedside manners. In a charm contest he would rate zero.

He leaned heavily on her as they wended their way through the living room. Once in the bedroom, he sprawled out on the bed gratefully and closed his eyes again.

Tracy, looking down at him, was struck by his sheer length and by the underlying effect of power given by those well-formed muscular arms and legs. Weakness, she thought dismally, seemed so alien to him.

Without opening his eyes he said, "You can go home now."

"I'd rather stay here with you," she answered.

The gray eyes flew open, and one dark eyebrow lifted ironically. "What is that supposed to mean?" he demanded.

She flushed. "Only that I don't think you should be alone just now," she insisted stubbornly.

"I'll do my own prescribing, if you don't mind," he told her coolly.

She shook her head. "Look," she said, "I know you seem to think I'm some sort of jinx. You made your feelings toward me very evident, down on the wharf . . ."

"Down on the *wharf?*"

"Yes, have you forgotten?"

"Totally."

"It was the day I came in on the ferry," she said. "You were with a dark-haired woman."

"Oh?"

"Yes. You saw me, and you stared across at me as if . . . as if you hated me."

He had closed his eyes again. He said, almost whimsically, "What a vivid imagination you do have! I didn't even notice you, if, in fact, you're not confusing me with someone else!"

"I am *not* confusing you with anyone else!"

"Then," he told her tantalizingly, "your memory is much better than mine."

She glared at him, exasperated, but before she could speak he said, "Another time, if you don't mind. I'm not in the mood for an argument."

Tracy couldn't help but be contrite at this. "I'm sorry," she said. "Again, all I wanted to do was help you. I mean . . . isn't there something I can get you?"

He moved impatiently, and she saw him wince as he did so. But he only said, "Not a thing."

"Not even a drink?"

He opened his eyes. "What is that supposed to imply?"

"Nothing, really," she stammered. "I just thought you might want a drink."

"Contrary to what you may surmise," he told her coldly, "I was not drunk when I stumbled over your bag of groceries."

"I wasn't inferring . . ." she began, but again he interrupted her.

"There's no need to get into it," he said firmly.

She didn't answer. She had forgotten all about the groceries which were still scattered outside over the step and the ground. "Excuse me," she said. "I'll go pick the things up, then I'll be back."

She left before he could tell her not to bother to come back. She hoped it wouldn't already be too dark to see, because she had forgotten to return the borrowed flashlight which was still back in Aunt Sally's cottage.

Twilight still lingered, though, and Tracy swiftly gathered the spilled items. Only the eggs had been a casualty, but they had fallen onto the grass so it wasn't as bad a mess as it might have been. She found the cardboard carton they had come in and used it as a repository for cracked and shattered shells.

The other things were remarkably intact. Tracy took them to the kitchen and put milk and butter in the refrigerator and a slightly dented loaf of bread on a side counter. Then she placed the tin of coffee she had bought to replace the partially filled tin he had given her next to his coffee container.

She stashed the torn brown paper bag and the egg carton in a trash can, then washed the sticky evidence of fractured eggs from her fingers, drying her hands slowly as she thought of *his* fingers and of his touch upon her arm. It was a treacherous memory, evoking a surprisingly sensuous feeling that made her shiver.

It took effort to seem totally composed as she returned to the bedroom, but she soon saw that it was an effort she hadn't needed to make. He was asleep, his breath rising and falling evenly. A shock of dark hair, which had fallen across his forehead, gave him an unexpected air of defenselessness, making him seem quite vulnerable.

Tracy stood for a long moment looking down at him, unable to restrain a sense of worry because there really could be something wrong with him. It was terrifying to go off and leave him here on his own.

Finally she went back to the kitchen and found some paper and a pencil, and wrote, *"Please* call me if you need anything." She put the message on the table by his bed, tucking the edge of it under the lamp so that there was no danger of it not staying in place.

Through the night, she kept waking at intervals, wondering if she was hearing the phone ring. But with dawn she conceded that this was wishful thinking, and she sighed deeply and turned over and went to sleep.

Chapter Five

The red car was back in front of the house next door the following morning. Tracy could see it from her bedroom window, and the sight spoiled her day.

She couldn't help herself. The thought of her haughty neighbor regaling the brunette with the story of last night's incident rankled, and she could well imagine what a tale he would make out of it. She would take the booby prize in his recounting, she knew. How easy it would be for him to make her seem totally inept!

She had intended to go across to his cottage before noon so that she could check on him herself. She had been wishing that she had curled up on his living room couch so that she would have been nearby in case he needed care during the night.

She knew that head injuries were tricky, and she had heard that doctors were notoriously poor when it came to treating themselves. They also made difficult patients. Her neighbor, she thought wryly, proved the truth of this latter adage. Still, he might be more sensible this morning if he woke up with a throbbing head, perhaps even to the point of agreeing with her that it would be prudent to go to the Nantucket hospital for an X-ray. Tracy had awakened ready to make the trip with him if necessary. Now, the sight of the red car made the idea seem thoroughly superfluous.

She took her paints and went up to the lighthouse

after breakfast, dabbling with different angles and reveling in the beautiful view as much as ever. But the zest was gone and the edge of her enjoyment had dulled, thanks to her recalcitrant neighbor, and she told herself she wished she had never met him.

The more she thought about it, too, the more she couldn't understand his refusal to admit that he literally had glared at her the other day down at the wharf. At least, she had considered it a glare, a hostile stare, especially striking because there had seemed no reason for it.

Didn't he want to admit that she reminded him of someone he knew? As she thought about this, the conclusion was inevitable that whatever memories she invoked in him dealt with a matter he didn't want to talk about.

After lunch she drove over to Nantucket Town, and wandered along the charming, cobblestone streets. The quaint little town was a delight, but, again, the zest had been taken out of exploring all by herself. She found herself wishing she had company.

She noted that there was an old Cary Grant movie playing at the local theater tonight. That, at least, was something to latch onto. Accordingly, she fixed an early supper and drove back across the island in ample time to park and get into the early show.

Cary Grant's physique reminded her of her neighbor's, and so did his dark hair. She decided that she'd made an unfortunate choice when it came to selecting a movie to see because this wasn't doing her any good at all. If anything, she felt lonelier than ever as she left the theater, and this sense of aloneness made it especially startling when she heard a man's voice calling, "Tracy!"

She turned to see Gerry Stanhope coming out of the theater behind her. It was so good to see someone she knew, even as slightly as she knew Gerry, that she gave him the full benefit of one of her very best smiles.

"I was beginning to think I'd imagined you!" he told her, beaming down at her. "I've driven all over the damned island trying to find you. You told me you were staying in a cottage, but you wouldn't believe how many cottages there are on Nantucket, and you never even gave me a clue to the section you were staying in!"

This, she knew guiltily, had been deliberate, but now she smiled up at him and said sincerely, "I'm sorry."

"You should be!" he chided her. "Hey, come on. Let's celebrate and have a drink together."

He took her to the bar at the Jared Coffin House, which was a beautifully restored 1845 mansion. "We'll have to come back for lunch one day," he promised. "The place is full of antiques that make even my aunt envious, and she has more than her share of them. Tracy, what have you been *doing* with yourself?"

"Not much," she admitted. "The cottage I'm living in is over in Sconset. It belongs to a friend of my mother's. I adore it, but I'm just about the only person on the lane and it does get a bit lonesome."

"And to think I've been right at hand, ready to take up every minute of your time," he groaned. "You've developed a touch of color, these few days on the island. It's very becoming. I think the sun has lightened your hair and deepened your eyes."

He had ordered frozen brandy alexanders, and Tracy sipped the delicious drink appreciatively, her sapphire eyes sparkling as she let herself enjoy his compliments. He was attractive, very attractive, she thought, and had a terrifically engaging personality. Briefly, she had a vision of her dark-haired neighbor. How different the two men were!

"How did you get to the theater from Sconset?" Gerry asked her now. "Taxi?"

"No," she said, "I drove."

"Damn," he said. "I wanted to take you home. Did you bring a car across on the ferry with you?"

"No. Aunt Sally—she isn't my aunt, really, but that's what I've always called her—keeps a car at her place, so she left the keys for me." She found herself actually laughing at the memory of something that had been anything but funny at the time. "I wish I'd known where you were," she confessed. "I couldn't get the car started when I arrived, and then when I went to phone for help the phone had been turned off . . ."

"And there I was, more than ready to ride my white horse to your rescue, had I but known," he mocked dolefully. "Tracy, before you disappear into the night again will you promise to have lunch with me tomorrow?"

"I'd love to, Gerry,"

"Great. Now, perhaps, I can relax. No, wait a minute. You'd better give me your phone number and also tell me what hidden little lane you're living on in Siasconset."

She obliged, and when he had written this information on the corner of a paper napkin and tucked it into his pocket he said, "You did mention you'd be here the whole month, didn't you?"

"Yes."

"And we've already lost precious days," he mourned. "I may have to leave before the end of September."

"Oh?"

"I go from here to Washington for briefing, and then to Madrid," he told her. "My last assignment was in Mexico City. I guess they're trying to keep me practicing my Spanish. I'm in the foreign service," he added. "I'll be an attaché at our embassy in Madrid."

"That must be fascinating," she said.

"It has its moments," he conceded, "but few things are totally fascinating, Tracy. My work has a full share of dull moments, and also certain obligations that can become trying. A bachelor is fair prey for all the diplomatic hostesses. I'm expected to escort everyone's sister, daughter, cousin, or old family friend, to say nothing of attending the various local government functions and the affairs at other embassies. It can become downright boring."

"I can imagine."

"My Aunt Emily tells me the solution would be to get married," he told her, grinning. "She says what I need is a 'sold' sign pasted on me, and maybe she's right."

His light greenish eyes were sweeping her with an expression that was a bit too appraising for comfort, but Tracy told herself that she mustn't start leaping to conclusions. She and Gerry Stanhope scarcely knew each other, and although they did seem to have achieved an instant rapport, that was all there was to it, certainly all she wanted there to be to it.

He was a fun person to be with, a delightful and witty companion, and this was exactly what she needed at the moment. She only hoped they could keep it that way.

He suggested another drink but she refused, and they went out together into a cool September night, the dark sky spattered with stars, the moon a silver sickle cutting clean.

Gerry walked with her to her car and lingered to say, "Sure you don't want me to drive behind you back to Sconset? There could be goblins, you know."

"It isn't time for Halloween," she laughed. "No, really, I'll be perfectly all right."

"Okay, then. I'll pick you up at noon tomorrow. If I

can't find your cottage on the first try I'll give you a ring from Sconset Village."

"I'll be ready," she promised him.

She was ready early, as a matter of fact, because she couldn't wait to get away from Scallop Shell Lane for a while. The red car was still parked outside the house next door. The dark stranger hadn't wanted *her* attentions, Tracy thought ruefully, but obviously he was more receptive to having his brunette friend play Florence Nightingale.

Tracy resolved not to think about either of them, but it wasn't easy. When Gerry pulled up in front of the cottage she lost no time in going out to his car.

She was wearing a skirt of deep, rich blue velour, with a gray turtleneck and a snug vest of matching blue material. She had brushed her hair down today and caught it back with a sapphire velvet band that nearly matched her eyes, and the painting excursions to Sankaty Head Light had brought a glow to her skin. Gerry gave a low whistle when he saw her and said, "You get better and better!"

"It's the Nantucket air," she told him. She settled down by him in the car feeling younger and more carefree than she had for a long time. As they passed the cottage next door she found herself wishing that her neighbor might be looking out the window at the moment. Not, she was forced to add reluctantly, that it would make much difference.

To Tracy's surprise, Gerry did not take her to the Jared Coffin House for lunch. Instead, he drove straight up the cobblestoned, elm-shaded Main Street in Nantucket Town. Then he curved left past the Pacific Bank building to continue on past several magnificent mansions which, he told her, had been built by whaling captains who had made their fortunes during the years of Nantucket's greatest glory.

He stopped at a brick mansion with a white-pillared entrance and turned to Tracy, his eyes sparkling mischievously. "I told my Aunt Emily you work with antiques," he confessed, "and she can't wait to meet you!"

There was an instant admiration on both sides between Mrs. Emily Stanhope and Tracy. The charming white-haired woman was pleased by Tracy's knowledge and appreciation of the beautiful glass and china objets d'art that filled her house. She graciously took her on what she called "the grand tour," regaling her with tales of Nantucket's whaling days as she showed her ginger jars, beautifully carved fans, jade figurines, and a string of perfectly matched Oriental pearls. All of her possessions had been brought back by her great grandfather to the wife he had been forced to leave for years at a time during the course of his voyages in search of sperm whales.

Mrs. Stanhope's great-grandfather had also been an artist in his own right. Like many other seamen of the day, he had spent lonely hours aboard ship carving whale's teeth with intricate designs which later were filled in with India ink, the blackness offering a stark contrast to the pale ivory surface. Among other things, he had made a filigreed ivory letter opener stenciled with the design of his own ship. There was a pie wheel also wrought from a whale's tooth, with which his wife could crimp the edges of her pastry strips when she made his favorite pie from Nantucket blueberries.

Even the table setting at lunch was an antique lover's delight. Mrs. Stanhope had decided to use her New England pineapple goblets today, made at the height of the famous Sandwich Glass Factory's fame. She explained that her silver came from the old Pairpoint

Manufacturing Company in New Bedford, while her china was hand-painted Limoges. Her great-grandmother had painted the china on "blanks" brought from France. Later, the china had been "fired" so that the designs became permanent.

During lunch, the older woman asked Tracy about herself. When Tracy said that she was occupying Sally Thorndyke's cottage a further accord was established. The two women had known each other for years, and now Emily Stanhope said, "Sally should have told me you were coming so I could look in on you."

"I didn't make up my mind until she was almost ready to leave for Europe," Tracy said, in defense of her mother's friend. "Otherwise, I'm sure she would have."

Mollified, Mrs. Stanhope went back to talking about antiques and about Nantucket and the whaling days.

It was late afternoon when Tracy finally said she had better be going. She left only after making a firm promise that she would come to visit Mrs. Stanhope again.

As they were driving back across the island toward Siasconset, Gerry said, "I knew you were a charmer but I didn't realize how *much* of a charmer you can be! You've mesmerized my aunt."

"She's a delightful person," Tracy said sincerely.

"She's also a difficult person to get to know, ordinarily," Gerry told her. "Oh, I'm not saying that Aunt Emily is a snob, but she *is* something of a grande dame. She can be pretty unapproachable."

"I didn't find her so."

"No, I realize that," Gerry said, his tone more serious than it usually was.

Tracy felt a brief twinge of discomfort. She didn't want Gerry getting heavy about things and much preferred him when he was using the light touch at which he was so adept. She switched the subject away from the personal, saying, "Your aunt lives in a regular treasure house."

"Yes, she does, doesn't she? She has an apartment in New York where she spends a good bit of the winter, but it's relatively contemporary. She keeps the things she really values here on Nantucket because it's such a perfect setting for them, and she loves the island. She was a Folger before she married my uncle; that's an old Nantucket family. Some of the things she has came down from my family but, as she told you, lots of them came from hers. I've never been too much for antiques myself, but when she weaves them into history and talks about the whaling days I have to admit it gets pretty fascinating."

"She has no children?" Tracy asked.

"She had one son who was a navy officer, and was killed in the line of duty," Gerry said soberly. "Now I'm her closest relative, as she is mine. I'm an only child, and my parents died when I was quite young . . ."

"I'm an only child, too," Tracy told him.

"Were you lonely?"

"No, not really."

"Neither was I," he said, and flashed a smile across at her. "Perhaps neither of us fit the general concept of only children."

"You mean being spoiled, self-centered, all of that?" she asked, smiling in return. "No, I don't think we do!"

It was impossible simply to dismiss Gerry at the cottage door. "Would you like a drink?" Tracy suggested. "I'm afraid all I have to offer is sherry, but . . ."

"Thanks, not this time," he told her, to her relief. "I promised Aunt Emily I'd go to dinner with her tonight at an old friend's house. It's going to be boring as hell, but I wouldn't hurt her feelings for the world by refusing."

He had come around to her side of the car and he stood looking down at her, his expression more tender than she wanted it to be. "I'll call you in the morning," he told her, then bent and kissed her lightly on the lips. "Take care," he added.

It was drizzling the next day and toward midmorning Tracy decided to make a hearty pot-au-feu. Her intention was to fill the container that had held the Portuguese soup with it, then take it across to the other cottage.

The red car still had been parked out in front when she had returned with Gerry the afternoon before, but it had left shortly thereafter and had not returned.

Tracy soon found that she lacked three or four ingredients for her specialty stew, so she drove across to the market in Nantucket Town to get them. The recipe was one that had to cook a long while, too, and it was late afternoon before she was satisfied that the flavors had "merged" as they should.

By then the sun was out again, a huge tangerine orb descending toward the west, spilling molten gold over the cottages along Scallop Shell Lane.

Tracy had a moment of trepidation before she lifted the brass knocker. She wondered if it would ever be possible to confront her neighbor without hesitation, without wondering how she was going to be received.

But she let the knocker bang, waited, let it bang again, and decided that this sort of response was getting to be a habit.

It was possible, of course, that he had gone off somewhere with the brunette in her red car. Or, that he had simply taken advantage of the change in the day's weather to get out of the house for a time.

Tracy hesitated. She had no intention of leaving anything on his stoop again, but she also didn't want to take the pot-au-feu back with her. Gerry had called early in the afternoon, having missed her in the morning while she was shopping. She had accepted his invitation to go for dinner at the Jared Coffin House, and to a late show at the movies. He was to call for her at seven and she wanted to bathe and take her time about dressing. This meant it was unlikely she'd have the opportunity to make a return trek until tomorrow, and who knew whether or not her neighbor would be home then?

Tentatively, she turned the doorknob and it yielded to her touch. Inside it was dim. She was at once certain he wasn't home, even though she called out "Hello" once, and then again to be absolutely sure.

Feeling like a true trespasser, she made her way out to the kitchen, and put the pot-au-feu on the counter. He should recognize the container, she thought, and so would know where it had come from.

She couldn't resist wandering as far as his bedroom door. There was the chance that the head injury might have been more severe than he had thought it was, and he might still be resting. The bed, however, was unoccupied, but he had not bothered to make it. The sheets and blankets were rumpled, the blue and white candlestick spread had been thrown back, and the imprint of his head still clearly marked the pillow. As she looked at it, Tracy swallowed hard, remembering much too vividly the contours of that dark head and the disarming lock of hair that had fallen across his forehead as he slept.

On her way back through the living room, her attention was drawn to the record player and the stack of records at its side. She loved music and now she wondered if their tastes were similar. Curious, she approached the record stack, lifted the top one, and was momentarily stunned. To her astonishment she saw that it was a "talking record" that had been made especially for the blind.

Swiftly, she scanned the other records. There were two Mozarts, some Beethoven, and the César Franck symphony, which happened to be one of her favorites. But most of the records were "talking records," oral versions of classics, plus a couple of fairly contemporary nonfiction books.

Records for the blind! Tracy stood very still, shocked by her discovery. Now she remembered a whole variety of things that gave credence to the thought that there was something wrong with her neighbor's eyesight.

She remembered the first time she had seen him walking down from Sankaty Light, and had thought he was drunk. Thinking back, she realized that something about his walk and his use of the stout walking stick had been nagging her all along, something about his stance. There had been an odd erectness to his shoulders as he stumbled along, using the stick as his guide; a blind man's gait.

When he had tripped over the grocery bag, she had again assumed he had had too much to drink. Now she wondered if it actually was possible that he hadn't even seen it? And, could it possibly be true that he hadn't seen *her* at the dock? That the bitter, hostile expression on his face hadn't been directed toward her at all?

She shook her head. This didn't make sense. There were any number of other indications that he *could* see. Puzzled, she was pondering this as the front door swung open so suddenly that she nearly gasped aloud.

Her neighbor stood silhouetted on the threshold looking, at the moment, larger than life. There was something so menacing about his shadowed figure that involuntarily Tracy shrank back, her hand knockin ashtray on the nearby table as she did so so that it clattered.

At once he rasped sharply, "Who is it?" and she stared across the intervening space between them, her sense of apprehension and shock deepening.

"Can't you *see* me?" she demanded shakily.

By way of answer he strode across the room, coming to stand so close beside her that she felt as if his silver gray eyes were boring through her.

"You're damned right I can see you!" he said contemptuously. "What are you doing here this time? How much of a message will it take to make you realize I want you to leave me alone?"

Tracy felt her throat thicken. "I'm sorry," she said abjectly.

"My God," he said, "are you *always* sorry about something?"

"No," she said. "I . . . that is, I had a feeling for just a moment, as you were standing in the doorway, that you might be . . . blind."

"I've already commented on your imagination," he retorted coldly. "It seems as if there is no limit to it. I can assure you I am not blind. Obviously I can see you, and yes, I know that you're blonde and beautiful and that you have big, hungry eyes. Is that what you want—to be looked at, to be admired? Or do you want more than that?"

Before she could answer she felt his strong arms about her, drawing her to him like relentless tentacles. His lips were equally demanding. There was pure sa— —y to his kiss as he crushed them down upon — —ing her so that she wanted to cry out from the — —orching pain. But he had captured her — — could make no sound. A searing flame — —, shattering in its intensity, as he drew — —e was pressed firmly against his hard, masculine body. Then, as he continued to kiss her punishingly, she realized that he was becoming as aroused himself as he was arousing her; the evidence of this could not be denied.

His closeness, the feel of him, swept aside her restraint. She felt as if she had no volition of her own as she was cradled against him, her arms rising to entwine themselves around his neck, one hand moving upward, the fingers of it becoming enmeshed in his thick, dark hair. His kisses still hurt, but now there was an ecstasy to the pain. She parted her lips so that he could explore her mouth, her hands moving over him and her body moving with them as she swayed against him . . .

It was he who brought the embrace to an end, thrusting her away so fiercely that she stumbled and nearly fell. She stared at him, shaken, her breath coming in gasps. A new kind of pain, a pain of pure frustration, came to take over in the wake of passion.

He was blazing with fury, and she recoiled from the whip of his voice when he said hoarsely, "Get the hell out of here!"

Ben Devlin was the first man who had ever made her feel cheap. Now there was a second one, and nothing he could have said or done could have hurt her more.

She flew out of the door, going straight to the bedroom at the cottage. She threw herself on the bed, her eyes hot with tears that couldn't be shed, her body burning with outrage and humiliation.

For a long time she lay there, aflame with hatred for the dark, arrogant, abusive stranger. Then she forced herself to get up because Gerry would be coming soon. It was too late to phone and postpone their date but the evening had been spoiled.

As she and Gerry sat across from each other at dinner in the exquisitely furnished dining room of the

Jared Coffin House, Tracy mused to herself that there must be something of the actress in every woman. She had been putting up a front all evening and evidently she had fooled Gerry thus far.

It was relatively easy to put other thoughts aside when in his company. He was entertaining and devoted his attentions entirely to her. She had worn a dress tonight of a soft, sand-colored material with a gold belt clasped around her slender waist that echoed the sheen of her hair, worn long around her shoulders. She had accented her eyes with turquoise shadow, and she was wearing an antique turquoise and gold necklace and matching earrings, both gifts from Florence.

After a time, she had begun to think about her neighbor more rationally, and over demitasses she told Gerry a little bit about him, being careful what she said. She described him as a man entirely intent on maintaining his privacy. In fact, she added, he seemed a rather hostile person, and she spoke of his reluctance to let her use his phone when hers hadn't worked.

Gerry grinned. "He must be a woman hater," he observed, and added, "Thank God for that." Then he said, more seriously, "I'll ask Aunt Emily if she knows who owns the cottage he's in. I think we should know who your next-door neighbor is. I don't like the idea of your being alone on the lane with just a solitary man in the vicinity."

"He's not interested in me, Gerry," Tracy said, and there was no need to feign anything about *that* statement. "I promise you he couldn't care less about having me around."

"More fool he, then," Gerry said, his eyes lingering upon her with an ardor she found disquieting.

Gerry was biding his time, though. Again, when he took her home, he was satisfied with a brief good-night kiss, but she suspected that this was a temporary interlude. Gerry had been trained in the ways of diplomacy, she thought wryly, and he was using that training. He was charting his course of action slowly, with deliberate intent and that intent, she sensed, was far more serious than she wished it were.

It was too bad, she thought as she went to bed that night, that she couldn't have managed to fall in love with Gerry. Marriage to him would bring the excitement of travel, of going to live in new and frequently exotic places. Gerry was the sort of man who would make a good husband. He'd had a long term bachelorhood, and although he looked younger, he had told her that he was almost thirty. Once men like Gerry decided to settle down they were more than ready for a life of domesticity and relative tranquillity.

Tracy had little doubt that any decision Gerry was making toward matrimony had been prompted to an extent by his aunt. Perhaps in part because of his aunt's endorsement—she knew he valued Emily Stanhope's opinion—she, Tracy, was undoubtedly his prime candidate at the moment.

Prime candidate. That was a strange way of thinking about becoming a man's fiancée and subsequently his wife, she told herself sleepily. But Gerry, despite his exuberance, would not be impulsive about such a matter as choosing a wife. She already knew him well enough to be certain of that.

She went to sleep dreaming about Gerry, imagining that she was in his arms and that he was raining kisses on her mouth. But then, in the inexplicable way dreams have of progressing, it became her neighbor who was holding her, and she moaned softly. In fantasy, his kiss was as savage as it had been in reality.

Chapter Six

Gerry phoned the next morning to say that his aunt had told him the cottage next to Sally Thorndyke's had been owned by a Boston family for years, but generally was used only in the summer.

"Maybe your neighbor knows the people and either borrowed or rented the place from them," Gerry conjectured. "I've been thinking about this, Tracy. Why don't I come out this afternoon and we'll go over together and pay a call on him? I'd like to find out more about him since you're living there alone."

The last thing Tracy wanted to do was to pay a neighborly call in Gerry's company! She said quickly, "He has a guest, Gerry. I don't think it would be a good time."

She didn't like to lie, but she consoled herself that although this was not quite truth, it was also not quite fiction. Glancing through the window, she could see that the red car was not in evidence today, but that didn't mean it might not be coming back. She couldn't imagine walking in on the mysterious Mr. Medfield and the brunette, with or without Gerry along for moral support!

Gerry went on to say that his aunt wished to invite Tracy for dinner the following night, and she accepted. When he started to outline plans for the balance of the day ahead, though, she drew back.

"I really want to do a bit of housework around here," she told him, "and I need to wash my hair, and . . ."

"Okay," he said agreeably, "how about dinner tonight, then? I understand the Chanticleer is still open and I think you'd like it. I'll check first, of course."

She sidestepped this, and she sensed his disappointment as he hung up.

She did do some housework over the morning, dusting and sweeping and mopping the kitchen floor. It was impossible not to glance out the windows at the cottage next door as she worked, and she noticed that Tim Sousa's pickup truck was out front for quite awhile. Later in the morning it was gone, but by lunchtime it was back again, and Tracy saw Tim carrying bags of groceries into the cottage. So, Tim did the shopping for her neighbor, among other things. It seemed strange to her that someone would come out to this section of Nantucket, especially at this season of the year, without a car. But then there were so many strange things about her neighbor that this became just another item to add to the list.

It had been a sunny morning, but by early afternoon it clouded over and soon rain began to spatter against the windowpanes. Tracy had intended to take her paints and go for a walk, seeking a stretch of moors, or one of many other eye-catching scenes that she could try to paint.

Instead, she picked up the mystery novel she had been reading sporadically and settled down in a comfortable armchair. A sense of loneliness soon swept over her, though, augmented by the grayness of the day, and she was giving thought to making a fire, if only for its cheery effect, when the phone rang.

She expected to hear Gerry at the other end of the wire. But this was a different masculine voice, deeper, with a crispness to the words that made it instantly identifiable to her. Even before he said, "This is Guy Medfield, Miss Graham," she found that her hands were shaking, the phone receiver wobbling between her fingers.

Guy Medfield. It seemed nothing short of ridiculous that it was the first time she had ever heard his full name. But it was even more surprising to realize that he had called her by hers.

"How do you know who I am?" she asked him sharply.

He chuckled. "An obliging friend at the telephone company," he confessed. "Miss Tracy Graham, isn't it?"

"Yes."

He hesitated, then said slowly, "I've an apology to make . . . and I'm afraid I'm not very good at saying, 'I'm sorry.'"

"Oh?"

"I didn't find the pot-au-feu you left for quite awhile, the other day," he said. "I had it for dinner, though, and it was delicious. It was kind of you to bring it over."

"It was intended as a return for the soup you gave me," she told him coolly. "I've been intending to get some firewood so I can return the wood you sent over, too."

"That's not necessary."

"I'd prefer to return it."

"I *am* an ogre in your book, I see," he said, with only a faint hint of mockery lacing the words. "I can't blame you, I . . ."

Again, there was that note of hesitation, and it had about it a quality that made her hold her breath. Then he said, "Look, do you have raingear with you?"

"Yes. Why?"

"I wish you'd come over and have a drink with me.

As I've said, I owe you an apology—more than one apology, actually. I think I owe you an explanation as well."

"You don't owe me anything, Mr. Medfield. Or, should I say, Dr. Medfield?"

He ignored this. "Come anyway, will you?" he asked her.

It was an invitation she couldn't resist. She quickly flicked a brush over her hair, added lipstick, and then touched *L'Air du Temps* to her throat and the back of her wrists. Then she slipped into the bright orange hooded slicker she was now glad she had brought with her.

He was waiting at the door for her and helped her off with her raincoat, spreading it out over a chair back to dry. As she watched him, Tracy again felt a surge of feeling that was almost a physical pain; it twisted like a coil, inside her chest.

Guy Medfield was disconcertingly handsome today in snug fitting brown corduroys and a beige turtleneck sweater. She suspected that he had shaved not long before, and the drifting scent of his woodsy after-shave lotion only added to her headiness.

He already had a fire going, and she saw that he had placed a table in front of it. A platter of cheese and crackers, plus the makings for drinks had been set out.

There was an armchair facing the fire on either side of the table, and he said, "Sit down, won't you?" motioning to one of the chairs. Then, still standing himself, he added, "I'm going to ask you to do the drink honors, if you don't mind. I'm not much good at measuring things out without spilling them these days."

She glanced up in surprise to find him staring at her intently, and his mouth curved in a rueful smile. "You were right, Tracy," he said. "My sight leaves a great deal to be desired. I'm recouping from eye surgery, and it still will be awhile before I get back my peripheral vision. So far, I can see clearly only if something is right in front of me—front center, I guess you'd say—and not too far away. It will all come back, of course, but, I'm not the most patient person in the world. Also, where you are concerned, it would seem I've become a victim of my own damned stubborn pride."

As he spoke, he sat down in the chair opposite her.

She said slowly, "Then you really didn't see the bag of groceries?"

"No," he admitted wryly. "I very definitely didn't see the bag of groceries."

"And you really didn't see me down at the wharf?"

"Do you think I would have forgotten so easily if I had?" he countered.

She felt herself flushing, but she managed to keep her voice steady as she said, "Why didn't you tell me you had an eye problem?"

"I suppose you could call it a display of pure masculine ego of the worst kind," he admitted. "When I came out here, I thought I'd be alone. This place has been in my family for years; now, my sister and I own it jointly. I get over as often as I can in the summer, and sometimes I manage a few fall weekends. I've always liked the fall best, because there are times when I enjoy being alone. This year, I especially wanted to be alone. My program right now is essentially one of rest, not using my eyes any more than is necessary, and avoiding bright light, which is why I take my walks so late in the afternoon, or on cloudy days. I expected to be by myself on the lane, so it was a jolt when I found there would be someone staying right next door . . ."

"And then I became an intruder," she said.

"Not exactly," he told her. "I think it would be more accurate to say that I became a damned fool. You can't imagine the curve you threw me when you came over here and asked me to help you start your car. You could as well have asked me to move a mountain single-handed, and of course, I should have had the guts to tell you so, but I didn't. Men and cars have a kind of affinity, I suppose. Almost any male thinks he can triumph over a motor, and I'm as guilty as the rest. I've been tinkering with car engines since I was a kid, like most American boys. So, if you had tried, you couldn't have thought up a request that could have been so ego-damaging."

He shook his head. "You don't have to say it," he told her. "I know I behaved like a rude idiot, and I've wished ever since that we could repeat the whole scene. Perhaps I wouldn't have reacted so intensely if you hadn't been young and beautiful . . ."

"Oh, please," she protested.

"No," he said quickly, "I knew immediately that you were young and beautiful, call it a seventh sense, if you like. It's true that other senses come to compensate when one is damaged. Anyway, I've since verified at close range that I was right."

Before she could comment, he added, "I admit I'm overly touchy about my poor eyesight. Thank God this kind of helplessness is only temporary because I also admit I've loathed every minute of it. Now, could we get on to something else?"

He smiled, and her heart skipped not one but several beats. Those gray eyes, she found, could be as soft as spring's first pussy willows, and his smile lightened a face that was apt to be almost stern in repose. She imagined that he must be in his mid-thirties, but he looked younger when he smiled; almost as young as he had looked while asleep with that lock of dark hair straggling over his forehead.

"How about fixing us both a drink?" he suggested. "I have only Scotch, I hope that's all right."

"It's fine," she told him. She put ice into glasses, added whiskey and poured in soda.

As she passed his drink to him, she asked, "Have you had to give up your practice?"

"Temporarily, yes," he said, then raised his glass. "To a better understanding," he suggested.

He leaned back in his chair, and after a moment he said, "I'm a surgeon, so obviously I wouldn't be of much use to patients at the moment. I'm on the staff of Commonwealth Medical Center in Boston, but they've given me a leave of absence for as long as I may need it." He frowned. "There's a slim chance my vision may not be good enough again for surgery," he admitted. "I've been thinking about the future, in the event this proves to be the case. There are several other fields of medicine I could go into and, as it happens, I have a built-in office. My father was a physician and he practiced in a wing of our house in Chestnut Hill, just outside Boston . . ."

"I know Boston," she told him.

"Do you? Do you live there?"

"Yes, I was born in Milton, as a matter of fact. Now I live with a friend in the Beacon Hill area."

"A friend?"

"She owns the antique shop I work in," Tracy explained. "She was a friend of my mother's and she gave me a job when . . . when I needed one."

He laughed. "I was afraid that you were going to tell me your roommate was male," he confessed. "That's pretty much the norm for people your age."

"Come now," she said, "you're not that much older than I am."

"Considerably," he informed her. "I'm thirty-six. What are you? About twenty-one?"

"Hardly," she laughed. "I'm twenty-six."

"It makes a ten-year gap."

"Not exactly a chasm!"

"I'm glad you feel that way about it. There is a man friend though, isn't there, even though you indicated to me that you were off men?"

"That depends upon your definition of 'friend.'"

"Well, Tim Sousa tells me you've been going around with a man here on the island," he reported to her astonishment.

"What a grapevine!" she exclaimed. "I can't believe it!"

"Yankees are born with built-in curiosity," he chuckled. "The communications system in most New England communities beats anything the African drums could ever conjure up."

"So," she said, "you found out my name from the telephone company, and you found out about Gerry from Tim Sousa . . ."

"His name is Gerry?"

"I'm surprised you don't already know that. Yes, his name is Gerry Stanhope and he's visiting an aunt who lives here on the island. She knows Aunt Sally Thorndyke."

"Convenient," Guy said, with just a touch of sarcasm.

"I met Gerry on the boat coming over here," Tracy told him. "Then we ran into each other at the movies the other night . . ."

She stopped short. There was no reason, no reason at all, why she had to make explanations about Gerry or anyone else to Guy Medfield.

"Well," he said, his humor returning, "obviously you struck it off with him better than you did with me!"

"The reason I didn't strike it off with you," she began hotly, "was because . . ."

"I know," he interrupted. "Because I acted like a total boor. We've already been through that."

He rose and put another log on the fire. It was only when one knew about his eye problem that it became apparent he was relying more on his sense of touch than on his sight. She could see that now. She felt a twinge of compassion for him. He must be at the peak of his career or close to it, she thought. How galling to be forced to give up his work, if only temporarily.

He sat down again, and his fingers were careful as they reached to touch the glass on the table between them. She yearned to help him, but had the sense to restrain herself. She didn't have to be told to realize that this handsome, dark-haired doctor would have no wish for pity. She could imagine the way he would castigate her if she were overly solicitous.

"Tracy," he said suddenly.

"Yes?"

As if he were able to read her mind, he said, "Stop feeling sorry for me!"

"I wasn't . . . " she began.

"Yes, you were," he contradicted. "You might realize it was largely because I didn't want that kind of sympathy that I tried to convince you there was nothing wrong with my eyes."

"Don't you think you're too sensitive?"

"Yes," he admitted, "I *am* too sensitive. This came upon me very quickly. I had no opportunity to prepare myself for it, to compensate."

"Do you want to tell me how it happened?"

His lips twisted. "You're not a psychologist in disguise, are you?" he teased her.

"Far from it!"

"Well," he said, "I'll tell you, but I'll make it brief. I have a married sister who lives in Wellesley and has two young sons. Last Thanksgiving I had dinner at her house, and afterwards the boys and I went outside and kicked a football around for a time. One of the kids sent off what we'll call a misplaced kick. The ball hit me in the head, and there was considerable optic damage as a result."

He was staring into the flames as he spoke, twisting the glass, still half full of whiskey and soda, around in his fingers. Tracy saw a muscle twitch at the side of his jaw, and she could imagine that thinking back must be a nightmare to him.

"For a time," he continued, "they were afraid I would be blinded permanently. But I had an excellent ophthalmological surgeon, with the result that now the prognosis is extremely positive. It's just a long haul, that's all."

The date he had mentioned suddenly clicked with her. "You mean that all of this happened to you nearly a year ago," she demanded.

"No, nine and a half months ago, to be more exact," he corrected her.

She said softly, "It must seem like nine and a half years to you."

"Nine and a half centuries, at times," he said grimly, and then sat up straighter, forcing a smile. "You're encouraging me to cry on your shoulder," he accused her. "Not that it wouldn't be a lovely shoulder to cry on, but let's talk about something else. Are you finding Nantucket lonely, or enjoyable?"

"Sometimes one, sometimes the other," she found herself telling him honestly.

"Your friend Gerry fills in some of the time, I take it?"

"Yes. I've been filling in a fair amount of it myself by trying to do some painting. I've always wanted to dabble in oils. I've been trying to capture Sankaty Head Light, among other things. What about you? Isn't it lonely for you, here?"

The memory of the brunette came to her only after

she had spoken, and she could have bitten her tongue. But he said only, "I suppose I'm used to being alone a good bit of the time. My mother died when my sister was born, and I was only four at the time. My father was considerably older than my mother and he never remarried. I was sent away to school at a fairly early age, as was my sister. We used to go back to the house on Chestnut Hill for holidays like Christmas, but I can't say they were very festive occasions. My father was always busy with his practice, and he had become something of a recluse. Once we were old enough, my sister and I went in our own directions, we had our own friends. My father died four years ago. My sister was already married, of course. I inherited the Chestnut Hill house, I have a housekeeper, but ordinarily my own schedule is pretty demanding so I limit my social life to a minimum."

"Haven't you ever married?"

"Yes," he said slowly. "I married when I was in my first year of surgical residency. The girl I chose was not cut out to be a surgeon's wife, though. She couldn't accept the kind of a life I had to lead, the schedule I had to keep. Finally, when I was on call and couldn't get home nights she began going out with other men, and before too long she asked me for a divorce. She married a man who became a banker, and they moved to San Francisco. I believe she has three children now, and is quite a society matron.

"After that experience," he said, "I wasn't about to drift off into the sea of matrimony again. I prefer my involvements to be structured on a completely temporary basis." He paused. "What about you?" he asked.

"I prefer not to be involved at all!"

"Would that indicate that you've been burned?"

"I suppose it might."

"Look," he said lazily, "you've gotten me to do my

share of confessing. Why don't you return the compliment?"

"There's not that much to confess."

"You've admitted there was a man."

"Yes," she said, "there was a man. He was a lawyer in the firm where I worked as a secretary, and we were very close for . . . for quite a long time. He had been wanting us to take an apartment together, but I'd held off because I lived with my father in our house in Milton. Since my mother died a few years ago my father had seemed to need me . . ."

"Then you found he didn't?" Guy Medfield asked discerningly.

"Yes."

"He met another woman?"

"Yes."

"A younger woman, I presume?"

"Do you have a crystal ball?"

"Would that I did!" he said ironically. "No. It's a rather stereotyped situation, that's all."

"I suppose everything about my life would seem stereotyped to someone like you," she said bitterly.

"Tracy, Tracy, don't jump to conclusions," he chided her softly. "Life patterns do sometimes seem to come in clichés, but that doesn't make them any easier to bear when the clichés happen to us. How about making me another drink, and then telling me about your father and your stepmother and the man in your life who let you down."

To her surprise, she did exactly this. She poured out her feelings about Ben, and about her father and Elise and their marriage in a way she had never done before, not even to Florence. She felt curiously purged once she was finished.

She had made herself a second drink midway through her discourse. Now she sipped it, then said, "If you don't go back to surgery, you could always take up psychiatry!"

"Thank you, no," he told her, with a hint of amusement. "For one thing, I'd have to put in some pretty long study hours in order to qualify, and for another thing I was never cut out to be a shrink."

"You're a good listener."

His left eyebrow shot upward. "Only when I'm interested in the subject," he told her.

It was raining harder. They could hear the staccato rhythm on the roof and it seemed to intensify the snugness of the low-ceilinged cottage room, warm with the glowing fire on the hearth.

Tracy had no wish to leave, and she hoped he might suggest they fix some supper together, but he didn't. So, finally, she told him she'd better be getting along.

He went with her to the door, holding her raincoat for her, and his hands lingered on her shoulders once she had slipped it on.

Then he turned her around to face him and said, his voice low, "When you came here before it was late in the afternoon. The sun was going down behind you as you stood in the doorway, and you seemed to me like a lovely golden shadow . . ."

His gray eyes darkened as he looked at her, and his hands tightened. But his kiss, when it came, was gentle. There was no savagery this time, there was, instead, a depth of feeling that evoked an entirely new emotion in her, something deeper, something different than she had ever experienced before.

Sensual, yes. She could not be touched by him without arousing *that* kind of feeling, without knowing desire in its most total definition. But *this* went beyond either desire or sensuality, plunging into something so basic that she knew everything within her, on every level of her being, was in danger of becoming involved.

She was shaken as she walked back to the cottage, lifting her face to let the cool, liquid raindrops touch the lips he had just possessed. Even as she felt herself drenched by crystal moisture, though, she knew that neither rain, nor anything else, could ever wash away Guy Medfield from her mind or, even more importantly, her heart.

Chapter Seven

It was difficult to be a good dinner guest when one's mind was eight miles away on the opposite side of an island. Emily Stanhope was a charming hostess, and her conversation was by no means limited to antiques and tales of old Nantucket. She was widely traveled and had many interests. She had kept up with the times; although she was close to seventy there was nothing "elderly" about her interests.

Still, Tracy found it hard to concentrate on the dinner talk until Guy Medfield's name came into the conversation, and then she was at once alert.

"I've met your neighbor," Mrs. Stanhope volunteered, as they lingered over a delicious blueberry cobbler. "I know his sister better, though, she comes here more frequently in the summer. Dr. Medfield's work seems to keep him close to Boston much of the time."

Gerry's eyebrows rose sharply. "Dr. Medfield?" he demanded.

"Tracy's neighbor is a famous Boston surgeon," his aunt explained. "He suffered an eye injury last fall, however, and I gather he's had a bad time of it. Patricia—his sister—was here with her boys during July, and she was quite worried about him. He'd had surgery, but he didn't seem to be responding as well as he should."

LOVE'S GOLDEN SHADOW

"Do you mean he's blind?" Gerry asked bluntly.

"No, not blind," Mrs. Stanhope said. "His vision has been severely impaired, though. He may not be able to operate again. Patricia said that he was very depressed because of this. She wanted him to come and convalesce in her home in Wellesley, but she says he's very stubborn. He wouldn't consider it."

At the word "stubborn," an involuntary smile caught the corners of Tracy's mouth. Stubborn, she decided, was a word that suited Guy!

Mrs. Stanhope said, "You probably know more about him than we do, Tracy. That is, you *have* met him, haven't you?"

"She's met him all right," Gerry interposed. "He was rude as hell to her the first day she came to the island. He . . ."

"That's not exactly so," Tracy interrupted, and Gerry scowled at her.

"It's the way you told it to me," he pointed out.

"I know. But I didn't realize then that Guy does have a problem with his eyes. When he explained, it made everything seem different."

Tracy could tell by the expression on Gerry's face that her use of her neighbor's first name had not gone unnoticed. He said darkly, "You seem to have come to know him better since the last time you spoke to me about him."

"He asked me over for a drink yesterday," she admitted.

"And you went over there *alone?*" Gerry demanded.

His aunt laughed indulgently. "Darling, which century are you living in?" she asked him.

"I don't think that's very funny," he retorted. "Tracy didn't even know who the man was when she went over there."

"Yes, I did," she contradicted him. "At least, I knew

he was a doctor. Tim Sousa, a boy who works for him, told me that."

"Are doctors necessarily saints?" Gerry asked coldly.

"Of course not. But . . ."

"I don't think that you should have gone by yourself," Gerry insisted stubbornly.

Mrs. Stanhope was viewing her nephew quizzically, but her next question was addressed to Tracy. "Since you've seen Dr. Medfield," she said, "perhaps you can tell us how he really is?"

"He's still recouping," Tracy said. "His vision remains limited, but he sees well enough to get around and I gather it's improving steadily. In fact he hopes to be able to return to surgery again."

"I'm delighted to hear that," Mrs. Stanhope said. "Patricia idolizes her brother, and she has been very upset by all this."

Tracy wondered if Emily Stanhope knew that it was one of Patricia's children who had caused Guy's accident, inadvertently of course. But she was not about to offer this piece of information.

"It would be a shame to have the talents of someone like Guy Medfield lost to the world when they are so badly needed," Mrs. Stanhope continued. "Patricia says he is a completely dedicated doctor, and some of the work he has done evidently has been nothing short of miraculous."

"I imagine he's made a fortune on his miracles," Gerry observed bitterly.

For a moment, Tracy thought that his aunt was going to chastise him, but she only said, "Dr. Medfield didn't need to make a fortune, Gerry. His parents both came from wealthy families. He and his sister inherited a great deal of money from his mother's estate which was held in trust for them until they were old enough to handle it wisely. They received a second substantial inheritance when their father died a few years ago. So money has not been a motivation in his career."

"I stand corrected," Gerry said, the note of sarcasm in his voice unlike him. "Now, do you suppose we could talk about something else?"

The balance of the evening passed pleasantly enough, but Gerry was silent on the drive back to Siasconset. Once they had parked in front of the cottage he sat behind the wheel, looking more thoughtful than Tracy had ever seen him look before.

He turned to say to her, "Aren't you going to offer me some of your sherry?"

She hesitated knowing very well that this wasn't the time to be alone with Gerry. She didn't want to be put in the position of having to repulse him either physically or verbally, and she sighed, a deep sigh that had an unhappy echo about it.

"May I give you a rain check?" she countered.

"You're tired? You have a headache?" he asked, that edge of sarcasm back again.

"I *am* rather tired, Gerry."

"And you don't want to be alone with me?"

"Not tonight," she said honestly.

Silence grew between them. Then he said, "All right, Tracy. I won't push it. Not tonight. But before very much longer you and I are going to have to have a serious talk."

He got out of the car to come around and open the door on her side for her. Tonight he didn't attempt to kiss her even lightly. She knew, as she let herself into the cottage, that he was still standing at the roadside watching her.

Life wove such an intricate pattern, she told herself

as she got undressed. It would have been so much simpler if she could have fallen in love with Gerry. As it was . . .

She shivered. There was no point in self-delusion. Even though she hardly knew him, she had fallen in love with Guy Medfield, and she couldn't imagine a more hopeless situation.

Tracy hoped that Guy might call her again, but he didn't, nor did she get so much as a glimpse of him the next day. Tim's pickup truck was in front of the cottage during the morning, but that was the only sign of life except for a single dim lamp burning in the front window in the evening, which indicated that the cottage's occupant had not gone away.

The following morning, Tracy decided to play neighbor. She baked a coffee cake, cut it in half, then while it was still warm and fragrant, walked with it across to Guy's cottage.

She had no sooner raised and lowered the brass knocker, however, than she heard the sound of a car motor behind her and, turning slightly, she saw to her horror that the red sports car was pulling up to the curb.

There was no chance of escape. Tracy watched the brunette get out of the car and come up the short path. Even from this distance she could see his magnificent dark eyes alight with curiosity.

Simultaneously, the door opened, and Guy peered down at her.

"Tracy!" he said, surprised but—at least so it sounded to her—not unpleasantly so. "I thought it was Gloria. I heard her car."

"It *is* Gloria, at least it's also Gloria," the brunette, now just behind Tracy, said with a hint of indulgent amusement in her voice.

Tracy noted that the other woman was carrying a brown grocery sack. "I had just run down to the store in the village to get some milk," she explained. "You must be Guy's neighbor."

"Yes," Tracy admitted awkwardly.

"Tracy Graham, Gloria Denton," Guy said, smiling at both of them. "Come in, won't you, Tracy?"

"Thank you, no," she said quickly. She thrust the coffee cake into his hands. "I was in a baking mood, and I couldn't possibly eat the whole thing myself," she explained

"It smells delicious," Guy told her. "How about sharing a piece with some coffee?"

"Thank you, no," she said again. "I have to get back. I'm expecting a phone call."

Something flickered in the gray eyes, something she couldn't define except that she knew it wasn't pleasant. But he said only, "All right then. And thanks for this," indicating the coffee cake.

As Tracy turned to go, the brunette added, "I'm glad to have met you."

Tracy mumbled something she hoped was appropriate in answer, and only wished that she had even a partial quotient of the other woman's poise under the circumstances. But then, Gloria Denton seemed supremely confident of her relationship with Guy. Tracy couldn't say the same about herself.

She had no desire to sample her part of the coffee cake once she was back in her own kitchen. On an impulse she walked up with it to Sankaty Head later in the morning, tossing it over the side of the bluff so that the seagulls could enjoy a feast. She wished, fervently, that she had never made it.

That afternoon she drove over to Nantucket's famous Old Mill and set up her easel. She had read that in older days there had been four windmills standing on a hill to the west of Nantucket Town, and this was the last survivor. It had been built in 1746 of wood salvaged from sailing vessels wrecked off these treacherous shores; this entire stretch of the North Atlantic was known as the Mariners' Graveyard. During the summer season, the mill, now the property of the Nantucket Historical Association, was open for the tourists. Despite its venerable age, it even ground corn into meal when the wind was right.

Now, though, Tracy had the mill site to herself, and since this was a stretch of high land, the unimpeded view of the surrounding countryside was spectacular.

Tracy's intention was to try to capture the mill on canvas, and she set up her easel and then began to sketch. Later, she began to apply her oil colors and was so interested in what she was doing that time passed quickly. Fading daylight, rather than fatigue, was what caused her finally to pack up her things. But she was pleased with the progress she had made. She resolved to return to the site at about the same hour the next afternoon when she could get a comparable effect of light and shadow.

The next day Tracy was so anxious to get back to painting that she packed a lunch and drove across to the mill earlier than she had planned. She began to work on details of the painting that could be put in without waiting for the sun to cooperate by giving her the right lighting.

It had begun to cloud over by midafternoon, so she was glad that she had taken advantage of the good weather while it lasted. Probably, now, she could finish the painting at home.

She was about to set up her easel in the kitchen, which seemed a likely place in which to work as she was not the neatest of artists, when the phone rang.

She was tempted to let it go on ringing because she was certain it would be Gerry, and just now she didn't want to talk to him. Curiosity got the better of her, though, and she lifted the receiver to find that it was not Gerry, but Guy.

"Did I interrupt something?" he asked. "I thought I heard your car door just a few minutes ago."

As if on premeditated schedule, her pulse started to pound at the sound of his voice. She said quickly, "No, you didn't interrupt anything at all."

"I tried to get you yesterday afternoon to thank you for the coffee cake," he said. "It was as delicious as it smelled."

"I decided to attempt painting something other than Sankaty Head Light," she confessed, "so I went across to the Old Mill."

"How did you manage with it?"

"Well . . . it's coming along. Let's face it. I'll never be Picasso."

"How about Rembrandt?" he suggested.

"No way!"

"If I were to take up painting just now I'd have to try to emulate Renoir," he said. "They say his eyesight was so poor everything looked fuzzy to him. That's why his work has that delightful, diffused effect that is so individualistic."

"So, then," she said, not intending to be flip, yet afraid once she had spoken that she must have sounded so, "there's a plus side to everything."

To her relief, he didn't seem to resent this. "The other side of the coin?" he asked lightly. "Perhaps. For example, if I could drive myself, I would have had no excuse to call you up."

"Oh?"

"I'm out of Scotch," he said, "and I covet a bottle

because I'd like to ask my beautiful blonde neighbor over for a drink with me. Any chance you might be going shopping?"

His beautiful blonde neighbor. It took a moment for Tracy to realize that he actually was referring to *her*!

As it happened, she'd had no intention of going shopping. But then, she would have built a space ship and gone to the moon for him if she were capable of it! So she said, "Matter of fact, I've been intending to buy some wine."

"Then you'll pick up a bottle of Dewar's for me—and help me initiate it?"

"Yes, to both questions," she said, and as she hung up she felt like singing.

She changed from her painting clothes into wool slacks of a deep rose color with a matching velour top. Feeling singularly carefree, she brushed her hair into a golden cloud around her shoulders, and used lipstick that almost exactly matched the color of her clothes.

She bought a bottle of chablis in the liquor store, thinking that perhaps she might fix swordfish for dinner one night and ask Guy to join her for it. The chilled white wine would go very well with her proposed menu.

The sun was again beginning its western travels as she knocked at the door of the neighboring cottage. As Guy swung it open she wondered if he were again seeing her as a golden shadow . . . a lovely golden shadow, he had said.

When she entered the cottage she was quite close to him. She looked up to find his gray eyes fixed appreciatively on her.

"Nantucket is agreeing with you," he said softly. "Maybe it's that pink color you're wearing, too. Whatever—you're quite a vision even for a man with bad eyes!"

Again, he had made a fire, and had set out glasses and ice on a table in front of it, and she poured drinks for both of them. There was an easy comaraderie between them today. She would not have imagined that she could ever feel so relaxed in his presence.

They talked about a variety of things as they sipped their drinks. Guy told her that he had always wanted to be a doctor, not merely because his father had been a physician but because the thought of working with the human body and trying to set something right that had gone wrong had always held a tremendous fascination for him. He told her about his years in medical school, highlighting some of the funny things that had happened so that before long he had her laughing.

She fixed second drinks for them, and now he drew her out about herself. She told him about her mother, whom she had adored. Her mother had died of cancer; that had been a very rough time. She told him about her father, remembering the good times they had shared before Elise entered the scene, and now she could even speak about Elise without rancor. She told him about Florence Anders and the shop on Charles Street, and how she loved dealing with beautiful old things, and looking up their histories.

Time passed, and finally Guy said, "You must be hungry."

"I hadn't noticed," she admitted. "Are you?"

"Now that I've thought about it, yes! Gloria made a pot roast yesterday, and there's quite a bit left. Shall we heat it up and share?"

Tracy stiffened. The thought of sharing something the brunette had cooked was an anathema, she decided instinctively, and then chastised herself for being foolish. It was more important to stay and have dinner with Guy, she told herself, than to question the source of the food supply!

"I've got a lot of canned stuff," he said. "We can add vegetables . . ."

"I'll stay if you let me play cook," she said firmly.

"I'm enough of a chauvinist to buy that," he told her, but he smiled as he said it.

Tracy was smiling, too, as she went out to the kitchen. As he had said, there was quite a bit of pot roast left, as well as mashed potatoes and some string beans. She heated the meat, made potato patties, adding a little chopped onion for flavoring, and found enough lettuce plus some ripe tomatoes in the fridge to make a salad.

She discovered that there was ice cream in the freezer, a can of peach halves on the shelf, and even some raspberry jam. For dessert she would be fancy and fix an "instant" peche melba.

She had to smile at this spurt of domesticity. But Guy complimented her on the potato cakes and the salad, and told her that the pot roast tasted even better than it had the first time around.

"You have a magic touch," he said, and she wondered how Gloria Denton would have reacted to that!

They continued to talk about all sorts of things as they ate, and Tracy was in a pleasant glow as she cleared off the dishes and went to make dessert. She decided to make coffee and put on a kettle of water to boil. She was prying the lid off the jam jar when the kettle began to whistle and as she reached toward the stove to shut it off Tracy failed to see the jagged metal corner edge of the kitchen counter. In a horrifying instant, she felt a slash of swift pain, and to her horror saw blood spurting out above her right wrist.

She gave an involuntary cry that was enough to bring Guy to the door. She had grabbed a dish cloth and wrapped it around the cut, but the cloth already was turning red.

Guy's face darkened as he looked toward her, and, suspecting that he couldn't see the blood-stained cloth, she hoped that she might get out of this without even telling him about it! Surely, the bleeding would stop!

Then she knew, sickeningly, that the bleeding wasn't going to stop easily. Guy, frustration underlining his voice, said, "Tracy, for God's sake, what is it?"

"I've cut myself, that's all," she said, trying to be calm about it.

"Cut yourself? Where?"

"On my arm."

"How?"

"There's a ragged piece of metal at the edge of the cabinet."

He swore under his breath, then he said, "I told Tim just a couple of days ago that something would have to be done about that. I know where it is, and I suppose I thought anyone else could see it."

He was coming across the kitchen as he spoke, "Here, let me look."

"No, Guy, really," she protested. "It's all right."

"The hell it is!" he contradicted her. He was standing within inches of her, and he peered down at her closely, studying her face. "You've gone white," he told her. "Switch on the light over the sink and let me see what you've done to yourself."

She knew very well that if she didn't do what he asked voluntarily he would make her do it by force. With her left arm she reached up and switched on the light over the sink, sending a bright beam cascading downward.

Guy, his fingers astonishingly gentle, unwrapped the dish cloth, then bent over her arm, studying the oozing laceration.

"Give me another cloth," he said then, "there are clean ones in the second drawer."

LOVE'S GOLDEN SHADOW

She did so, a bit sickened by the sight of her own blood.

"Hang on," he said. "Hang on just a little bit longer, Tracy. Look, it will be quicker if you do this than if I try to fumble around to find things. There is Zephiran Chloride in the bathroom cabinet which will serve as a first-aid antiseptic. Bring it out here, but first look in the right side of my bedroom closet. You'll find my medical bag there." He hesitated. "I want to wash this off," he told her, "then we'll see what's to be done about it. Hold that cloth tightly around your arm meantime."

She did as she was told, which wasn't easy, but she placed the antiseptic inside his black leather medical bag, and then tucked the bag under her arm to make the return trip out to the kitchen.

He took the bag from her, swiftly extracting the antiseptic and a roll of cotton. Then, while she held her arm over the sink, he cleansed it gently but thoroughly. Watching his face as he worked, Tracy was so mesmerized by his intense expression that she almost forgot about her stinging arm.

Then she saw he was frowning, and he said, "It's going to need suturing, Tracy. Just a few stitches, but it's not going to heal well by itself." He bit his lip. "I hate like hell to have you drive across to the hospital," he said, "and it would take much too long to get Tim Sousa to come out here to take you. I . . ."

"Yes?"

"I have everything necessary to do it," he told her. "However, there *is* my eyesight to be reckoned with. I'm sure I can see well enough to do the job, though, if we take that gooseneck lamp in the corner of the living room and focus it directly on your arm. It has a very bright light, which is why I never use it. We can work on the kitchen table, I'll pad it with some bath towels. That way I'll be able to get close enough to you to see what I'm doing."

He straightened. "That is," he said carefully, "if you feel you can trust me . . ."

"I trust you completely, Guy," she told him swiftly.

"Okay. Keep the towel tight over the cut, and go get the lamp. I know I'm asking you to manage a hell of a lot under the circumstances . . ."

"I can do it," she said staunchly, but the fact was that she was feeling more than a little giddy, and only hoped that she wouldn't suddenly collapse at his feet.

By the time she brought back the lamp he had set up a small emergency surgery area at the end of the kitchen table, padding it thickly with towels. It was only when he actually had switched on the lamp, which was indeed dazzling in its brightness, that she remembered he had told her that his eyes were not supposed to be subjected to too much light.

"Guy," she cried, trying to fight off a wave of giddiness, "You shouldn't be trying to do this!"

"Why not?" he demanded. "Have you lost your faith in me so quickly? Not that I'd blame you!"

"I'm thinking of your eyes," she said weakly. "You told me that bright lights . . ."

"To hell with that," he said roughly. "It's not going to matter. Not for such a short time as this will take. For God's sake, Tracy, sit down before you fall down!"

Then his tone became gentler. "Look," he told her, "I'm going to give you a shot first so that it won't hurt so much." He had taken a hypodermic syringe out of the medical case, and he said, "This will take only a second, darling."

Involuntarily, Tracy closed her eyes, but his touch was so expert that she scarcely felt the needle. After that, she kept her eyes closed, opening them occasionally not to look at her arm, but at the dark head bent so closely over it.

His skill was consummate. Even though she had had very little experience with such things, Tracy recognized his expertise. What a marvelous surgeon he must be! She remembered Gerry's aunt saying that it would be such a loss, were he not able to return to his work. Before, she had not fully realized Guy's potential tragedy. Now she could see why he was at moments hostile and irascible. Life had dealt him a severe blow, a very severe blow, even more disastrous to him than it would have been to most people.

She heard a click, and opened her eyes to find that he had switched off the lamp. As he began to bandage her arm with deft fingers he said, "I don't need to see that clearly to do this. It's been awhile since I've done much bandaging myself, but it's a technique, shall we say, that you don't forget."

After a moment he stood, and she found herself being drawn erect by two strong arms then, to her surprise, scooped up in them.

"I don't need to be carried," she protested.

"I disagree," he told her firmly, "and I'm the doctor, remember?"

She realized that he was taking her in the direction of his bedroom, and a moment later he lowered her onto the blue and white candlewick spread. Then he was smoothing a patchwork quilt over her, very much like the one in Aunt Sally Thorndyke's bedroom.

He wedged a pillow beneath her arm so that it felt surprisingly comfortable, then he sat down on the side of the bed, taking her left hand between his.

"You were very brave," he said softly. "Beautiful and brave. It's quite a combination!"

"You were wonderful," she said sleepily. The shot he had given her was taking full effect. There was pain in her arm but it seemed distant. She felt as if she were drifting away on a cloud.

"Get some rest," he told her, and bent to kiss her. But when she involuntarily made a move to reach up to him he said sharply, "No! You've got to keep that arm down for a while, Tracy. Anyway, I want you to get some sleep."

"Will you be near?"

"I'll be listening for you," he promised her. "One sound, and I'll be in here."

He was true to his word. Much later she awakened to find that it was dark in the room, except for a single small light on a corner table that he must have switched on while she slept. Her arm had begun to throb, and she called restlessly, "Guy."

He was at her side almost immediately, asking, "What is it, Tracy?"

"It hurts," she said. "I don't mean to be a baby about it, but it *does* hurt."

"You're not being a baby," he assured her. "You've had some good sleep, though, which was the best thing for you. Now it's bound to hurt, darling. I only wish I could tell you otherwise. I've brought a pill that will help, though, and later I'm going to give you a supply of them to take home with you."

He held out a white tablet and a glass half full of water. She responded like a child, putting the pill in her mouth then obediently swallowing the water. When she had finished, she automatically held the glass out to him, and couldn't help but notice that he first explored an empty place on the bedside table with his fingers before setting the glass down on it.

Seeing him fumble like this couldn't fail to evoke pity

in her, and she said, "Guy . . . I should never forgive myself if you have a setback with your eyes because of using that light today."

"I won't," he promised her. "And stop worrying about my eyes, Tracy. What's *your* visual acuity?"

"I'm just slightly farsighted," she admitted. "I suppose I'm one of those people who will have to hold a book ten feet away to read it when I get older."

"Well," he said, "I had twenty-twenty vision until this happened, so you just wait! One of these days I'll be seeing so well you won't be able to hide a thing from me!"

"I don't want to hide a thing from you now," she found herself telling him.

"Are you sure about that?" he teased. "What about your rising young diplomat?"

"How did you know Gerry is a rising young diplomat?"

"Tim Sousa's mother came over to do some washing and ironing for me, and she told me," he said, with a surprisingly impish grin. "She also works for your friend's aunt."

"Honestly!" Tracy said, dismayed.

"Put out because you can't keep any secrets on Nantucket?" he asked lightly.

"No, but I'm not used to having everyone know everything about me."

"I'd like to think I could ever know everything about you," he told her. He shifted slightly, and she could feel his hip taut against her leg. She became so intently aware of his nearness that she shivered.

Instantly he asked, "Are you cold?"

"No. I . . ."

But he didn't let her finish. He turned slightly, very gently touching her shoulders as he bent closer to her. His lips first brushed her forehead at the hairline, then moved to her eyelids, and on, finally, to her mouth. Now he drew back the patchwork quilt, his hands finding their way beneath the edge of the rose velour top, working to the back where he unfastened the clasp of her bra, his fingers moving on to touch her breasts so that her nipples swiftly became erect.

"You have too much on," he groaned hoarsely, and she couldn't have agreed with him more. As if to get closer to her, despite this, he lay along the side of the bed, drawing himself toward her but mindful still, of her injured arm. But, as desire mounted, she came close to forgetting about it herself.

He had thrown off the quilt, and as he molded his body alongside hers she could feel his hardness; his masculinity was as tangible as it was potent. A wave of intense yearning swept over her, burning like an unquenchable flame, and she felt consumed by her need for him.

He had pulled up the velour top. Now his lips found her taut, rosy nipples, holding first one then the other between them, his mouth describing a tantalizing arc augmenting the frenzy of her feeling.

"Tracy!" he moaned. But then she turned toward him, and the surgeon surfaced. "You mustn't move that arm," he cautioned, but she knew the words had been wrung from him and that this was not what he wanted any more than she did.

She looked at him to see that his face had gone white, and the sweat was standing out on his forehead. He, too, was swept up by passion. She felt as if they were both on a beach, actually, yearning to be caught within the vortex of a tidal wave only to have fate intervene so that the wave broke while it was still at sea and thus couldn't reach them.

"Oh, my God, Guy," she said helplessly.

"Don't, Tracy," he whispered, and his eyes had

never been more silvery. They gleamed in the wetness of his face. "Don't make it any harder for us. You could get into something nasty if that cut reopens. I don't want to put you through anything like that."

"You *would* have to be a doctor!" she said shakily, trying to rally. And the moment was over.

She would have given a great deal to have been able to summon it back again.

Chapter Eight

Tracy's arm was sore when she awakened the next morning, and she found, as the day drew on, that she was unusually tired. This was merely a reaction; from the injury, to be sure, but also from the tremendous letdown that had followed the lovemaking between Guy and herself.

When Gerry called, to complain that he had been unable to get her on the phone the day before, she fibbed and told him that she had a slight sore throat that might presage a cold, and intended to rest for the next twenty-four hours and take care of herself. Gerry at once cheerfully offered his services as a male nurse, but she managed to sidestep this.

After she hung up, she wondered why she hadn't told Gerry the truth about cutting herself while fixing dessert at Guy's house. With the bandage on her arm an advertisement of the injury, she could scarcely expect to be able to keep Gerry from finding out about it sooner or later. What would she offer in defense of having told him a white lie, then?

She thought of the old poem about weaving "tangled webs" when one first practiced to deceive. How true it was!

Guy called after a time and suggested that she rest as much as possible for the next twenty-four hours, after which he wanted to take a look at her arm and change the bandage. She was intensely disappointed by the fact that he didn't ask to see her sooner, but this was explained when the red car again drove up next door early in the afternoon.

The sight of it was a bitter one to Tracy. It seemed unbelievable to her that Guy could welcome the brunette into his house after last night's episode. She recalled the way he had looked when he let her go, remembering her injured arm. He had been as tormented as she was, she felt sure of that.

Now, though, she wondered if he was one of those men who seemed able to eternally play the field, dispensing his affections with equal ardor when motivated by the spell of the moment? Had Guy's early, unhappy marriage made him incapable of a really deep relationship with a woman?

It was hard to believe this when she remembered his tender kisses, and the way he had tucked her in after putting her down on his bed last night. Every move he had made, everything he had done for her, had denoted an intensely caring sort of person. Yet the red car certainly was evidence to the contrary, and it could hardly be negated.

Gloria Denton didn't stay overnight this time, though. The car was gone by late afternoon. As she heated a can of soup and ate a solitary supper, Tracy could imagine that across the way Guy was probably finishing up the pot roast, and it was not a happy thought.

She took one of the painkillers he had given her and went to bed early, but it was a dream-filled sleep and she was not at all refreshed when she awakened. Though her arm had stopped throbbing, it had begun to itch and that, of course, was supposed to be a sign that the healing process had started.

Guy confirmed this when, after a call from him, she went over to his cottage late in the afternoon and he examined the cut and put a new bandage on it.

"Coming along very well," he told her, smiling. "You must have had a good doctor!"

Tracy could not resist smiling back at him. "I had the best," she said.

"Shall we drink to that?"

She made their drinks out in the kitchen, this time, and she noticed that the ragged corner of the counter had been hammered down to a somewhat dented but nevertheless safe smoothness.

She commented on this, and Guy said, "I did it myself, this morning. It was incredibly stupid of me not to take care of it sooner. As a result of my carelessness, you're going to have a scar on your arm. A very neat scar, but still a scar."

A scar. A brand. His brand. Every time she looked at her arm for the rest of her life—even when the scar had whitened to a thin line as, in time, it undoubtedly would—she would be reminded of him!

For that matter, she didn't need a scar on her arm to remember him. In such a short space of time, he had become woven inextricably into the very fibre of her emotions. Casting out Ben Devlin had been one thing. Casting out Guy Medfield would be something else entirely.

The subject of her thoughts said, "Shall we go sit by the fire?"

"If you like," she said.

That telltale eyebrow twitched upwards. "It's not like you to sound so indifferent," he commented mildly. "Is something the matter?"

It was a question that could have unleashed a flood of words, but she restrained herself. *Was something the matter?* The fact that Guy could ask her such a thing made him seem incredibly blind in a way that had nothing to do with his eyesight.

Did he imagine that she had failed to notice the red car at his door overnight? Or that she failed to connect the red car with Gloria Denton? How stupid did he think she was?

Resentment stabbed her. Was he *really* so supremely sure of himself that he believed he could get away with handling two women in the way he was dealing with Gloria Denton and herself?

The answer came involuntarily. He actually *was* getting away with it and the idea was humiliating. True, she'd had to come over this afternoon to let him look at her arm, but afterwards she could have picked up the pieces of her pride and gone home! When he had suggested they have a drink, though, she had not thought of refusal. Now he was asking her to go sit by the fire with him, probably in the very place where Gloria had been sitting not long before.

"What is it, Tracy?" he asked quietly.

She didn't know what to answer. This wasn't something she could make a simple statement about. In fact, anything she said was almost certain to sound like an accusation, and she was not prepared for his inevitable reaction. She had seen enough of Guy in a caustic mood to imagine how he could turn her words, if he wished to do so. He undoubtedly would be the first to tell her that his relationship with Gloria, or anyone else, was essentially none of her business.

Was he trying to prove himself in some misguided way? She wondered. Was making love to a woman and feeling her sway beneath the impact of his sensuous mastery something that stemmed from an inner need to prove that he could triumph, to compensate, insofar as his ego was concerned, for this temporary problem with his vision?

She had been staring down at the drink in her hands. Now she became aware that he had moved to her side silently. Slowly he cupped her chin between his long, slender fingers, tilting her head up so that he could gaze directly down into her eyes.

"What is it?" he asked her gently. "And please don't answer 'nothing.' I find it supremely irritating when women take refuge in that eternal 'nothing' response when you ask them a question that definitely must have an answer."

"I—I've been thinking about things," she said lamely.

"Would it be presumptuous to ask if those 'things' involve me?"

"You?"

"Yes," he said, just a trifle impatiently. "Where *do* I rate with you, Tracy?"

"Am I supposed to measure people on some sort of numerical scale?" she evaded.

"You know what I'm talking about. I've come into your life very recently . . ."

"True."

"But, then, Gerry Stanhope has only come into your life recently, too. Sometimes, though, I think that of the two of us he's made the deeper impression on you!"

How wrong he was! Deliberately, she turned away from him because she wanted to place herself out of his range of vision. She didn't want him to be able to read her face.

"Gerry is a friend," she said.

"Friend!" He scoffed at the word. "Your generation uses that term 'friend' to cover a multitude of relationships."

"You consider yourself in a different generation?"

"I *am* in a different generation. I'm ten years older than you are."

"Such a chasm!" she mocked him.

"There are moments when I probably feel a hundred years older than you do," he said soberly. "There's a quintessence of youth about you. Sometimes I feel that you've never really been touched, although you tell me you and your friend Ben had a long, intimate relationship."

She had told him a great deal about herself the other night. Now she wished she hadn't been so revealing. But he had been equally frank; he hadn't tried to hide the fact that his marriage had left emotional bruises from which it had taken a long time to recover. He had admitted that one reason for his unusually intense dedication to his work was because he had put all the energy that might have gone into love into his surgery.

"Why don't you want me to look at you?" he demanded now.

She was flustered. "Look at me all you wish," she told him.

"I can't when you move out of my very limited field of vision, and I think you know that," he said, and she sensed the effort he was making to control both his voice and his emotions.

"So," she said, wanting to hurt him, even as she recognized this as pure perversity. "What am I supposed to do? Stick my face right up into yours?"

He stepped back, and she saw his hands clench, the knuckles whiten. But he forced a smile and said coolly, "I'm sorry such proximity offends you."

She was instantly contrite. "Guy," she said, "I didn't mean that!"

There was sadness to his smile as he said, surprisingly, "I know you didn't. I've done something that has made you madder than hell. I know that too. But I haven't the vaguest idea what it was, and I'm sure you're not about to enlighten me. If you want that kind of impasse, Tracy, there's not much I can do about it."

Silence stretched between them to be shattered by the telephone's ringing. Guy made his way across to the wall phone, his fingers seeking the receiver, finding it and lifting it off the hook.

"Oh, hello," he said. And then, "No, Gloria left on an afternoon boat. I'm here alone."

Alone. The word was a cold slap under the circumstances. Was her companionship of so little value that he forgot about it the moment someone called him up? Tracy asked herself, indignant. At once, her own intelligence prodded her to admit she was unquestionably reading his remark in entirely the wrong way, but she didn't want to listen to the voice of reason. Just now, she was not prepared to give him any room for doubt.

She put her unfinished drink down on the kitchen table and left the room. His voice, talking to an unknown someone at the other end of the line, still echoed in her ears as she let herself out the front door and went home.

It was ridiculous not to have told Gerry the truth about her arm. She would have welcomed his company after leaving Guy's house and she was more than a little tempted to call him up and ask him to come out to dinner. Yet she knew that encouraging Gerry would only add to her own emotional complications. And this, certainly, was an area in which she needed no more problems!

Nantucket during the off season was too small a place in which to practice subterfuge, though. Tracy had read that the house on Vestal Street in Nantucket Town which had been the birthplace of Maria Mitchell,

America's first woman astronomer, was still open afternoons. So the next day she decided to drive across and visit it. She had just gotten out of her car when she saw Gerry Stanhope walking down the street.

There was no chance for retreat. He covered the distance between them with a long stride, then stood looking down at her accusingly.

"You've evidently made a miraculous recovery," he commended.

"Gerry . . ." she said, and then plunged into the truth. "I didn't have a sore throat," she admitted.

"Somehow I didn't think you did," he told her. "Next time you want to dissemble about something like that make your voice a bit hoarser, as if you're having difficulty in speaking."

"Gerry, really . . ."

"Why did you feel you had to lie to me?" he asked her bluntly.

"It wasn't that," she said. "Not exactly. Actually, I had a sore arm."

"Tracy, for heaven's sake!"

"It's true, Gerry. I know it was silly of me, but I didn't want to talk about it. I cut my arm on a ragged piece of metal in Guy Medfield's kitchen. He had to put in a few stitches."

"*He* put in a few stitches!"

"He *is* a doctor, you know," she reminded him. "It was foolish of me, but I didn't want to tell you about it."

A faint smile lit his greenish eyes. "Were you afraid I might be jealous?" he asked her.

"Jealous?"

"It's entirely possible, you know, Tracy. I could be as jealous as hell of you."

"Gerry, please."

"I am not about to make a nuisance of myself, if that's what you're afraid of," he said stiffly. "I do possess a talent for patience, especially if it's in regard to something I really want. And, yes, I really want you, Tracy. For the moment, I'll say no more than that."

He drew a long breath. "What are you doing here?" he asked her.

"I came over to see Maria Mitchell's house," she told him. "I read a book on her a few years ago, and I was intrigued by the story about her discovery of a comet."

"Funny," Gerry said, "but some friends of Aunt Emily's were talking about the Mitchell comet the other night. One of them is a professor of astronomy at Boston University. He'd come over to close up his summer place on the island."

"I find all of astronomy strange and fascinating, but comets particularly so," Tracy mused. "What especially intrigues me is that Maria made her discovery with a very simple little telescope. It had belonged to her father, who made a hobby of astronomy." She caught herself short. "I'm sorry," she told Gerry. "I must be boring you."

"Not at all. As I understand it you can still see the telescope she used in the Mitchell Association Museum in that building across the street. Then there's another telescope in an observatory that's been built back of the house. I don't think she was living in this house, though, when she discovered the comet."

"That's right," Tracy concurred. "This little gray house—they call houses like this 'single dwellings' here on Nantucket, incidentally—is where she was born, and she spent most of her girlhood here. The house was built not long after the American Revolution. I believe 1790 is the right date. And that long, wooden latch on the front door is typical of Nantucket houses of that period. This one is made of mahogany that was taken from a wrecked ship."

Gerry was regarding her admiringly. "You have a mind like an encyclopedia!" he said.

"Not really," she demurred. "I brought a couple of books on Nantucket to the island with me, and I read up about Maria Mitchell today before I came over here."

"You're the most honest woman I've ever met," he teased.

"Sometimes my honesty gets me in trouble," she said ruefully.

"Deceit can get you in even more trouble," Gerry told her. "Tracy, may I come see Maria Mitchell's observatory with you?"

"Of course," she said. "Actually though, it never really was Maria's observatory. Shortly after the turn of the century a number of people who admired Maria formed an association and bought the house, and later they built the observatory. The telescope in it is one that was given to Maria in 1859 by the women of America. Maria's work has been carried on here, via research—they've done a lot on one particular cluster in the Milky Way—and also as a sort of astronomical center, especially for schoolchildren. The museum across the street has the original, small telescope on display. You probably know the building was once a school, in fact Maria went to school in it. I understand there are natural science exhibits to do with Nantucket, as well as all sorts of things to do with astronomy."

"Want to go there first?" Gerry asked her.

"No. I'd like to go look at the observatory first."

Tracy was fascinated by everything she saw. Although it was the better part of a century since Maria Mitchell had lived—her life span had covered the period from 1818 to 1889—it seemed remarkable to

Tracy that a woman in that faroff day had been able to make such a name for herself in science.

Maria's father had wielded quite an influence on his young daughter. One of his tasks had been to prepare a nautical almanac used by the whaling captains of the day. By the time she was twelve Maria was helping him in his calculations for this and also helped him to correct the navigating instruments used by the whaling men and, of course, precision was vital.

Maria and her father had shared a small observatory where they spent endless nights studying the stars together. This was an avocation carried out even in the dead of winter. Friends of the Mitchells had recorded the fact that Maria and William Mitchell would be in the observatory studying the skies when the temperature hovered at zero outside, and they were certain it had been equally cold inside!

Maria's great discovery was made on October 1, 1847. As Tracy browsed with Gerry among the scrapbooks, letters and souvenirs now in the museum honoring the astronomer, she could imagine how it must have been on Nantucket on that crisp evening at the beginning of fall.

Willliam Mitchell was holding a position as cashier in the bank at the time, and the family had moved to an apartment on the upper story of the bank building. This proved to be a perfect move for Maria because she and her father promptly set up an observatory on the roof.

On that first of October evening, the Mitchells were having a party in their apartment. Maria, though, could not resist the temptation to slip up to the roof and take a look at her beloved heavens through her small telescope. She came back, outwardly quiet but inwardly brimming with excitement.

As soon as it was possible, she whispered to her

father that she was certain she had discovered a new star.

Mr. Mitchell promptly followed her up to the roof, and she showed him the comet that would forever after bear her name. The Mitchells immediately posted word of the discovery to Harvard University, and it was a good thing that they didn't delay, Tracy mused. Only two days later an Englishman saw the comet and recorded this, and other astronomers followed. However, twenty-nine-year-old Maria Mitchell of Nantucket had been the first, and so the honors went to her.

The king of Denmark had offered a gold medal for the discovery of a heavenly body by telescope, and so the medal was given to Maria. Even in a day when there was no radio, no television, no "media" coverage of an event in the contemporary sense of the word, Maria Mitchell soon learned what it was to become famous virtually overnight.

She was working at the time as librarian of Nantucket's Athenaeum, and she continued with her job despite her fame, staying on Nantucket until 1861. Meantime, she had become the first woman to be made a fellow of the Academy of Arts and Sciences, and finally, in that initial year of the Civil War, she gave up Nantucket as her place of residence to go to Poughkeepsie, New York, where she became the first professor of astronomy at Vassar College.

"She must have been quite a person," Tracy said as she and Gerry finally left the Mitchell birthplace. "Most of the people on Nantucket were Quakers in her day, and they were very strict. Did you see that bit about her being 'disowned' by the Friends because she didn't go to meetings?"

"No," Gerry said, "I missed that one."

"She wrote them that her mind was not settled on

religious subjects and she had no wish to retain her membership anyway," Tracy chuckled.

She sobered. "How fantastic it must be to do something like she did," she said, "and then to go on to become tops in your profession. The odds were so much more against her than they are against women today."

Gerry smiled at her indulgently. "I can't see you as a woman scientist," he told her.

"I can't see myself as a scientist either," she said sharply. "I would like to think, though, that I might contribute *something* to the world. I'd like to do something worthwhile . . ."

"I think most people make a contribution," Gerry said slowly. "Not as dramatic a contribution as Maria Mitchell made, to be sure. On the other hand, there was an element of luck working for her. If she hadn't slipped away from her family's party that night . . ."

"Gerry!"

"Don't look so indignant, Tracy. It's true. Suppose she hadn't gone up on the roof? The Englishman, whose name has been lost to history except, probably, in professional astronomical circles, would have gotten all the glory. Maybe *he* would have been asked to teach at Vassar!"

"You're impossible," she said. But she had to smile as she said it.

"That's better," he told her. "I had visions of you escaping me entirely by deciding to dedicate your life to a worthwhile cause." He grinned. "Maybe one of these days I can convince you that *I'm* a worthwhile cause," he suggested.

"You're hopeless," she told him. "Incidentally, what were you doing here on Vestal Street, anyway?"

"Not looking for virgins," he said wickedly. "Not

even vestal virgins, okay? Actually I was taking a walk, believe it or not. Nantucket always has a fascination for me. I like browsing around the streets. There isn't that much else to do, to tell you the truth. Aunt Emily has some of her cronies in playing bridge this afternoon, and so the matter of escape from the premises became urgent. You wouldn't like to take pity on me and take me home for dinner with you, would you? Or, we could check and see if the Chanticleer is open."

"Gerry, I hate to always be saying no to you."

"But you have an appointment with your doctor, is that it?"

"No," she said, "I do not have an appointment with my doctor. Guy checked my arm yesterday and said it's healing well. I'll have to find out when he wants to take the stitches out, but I'm sure it won't be for a while yet. That's the only reason I can see for our getting together again."

"Storm clouds?" Gerry asked.

Inadvertently she glanced skyward, and he said, teasingly, "Don't be so literal, Tracy. Sometimes you do tend to take things much too seriously, do you know that? I wasn't talking about the weather, I was talking about matters between you and your neighbor."

"Let's just call it a modern-day variation of the Hatfields and the McCoys," she said flippantly, and refused to discuss the matter further.

Gerry persuaded her to walk over to the Jared Coffin House with him where they had a drink in the bar. She refused his invitation to linger for dinner, though, but agreed that she would do so before the week was up.

Alone in the car, driving back across the island, she felt a pang of loneliness and almost wished she *had* let Gerry come home for supper with her. But she dreaded the potential pitfall inherent in his subsequent leave-taking. She couldn't always expect him to be restrained.

In his own way, he had been making his feelings toward her quite clear.

Unlike Guy Medfield, she thought dismally, she felt completely unable to cope emotionally with two relationships at the same time.

The dim light was on in Guy's living room as she pulled up in front of her cottage. She wished there were a valid reason to go across to see him, but couldn't think of one. There, too, she would only be inviting trouble.

Unquestionably, he must have been annoyed if not actually angered when he finished his phone conversation yesterday to find that she had left without even waiting to say good-bye to him. Leaving so abruptly had been a rather childish display on her part, she could see that now and she wished she had mustered up a bit more sophistication. It was extremely difficult, though, to be casual where Guy was concerned. Gerry was right. She did tend to take things too seriously. Now she was convinced she had taken Guy's ardent lovemaking *much* too seriously, and she didn't even want to begin to think about his touch, his kisses . . .

Stop it, Tracy, she told herself impatiently. For God's sake grow up!

She scrambled eggs for her dinner and ate at the kitchen table. The night that stretched ahead seemed long and empty. She couldn't concentrate on reading, nor was she in the mood to write letters, and there was nothing else to do.

Thoughts of the man next door who just might be every bit as lonely as she was could not be banished. She tried to brush them aside by thinking about Maria Mitchell and the heartwarming story of her comet discovery. It came to her that Maria Mitchell and Guy had something in common. She could imagine his amusement were she to tell him this. Yet, just as Maria had contributed in her area of science, so had Guy contributed in his.

She found herself wishing, more than she had ever wished anything before, that nothing would go wrong for him in his progress toward regaining his eyesight.

Chapter Nine

Tracy had noted that the Jethro Coffin House, the oldest dwelling on the island, having been built in 1686, had been completely restored. It could be visited in summer and now had been closed to tourists, but she was primarily interested in the exterior anyway. She wondered if she might manage with her oil paints to capture the old house, which was said to be a classical example of a late-seventeenth-century lean-to.

The morning was bright and clear, and when she had finished breakfast and washed the dishes she told herself there could be no better time than the present for some exploring.

She changed into jeans and the faded top she had been using for painting, and was gathering together her easel, paintbox, and some canvasboards when there was a sharp rap at the kitchen door.

Thinking that it might be Tim Sousa, as he stopped by occasionally to ask if there were anything she needed, she opened it and was astonished to see Guy Medfield on the doorstep.

He was wearing dark glasses that banded around the sides of his eyes, and he was carrying the stout walking stick. As he surveyed her cheerfully, he said, "Well, since the patient doesn't seem to be showing any indication of visiting the doctor, I thought maybe the doctor should make a house call!"

She was speechless, and after a moment he said teasingly, "Aren't you going to ask me in?"

"Of course."

She shut the door behind him, staggeringly aware of the scent of his shaving lotion. The woodsy aroma saturated her, underlining the fact of his presence, his nearness. A provocative, tingling sensation of pure desire began to course through her, which was, at the least, annoying. There was no *reason*, she told herself angrily, to permit him to have this kind of effect on her!

"I don't suppose," he suggested, with a slight smile that seemed to her much too knowing, "that you might have some coffee around?"

She did, as a matter of fact, and it was still hot. She had left the pot on the stove, thinking she might reheat the contents when she got back from her painting session.

"Yes," she said, "I do."

He pulled out a chair at the kitchen table and settled himself into it comfortably, propping his walking stick up against the wall. "What have you been doing with yourself?" he asked. "Or do I stand in danger of getting bitten if I question you?"

"Don't be silly," she told him shortly, pouring coffee for both of them. "Actually, I haven't been doing much of anything. I did go over to see the Mitchell house yesterday. It's still open weekday afternoons."

"Ah, Maria," Guy said. "She was quite a girl. Probably every bit as ornery in her way as you are, from what I've heard about her."

She knew that he took a spoon of sugar and a dash of cream in his coffee, and she fixed it for him automatically. He sipped and said, "You have a good memory."

"Thank you," she responded drily.

His eyebrow quirked above the rim of the dark

glasses. "Your tone tells me that I'm still in disfavor," he observed.

"What makes you think you were in disfavor in the first place?"

"Well," he said, "do you make it a habit of walking out on people when they have their backs turned?"

"You were speaking on the phone," she pointed out. "I had no desire to eavesdrop."

"Then you could have gone in the living room and put on some music or *something*, couldn't you?" he asked logically. "Anyway, I was only talking with a friend of mine in Boston. He's a doctor, an anaesthesiologist. Gloria . . ."

Inadvertently, she drew in her breath and he chuckled. "Ah," he said, "now things begin to come clearer. So that's what it is! Well, Gloria . . ."

"You don't need to explain anything to me, Guy," she interposed quickly.

"No, I don't," he agreed. "It's been many a year since I've felt I *needed* to explain anything to any woman, if you must know. I value my independence, Tracy. I make no secret of the fact. However, if I *wish* to explain something, then that puts a different complexion on the matter."

"There is no need for you to explain anything about your friend Gloria to me," she said stiffly.

"You're quite sure of that?"

"Of course I'm sure of it!"

"Very well, then," he said diffidently, "I won't."

With his gray eyes hidden from view by the dark glasses his expression was unfathomable, and she found herself disconcerted by her inability to read him at all. Was he disappointed because she didn't want him to tell her about Gloria, or was he relieved? It was impossible to say, and she was not about to get into the subject again.

"You were here last night, weren't you?" he asked suddenly. "I mean, fairly early in the evening."

"Yes, I was."

"Alone?"

"As a matter of fact, yes."

"I nearly called you," he confessed. "I heard your car, at least I was quite sure it was your car. It was about the time I was putting together some stuff for dinner and I had enough for two. I thought, though, that your diplomat friend might be with you."

"Gerry and I had a drink at the Jared Coffin House," she said, "and he did ask me to have dinner with him, but I wanted to come home."

"The arm isn't bothering you, is it?"

"No. Oh, I know it's there . . . but it itches more than anything."

He nodded. "I should be able to take the stitches out in a few days," he said, "and after that you'll be as good as new . . . except for the scar I've already spoken about." He finished his coffee and carefully set the cup back in its saucer.

"Well," he said then, stirring restlessly, "I can't think of any excuse to offer for keeping you any longer from whatever you were planning to do."

"I wasn't planning to do all that much," she admitted. "I thought I might go take a look at the old Jethro Coffin House and if it seems like a subject I'd be capable of tackling I might try to paint it."

"You wouldn't consider taking a picnic out to the Jetties instead, would you?"

"The Jetties?"

"It's a beach on Nantucket Harbor, past Brant Point Light. You go right by it when you're coming in on the boat."

"Oh," she said remembering. "There were people swimming the day I arrived."

"The water's still relatively warm on the Sound side," he told her. "The air would be cool, though, once you came out, and I don't want you to get that arm wet. But we could roll up our jeans and wade, or just get some sun. You could bring your paints along and try a beach scene, or we could stop at Brant Point. That would be a good subject unless Sankaty Head has made you feel over-lighthoused."

He was speaking with an eagerness that surprised her, and she realized that evidently this was something he really wanted to do. He was such a dominant sort of person, so essentially masculine and usually in such complete command that she tended to forget he couldn't go very far from the cottage by himself. Just now, physically, he was limited, and she could only dimly appreciate the frustration this must be to him.

Before she could speak, though, he said with that seeming divination of her thoughts so disconcerting to her, "Now I have you feeling sorry for me again, and that's not what I wanted at all! To be honest, I came over because I was so damned restless I thought I'd go crazy if I didn't get out for a few minutes. Call it a bad case of cabin fever, but I've really had it lately! My work has bogged down completely, there's something about talking into a recording machine that seems to set up a mental barrier. I'm used to dictating letters to my secretary, but this is entirely different. I mean, when it's a matter of trying to express your thoughts . . ."

"What thoughts?"

There was irony to the twist of his mouth. "I do have some," he told her. "Quite a few, matter of fact. Some good, some bad . . . some that I guess you might call forbidden."

"Guy, what work were you talking about?"

"I'm trying to write a book," he said dismally, "though I've about come to the conclusion I was a fool to agree to make the attempt, and I think I should call up my publisher and admit it."

"A book about what?" she asked, surprised. "Something technical about medicine?"

"No," he said, "nothing really technical at all. Surprised?"

"Yes," she said frankly, "I am."

"I don't strike you as being the author type, is that it?"

"Will you please stop putting words in my mouth," she told him testily.

"I'm not. I'd be very much interested in knowing what type of person you think I am, even though I realize I'm leaving myself wide open when I say that."

"I haven't analyzed you, Guy," she fibbed. She had been trying to do nothing else ever since she had first seen him down at the ferry dock.

"You don't believe in flattery, do you, Tracy?" he asked edgily. "Not that analyzing me would be cause for flattery on your part. I would never think of presuming anything like that."

"There's no need for you to be so cynical!"

"Isn't there?"

She sighed. "Must we always get into arguments?" she asked him.

"It would seem," he said wryly, "that only one thing keeps us from it. And don't worry, Tracy, there's no need for you to recoil. Even I know better than to attempt to make love to you when you're in your present mood."

The dark glasses, she decided, gave him a decided advantage; he was shielded by them. She said irritably, "Must you wear those things indoors?"

"The glasses?" he asked. "Yes, I'm afraid I must in this kind of situation. In case you haven't noticed, it's a very bright day and your kitchen takes full advantage of the sunlight—as it should, especially in this climate. Why? Are they so ugly?"

"They're not ugly at all," she snapped, "as I think you very well know."

"I haven't exactly been staring at myself in the mirror," he retorted, and she knew she had put him on edge.

She said, "I hadn't seen you with dark glasses on, that's all."

"I know," he agreed. "I haven't had them long. Gloria brought them over to me on her most recent visit. Evidently the medical opinion is that the less my eyes are subjected to direct light the faster they'll respond. At least it's a theory to try out, and I'm agreeable." He stood, reaching for his stick. "Look," he said, "I'm intruding, and I apologize. I shouldn't have come over in the first place. Enjoy your day painting the Jethro Coffin House."

The band of tension that had begun to stretch between them seemed to snap suddenly, on Tracy's part. She said impishly, "I'd rather go to the Jetties!"

"Well, then, enjoy yourself at the Jetties!"

"You won't come with me?"

"I think not."

"Why not?"

"Because I realize it was a stupid idea," he told her tersely.

She risked it. "Are you by any chance feeling sorry for *yourself?*" she asked him.

That telltale muscle in his jaw twitched. His face, already made inscrutable by the dark glasses, momentarily seemed carved from stone. "Damn you!" he said softly. Then, while she held her breath, the tension seemed to go out of him too. "Very well," he told her, "you win, Tracy. Yes, I am feeling sorry for myself. I'm feeling sorry as hell for myself, and it's not a healthy state to be in. At some point in my career I should have taken a course in touch typing, but I didn't. So I have to try to use the damned recorder, and it isn't working for me. Also"—a quick smile transformed his face—"I'm being nothing short of a clod trying to unload all these problems on you."

"I'll pack the lunch," she said. "I've plenty of things in the house for sandwiches, and I can fill a thermos with coffee. On second thought, maybe I'll make cocoa for us."

"Look," he said, "seriously . . . I'd be a liability just now. You'd practically have to lead me around by the hand in strange territory. I hadn't thought that out when I made the suggestion."

She laughed. "I don't think it would be so much a question of my leading you around as trying to get you to follow," she told him.

"You *do* consider me completely recalcitrant, don't you?"

"Do you blame me?"

There was chagrin to his laugh. "I can't say I do," he admitted.

He was wearing snug-fitting jeans and a long sleeved blue knit shirt. She said, "Will you need to get a jacket?"

"I don't think so. It's pretty warm in the sun."

"Then why don't you sit down and talk to me while I make our lunch?" she suggested.

To her surprise, he did so without argument—it was rare for much of anything to happen between Guy and herself without some sort of disagreement. She began to see that, on her part, this was a kind of protective device. She was tremendously vulnerable where he was concerned. Just being near him was so tantalizing that it was extremely difficult to concentrate on spreading bread with a deviled-ham filling, and then topping the filling with slices of Swiss cheese with mustard.

She knew that if she were not careful she'd be cutting herself again, or burning her fingers while making the cocoa, or doing something else equally stupid. But having Guy so near was an overwhelming distraction.

"Are you always so silent when you're concocting sandwiches?" he demanded.

"No," she told him. "I hope you like mustard," she added.

"I adore mustard. But I'd adore having a glimpse of your thoughts even more."

"No way," she told him. "As it is, you seem to be reading my mind half the time. That's bad enough!"

She concentrated for a moment on filling the thermos with cocoa. Then she said, "What's your book about, Guy?"

"It's a personal story," he said. "I don't mean it's autobiographical, but it does draw on my own experiences . . . with others, though, rather than myself. I suppose you could say it's about fear. A surgeon sees a great deal of fear, and of course it's something impossible to alleviate entirely. One wouldn't be human if they didn't have a certain amount of anxiety when facing a crisis, and surgery is always a crisis." He paused, then added wryly, "I found that out for myself."

After a moment, he said, "Some of the fears that haunt people the most are unnecessary. Sometimes it's apprehension about the unknown more than anything else. There is still a mystery to medicine. I think there always will be because there's mystery not so much to the human body as to the human mind and spirit, and medicine deals with all of these things. I'm not attempting to dispel a myth in my book, but I *would* like to be able to offer a combination of practical advice for facing surgery, and something that I suppose comes close to inspiration. An admittedly positive philosophy."

He smiled ruefully. "It's all in my head," he confessed. "The problem is that I can't seem to find a way to get it down on paper."

"Maybe I could help," she ventured.

"You?"

"It isn't *that* incredible, Guy. You don't have to sound so skeptical."

"How could you possibly help me, Tracy?"

"By taking your dictation," she told him. "I think you'd find that talking your story out to another person would be quite different than trying to record it by yourself. I'm a good sounding board, believe it or not. We could go over the parts where you tend to get stuck. I think if you talked about the tangles they might all come unraveled. It's like having someone else help you straighten out a hank of yarn when you've gotten it all twisted together."

"I don't know whether I *could* talk my thoughts out with someone else," he admitted.

"You might try."

"Possibly. But not with you, Tracy."

He said this so flatly and with such complete certainty that she was stung by it, stung to the point where tears came to fill her eyes, and she brushed at them angrily.

After a moment, he said, "Tracy?"

"What?"

"That must have sounded pretty rotten," he told her.

Her voice was muffled. "Yes," she said, "it did."

"You're crying," he said, and instantly he was on his feet. Before she could protest he had come to her side, and he was bending to look closely at her. Then he touched a teardrop, tentatively, with one finger.

"Oh, hell," he said bleakly. "Why do I always make you miserable?"

"You don't. But . . . you can be quite rough on a person."

"And you're the last person in the world I want to be rough on at all," he said. He grasped her shoulders. "Oh, God, Tracy," he said, and then his mouth descended to find hers and once more she knew what rapture really meant as her emotions soared.

It was a glimpse of a red potholder hanging over the stove that jerked her back to her senses. Red. The color brought to mind the car that was parked out in front of his cottage much too often and the brunette who came so frequently to spend the night with him.

She drew away, and he asked, puzzled, "What is it now?"

"Nothing," she said, then realized this was the response he hated the most and quickly added, "It's time to go, that's all."

"Very well."

He spoke quietly and she was surprised at his tone. He actually sounded as if she'd hurt his feelings. She glanced at him swiftly, but the black glasses still provided a kind of mask to his face. It was impossible to read his expression accurately when he had them on.

"Can I carry anything?" he asked now.

"Thanks, but I've put it all in one small hamper, so I can manage."

"What about your paints?"

"I don't think I'll take them this time. I'll get familiar with the surroundings first."

"You're not leaving them behind just because of me?"
—"Of course not."

As they started out, he was silent, almost morose, and finally she asked, "Cat got your tongue?" trying to be light about it.

"Sometimes I don't feel much like talking," he said.

"Okay," she told him agreeably. "Just pretend I'm not here."

"That would be impossible," he told her. "Your presence exerts a definite effect, I assure you. To erase it, I'd have to blot out all five senses . . ."

They were driving through Nantucket's stunted forest. Again, the weather was perfect. September had painted the sky, the trees and the moors with wonderful colors Tracy only wished she were able to match with her oils.

She said almost absently, "It's such a beautiful day, a beautiful time . . ."

"What?"

"A beautiful time," she repeated.

"Yes, I heard you. You're right, of course. It *is* a beautiful time. When winter comes we can both look back to today . . ."

When winter comes. The words had a forlorn quality, and Tracy was brushed by a sense of depression. When winter came where would he be, and where would she be? There was not a chance, she thought sadly, that they would be together.

This time on Nantucket was like an interval set apart by itself, and she didn't like to think beyond it, she didn't like to contemplate living the rest of her life without him.

"When are you going back to Boston?" she asked him suddenly.

He had lapsed into a private reverie. Now, startled, he said, "I'm not sure. Why?"

"I wondered. I've only about ten days left on Nantucket. The time slips by so smoothly . . ."

"Time has a way of doing that, out here."

"Maybe it's because it's an island," Tracy said. "Islands are little worlds unto themselves. They don't seem to be governed by ordinary things."

"Then that should mean the people staying on them needn't be governed by ordinary things either," he told her. "That gives us freedom, wouldn't you say? Freedom to live, and to love."

Love. She tensed at his use of the word. How, she wondered, could he speak of love to her! Passion, yes. They shared that, there was no doubt of it. But *love* . . . love was entirely different. Love was, in part, this wrenching thing she felt for him . . . a feeling that she was very sure was not reciprocated.

They came to Nantucket Town, and he directed her along the streets that led to the Jetties. With summer a memory, the parking lot was nearly vacant. A few late vacationers were sunning on the beach, but Tracy and Guy virtually had the lovely stretch of beige sand to themselves, and she sighed luxuriously.

"It's almost too much," she said. "Perfection."

She kept an old blanket in the car trunk, now she got it out and said, "You can take this, I'll manage the hamper."

He slung the blanket over his arm and started out using the stick, but he stumbled almost at once. Tracy saw his mouth tighten and heard him swear softly. She was afraid that if she offered to help he'd cut her off, but she couldn't help trying.

"Take my hand," she said.

"Blindman's Buff?" he commented bitterly.

"Look, Guy," she said impatiently, "if there were something wrong with my eyes you'd help me, wouldn't you?"

"Yes."

"Then stop making such a big deal out of it!"

He laughed. "You do have a way!" he said. "You manage to strip away the nonessentials, Tracy. Okay, I'll take your hand. In fact, even if I could see perfectly I'd thoroughly enjoy taking your hand."

His clasp was warm, his touch as treacherous as ever. But she soon saw that just a handclasp was not enough.

"I think it would be easier if we walked arm in arm," she decided.

"Like two lovers strolling on the sands?" he suggested. "All right, but let me get on the other side of you. I don't want to press against that cut."

She had read somewhere that one should let a blind person take the sighted person's arm, rather than the other way around. Now she said to Guy, "You take hold of me."

"What an invitation!" he laughed as he put his arm around her and they moved across the beach.

"Excellent teamwork," he said, when Tracy found a spot where she wanted to stop. "We work well together."

"You think so?"

"Yes, don't you?"

As he helped her spread out the blanket and they both settled down on it, she said, "That was a trap you just fell into, doctor!"

"What are you talking about?"

"If we work well one way, don't you think we might work well another?"

Guy grinned. "What sort of suggestion are you making?"

"Honestly!" Tracy protested, reading *his* mind this time. "I was talking about *work*."

"There are all kinds of work, didn't you know that?"

He was lying on his side, his head propped up on one hand and again she could smell the tantalizing, woodsy scent of his after-shave lotion. He was very close. The knit shirt he was wearing was open at the neck and she could see his pulse throbbing in the hollow of his throat.

She deplored the effect he had on her. Jelly, she nearly said the word aloud. He turns me to jelly!

"I was talking about your book," she told him.

"Tracy, you've said yourself it's a beautiful day. Let's try not to get into an argument, agreed? Let's really *try!*"

"I don't intend to get into an argument. The thing of it is, I'd like to work with you on your book, Guy. It wouldn't be doing you any favors, if that's what you're afraid of . . ."

"Bring out your sandwiches," he interrupted. "We'll talk about the book later."

Chapter Ten

It was an afternoon to be treasured, to be filed in her memory—a small, perfect slice of time. For once they didn't argue about anything. They spoke when they wanted to speak, telling each other intimate little things about their respective childhoods. Tracy had cherished a passion for maple walnut ice cream cones, while Guy had possessed a seemingly insatiable appetite for chocolate-covered cherries. Tracy had taken ballet lessons when she was eight, and this had proved to be a dismal failure. Guy's mother had wanted him to play the violin, and he was still sure he'd been the cause of his teacher's high blood pressure.

There were golden moments when they were silent; for even in silence there was total rapport. He reached out to find her hand and held it loosely in his and love for him flowed through her in sweet intensity.

They dozed for a time, to be wakened by the blast of the ferry rounding Brant Point. Seagulls soared behind the boat, their flight graceful, seemingly effortless, and Tracy said, "It would be great to be a bird."

"What would you do if you were a bird?" he asked indulgently.

"I think I'd feel so free. Wouldn't you?"

"No," he said. "There would always be predators."

"Must you be so practical?"

"I don't feel very practical," he admitted. "Just now,

I feel as if I've been shipwrecked on a desert island. You and I are alone in our own small world." He grinned. "Maybe I'd better go find us some coconuts for dinner," he suggested.

"You're insane," she told him.

"I agree," he said calmly. "Quite insane, about you."

Caution came to prick her. She said, "It's getting late. I think we'd better be starting back."

"What are you afraid of, Tracy?" he asked her. "Me?"

"Why should I be afraid of you Guy?"

"That's not what I asked you."

"I just think we should be getting back, that's all," she said stubbornly.

"Okay. I refuse to be the one to precipitate a quarrel."

He got to his feet, reaching down for the blanket and shaking it gently before folding it over his arm. Without waiting to be asked this time, he reached for her arm and they made their way back to the car in companionable silence, even though Tracy had lost the utter sense of peace that had possessed her earlier.

She had bought a bottle of Scotch, and when they got back to the cottage she asked him to come in for a drink even though she expected him to refuse. He surprised her by accepting, and this time they settled at her fireside.

Finally, he took off the dark glasses. He closed his eyes and she saw that his face was etched with weariness.

"Would you have any aspirin?" he asked her.

"Yes, of course. I'll get you some."

"I still get these damned headaches," he explained. "It's not a great idea to mix aspirin with alcohol, but fortunately I have a pretty sound stomach."

She poured a little milk for him to take with the aspirin and he smiled. "Playing Florence Nightingale again?" he demanded.

"You've never given me the chance to play Florence Nightingale at all!"

"Would you like the job?"

"Do you think I'd qualify?"

His ironic eyebrow tilted upwards. "Someday," he said mockingly, "maybe you'll shock me by answering directly when I ask you a question. You're a master at the art of evasion, Tracy."

"Self-defense," she quipped.

"My God, do you *need* to defend yourself from me?"

"Perhaps. Speaking of jobs, have you given any more thought to my helping with the book?"

"There you go again!" he protested. "Skirting the issue. Yes, I have given further thought to your helping me with the book."

"Well?"

"You came out here to get a rest," he pointed out. "Working with me would not be restful. Most of my associates tell me I tend to be a tyrant."

"Yes, I can imagine that," she said. "Certainly you're not what one would call a meek and mild type."

"What am I, then? Arrogant, overbearing?"

"At moments," she said, but not without a smile. "I think I could cope with working with you, though."

"And go back to Boston a frazzled wreck? What would your employer say?"

"Florence wasn't advocating that I take a rest cure," Tracy said. "She thought I needed . . . something."

"Something or someone?"

"We're getting away from the subject," she told him firmly. "You're the one who is hedging this time, Guy. Do you, or do you not, want me to work with you?"

"Such directness!" he said mockingly. "Very well,

since you put it so precisely, I *do* want you to work with me, but I don't feel I'd have the right to take up so much of your time. It would require hours each day, Tracy."

Hours each day in his company—Tracy could think of nothing more desirable. Hours to be stored up against that winter he had spoken about; an emotionally frigid winter that she didn't like to contemplate.

"I think," he said, before she could answer him, "that you need to get out and do other things. You have your painting, your diplomat friend. I can't ask you to give up all your other activities."

She stared at him. How could a man be so obtuse, she wondered, especially a man as clever and intelligent as Guy Medfield!

A week ago she would have given up. But now she had come to know him better and to realize that a lot of his behavior was due to his own frustration, plus a staunch pride that was forever being dented by his temporary helplessness. She knew he wouldn't come out and ask her to aid him, whether it involved his book or anything else.

"Guy," she said firmly, "I really want to do it."

This was the truth, and she could only hope he would recognize it.

He nodded and said almost lazily, "Okay, then, when shall we start? Tomorrow?"

They started to work the next morning. Guy had called Tim Sousa the evening before and by the time Tracy walked across to the cottage next door Tim had managed to procure an antique but usable typewriter for her. This was set up on the kitchen table, her work area where she would transcribe Guy's dictated notes.

They worked together primarily in the living room where Guy could sit in the shadows as he dictated to her, thus sparing him the need of wearing his dark glasses. She sat by the window, and the first morning they spent a good amount of time talking about the book. He elaborated on his theme and she found that he already had managed to map out a comprehensive outline. He had been right when he said it was all in his mind, and he had progressed as far as setting the basic structure down on paper. It was beyond that, he confessed, that he had gotten bogged down.

Tracy made sandwiches for their lunch, but they didn't linger over them. They were both anxious to get back to work. Now he started to dictate to her and by midafternoon they were well into the first chapter.

Toward four o'clock, Guy stood up and stretched. "Time for a break," he told her. "Let's walk up to Sankaty Head Light."

She was agreeably surprised, especially when he took her arm without being asked. He still brought the walking stick with him, but he seemed content to let her guide him. There was an easy camaraderie between them as they walked along together. She had never felt so close to him.

Even so she sensed a certain restraint on Guy's part, but it wasn't until she was alone in her own cottage that evening that she recognized the difference in him. He had made no attempt to touch her today aside from taking her arm on the walk to Sankaty Head. There had been no kisses, no attempt at an embrace. He had been *friendlier* than before, so agreeable that she had not at once realized his attitude toward her had become almost brotherly.

Had he thought matters out? she wondered. Had he decided that now that they would be working together on a daily basis he had better cool his ardor? It was the more discreet course, she had to admit that; had he come close to her, had he touched her as he usually did, she could not possibly have concentrated on his dictation.

Yet, this change in his attitude gnawed at her. She couldn't possibly feel like a sister toward Guy, she thought ruefully. She didn't want to be his sister!

What *did* she want to be? A part of his life, she found herself thinking. She wanted to be a necessary, vital part of his life.

This, she warned herself, was a dangerous line to follow!

She got up early the next morning, ate breakfast, then waited impatiently until it was time to go next door. He was ready for her and they quickly settled down to work. Again they took a short lunch break and in the afternoon went for a walk. Then they came back to work awhile longer before calling it a day.

She offered this time to make supper for him, and was not at all surprised by his answer, which was a rather short, "That's not necessary, Tracy."

"You have cheese in the fridge which is going to waste," she pointed out. "I could make you an omelette and a salad."

"If you like," he said indifferently.

She could have shaken him until she noted the taut line around his mouth and knew, without being told, that he had a headache again. Without being asked, she went and got aspirin and a small glass of milk, only to be met with an icy stare when she handed both to him.

"You *are* a frustrated nurse, aren't you!" he commented coolly.

"I am not!" she snapped. "Don't be such an idiot! The least you could do is to tell me when you need something."

His mouth twitched. "That's a dangerous statement," he pointed out, and for just an instant the brotherly mask slipped.

When she served the omelettes, he was listening to the radio. As he switched it off he said, "There's a powerful hurricane starting up the coast. They say it's one to keep an eye on. It could eventually head this way."

It had been another perfect day; the thought of a storm seemed remote and she said so. "True," he agreed. "But we won't be feeling its effect for quite a while, if it continues in this direction at all. There's always a good chance it will go out to sea and miss us."

"Should we get in some extra supplies, just in case?" she asked.

"It might be a thought," he conceded. "Candles, especially, and flashlight bulbs. Maybe some jugs of drinking water in case we were to lose our power. I have a gas stove, though, so we could still cook. In any event, it's nothing to worry about at the moment." He finished the omelette and put his plate aside. "Added to all your other talents, you're a good cook," he observed.

"Thank you, sir."

"Demure, too, eh? Are you tired, Tracy?"

"No. Why?"

"I worked you awfully hard today. You mustn't let me be a slave driver, you know. But I can't believe how easily it's all coming along, thanks to you. Too bad you have to go back to Boston so soon, though I think we can get quite a bit of the book down before you leave, provided I don't wear you out in the process."

"No danger," she assured him. "For that matter, I imagine Florence wouldn't mind my taking another week if it would help."

He shook his head. "No," he told her. "I want to get back to Boston myself the first part of the month. Anyway, we've time enough."

Time enough. Could there ever be time enough,

where Guy was concerned? Tracy wondered. She needed time in which to come to a full understanding of him, for he was in many ways still an enigma to her, an impossibly hard person to read.

Gloria Denton hadn't visited him again. But each morning when she got up Tracy knew a brief moment of fear before she looked out the window, dreading the possibility of seeing the red car parked down the street.

Maybe he talked to Gloria on the phone at night after she left. There was no way of knowing. Maybe, on the brunette's last visit, he and Gloria had quarreled. There was no way of knowing about that either.

As it was, Tracy didn't have too much time in which to think about it. They were in a habitual pattern now. She transcribed the notes she had taken the day before first thing in the morning. Then she took dictation till lunch, resuming again in the afternoon. After their walk, she would read to Guy what she had typed in the morning. At the end of the day she usually fixed dinner for both of them.

He insisted on helping her clean up, saying that the least he could do was dry the dishes. He managed this with surprising efficiency seeing that he was working primarily by a sense of touch. Watching him one evening, Tracy frowned. It didn't seem to her that his vision was improving and she wondered if things were going for him as they should be going. Probably the process of regaining his sight was a very slow one, she conceded; at least she hoped this was the case. She wished she had the courage to come right out and ask him about his eyes and how long it was apt to take before there would be positive results. But she knew instinctively that this was a forbidden area.

They were so immersed in the book that they seldom spoke about anything else. She was discovering that the book was revealing in many ways insofar as Guy's character was concerned. In it he showed wonderful qualities of humor, compassion, and a deep love for humanity. He understood people and their fears; he made it clear that he did not consider fear a weakness and had, in fact, experienced a good deal of it himself.

A philosophy that she found extremely positive shone through everything he said, yet he didn't dodge issues. Rather he faced them squarely, even when confronting death, which was no stranger to him. There was real beauty to much of what he had to say. Yet, he could at times be totally scientific, detached, his words incisive and laced with a logic that couldn't be disputed.

The book was as variable and fascinating as he was. There was no pretense in Tracy's statement to him that she couldn't wait to get back to it each day.

She wondered how much he might say in it about his own injury and the depression that must have overwhelmed him when, for a time, he feared he was going to lose his sight. She soon discovered, though, that he had no intention of becoming that personal in his writing by detailing his own feelings, and she couldn't help but be disappointed by this. She yearned to understand Guy better in every way possible.

Late one afternoon, as they relaxed with a drink after having put in an especially good day's work, she asked him about this aspect of the book.

"If you told people about what you've been through yourself, I think it would have a great impact," she said, trying to be casual about it. "You wouldn't seem like just another doctor prescribing for the public."

He eyed her narrowly. "Is that how I seem?"

"No, of course not," she said quickly. "The book is excellent, as far as it goes. But I think it would be even better if you could bring yourself to talk about your own doubts, your own suffering, and how you came through it all."

"Came through it all?"

"Yes."

He laughed shortly. *"Have* I come through it, Tracy?" he asked, an odd note to his voice. "You should know better than most people that I'm still not the easiest person in the world to deal with."

"I doubt you ever have been," she said firmly. "I don't think your disposition has all that much to do with your eye problem!"

"You're right, I suppose. Other factors in my life that came long before the eye problem helped to fuse my disposition," he admitted. He stared ahead of him seemingly lost in memory, and Tracy felt a pang of jealousy. She suspected that he was brooding the girl he had married, and for the first time she wondered if he might still be in love with his ex-wife. This was a daunting thought. It was bad enough to know that somewhere offstage Gloria Denton was lurking and might drive up in her red car at any moment!

Had Guy, perhaps, suggested to Gloria that she not come to the island while he was working on the book?

Questions, questions—most of them without answers. Tracy sighed deeply.

His voice interrupted her thoughts. "Am I such a problem, Tracy?" he asked her. "Don't tell me I'm making *you* morose!"

"No," she said flatly, "you don't make me morose. But sometimes I *do* wonder about you."

"Wonder about what, specifically?" He shrugged. "Don't bother to answer that question. The last thing I want to discuss just now is myself. Look, would you mind taking dictation for another hour or so? I've been thinking about some things I'd like to get down."

He had switched the subject away from himself, and she was annoyed. Sometimes the wall Guy hid behind seemed unscalable, she decided, then swiftly corrected herself. Guy didn't *hide,* that was the wrong analogy. He simply *put* himself behind the wall when he wished to, thus out of reach.

Tracy had not forgotten about Gerry, and her promise to have dinner with him again at the Jared Coffin House. Each morning she was mindful of the fact that the days were passing and Gerry would be leaving very soon.

She liked Gerry and there was an edge of guilt to her thoughts of him. But she feared that before he left Nantucket he was going to make a definite declaration toward her and this was something she really didn't want to handle just now.

Also, there was the matter of his aunt. Tracy had found Emily Stanhope charming; she was a woman she would like to get to know better. Yet she knew Mrs. Stanhope wanted her nephew to settle down and find a wife, and—thanks in part to her appreciation of antiques—she had qualified almost immediately as a possible candidate.

The last thing she needed, Tracy told herself, was a matchmaker on her scene. Further, she suspected that Emily Stanhope was more than a little used to getting her way. She didn't want to have to sever her relationship with either Gerry or his aunt, and hoped that matters would not progress to a point where she would have to do so.

She and Gerry had talked on the phone the day after Tracy had started working on the book with Guy and she determined not to hedge with him again as she had about her arm. Instead she had told him of this "temporary job" she had taken and then steeled herself, prepared for his protests.

He had been surprisingly accepting of it, and she began to realize why he was successful as a diplomat.

He said, "Well, I can imagine he really does need someone to help him, under the circumstances, and he's lucky to find such a lovely candidate. I can see that time probably drags a bit for you, too. There's not that much to do here at this time of the year, and you're not the type to lounge around. Just save a few hours now and then for me, will you?"

Thus far, she hadn't. But this evening, when she finally walked back to her cottage, she was feeling more than a little discouraged. Guy had been aloof. When they went back to work after their drink together, he had been all business. Theirs was strictly an employer-secretary relationship as he dictated to her, and she began to wish she had never mentioned to him putting some of his own experiences into his book. Evidently her doing so had started a train of thought that he was not about to share with her. He had been dour the balance of the time she was with him.

She had fixed a quick spaghetti supper for them, but they had eaten in silence. Afterwards, when they had settled down in front of the fire with coffee, Tracy prepared to read to him the notes she had typed up earlier in the day only to have him say to her ungraciously, "You don't need to stay around and do this if you don't want to. I could go over it myself later."

Her "Oh?" betrayed her surprise and she saw him frown.

"I'm *not* blind, you know," he said testily. "Sometimes I feel you think I don't have much vision . . . about anything."

She knew that he was challenging her. But she realized exactly where this would lead if she responded to it. They would plunge into yet another fruitless argument, and she could see no point in this.

She said slowly, "I didn't think you were supposed to read, that's all."

"Don't jump to conclusions!" he told her coldly. "It tends to be a habit of yours."

Again, she refused to rise to the bait. He was in a bad mood tonight and she felt she had precipitated it, bringing back memories when she had inferred that he might make his book a bit more autobiographical. Now she knew of only one way in which she might be able to snap him out of it, and she could imagine what his reaction would be if she were to go over to him and entwine her arms around his neck and kiss him as she wanted desperately to kiss him! Thinking about it, she could almost feel the warm touch of his mouth. A sensation of pure desire was born within her, so tantalizing that it was close to impossible not to yield to impulse.

But he had not so much as touched her since they had started on the book. He hadn't blatantly ignored her, true, but it was obvious to her that he had been avoiding physical contact except for the times when they walked together and he took her arm.

Why? she wondered. From the beginning a kind of wildfire had burned between them. How could it have died so completely on his part for no valid reason that she could think of?

This she pondered, as she went back to her cottage that night. So when the phone rang and it was Gerry she was more responsive to him than she might have been otherwise. She agreed to be ready at six the next evening for cocktails and dinner.

Guy was waiting for her at the kitchen door the following morning. Sunlight was streaming through the yellow curtains but he wasn't wearing his dark glasses. She started to say something to him about this, then thought better of it. There was no point in sparking off a reaction that would start their day on a bad note.

He said impatiently, "Before we get started I want to take out your stitches."

It had been a deep cut. He had examined it once or twice and decided to leave the stitches in a bit longer. Now she shuddered slightly because she tended to be a bit squeamish about things like this, but he paid her no attention.

"We can do it at this end of the kitchen table," he said. "The light is best out here."

She helped him get towels to make a padding for an arm rest. Then despite the brightness in the room he directed her to get the lamp with the bright light from the living room which he had used at the time of her accident.

It seemed to her that his dark head was bent so close over her arm that his forehead was going to touch her skin as he worked. Had he been *this* close before when he had put in the stitches? It hadn't been that long ago, but it seemed to her that there had been a bit more of a gap that first time, and she felt a fresh pang of anxiety for him. She couldn't repress the thought that his vision was getting worse rather than better.

Despite the fact that he had to bend so low, he worked quickly and expertly. To her astonishment she didn't even feel a twinge. Finished, he sat back surveying her, those arresting gray eyes like quicksilver.

"That does it," he said. "It has healed very nicely. The eventual scar will be minimal." He added, almost reluctantly, "You've been a very good patient, Tracy."

"Probably," she said, "because you're the best doctor I've ever had in my life."

He was still very close to her, and that quicksilver glance blazed briefly. Then she could see him swallow hard, and he said thickly, "We'd better get to work."

A sense of triumph shot through her. She *knew* in that instant that he wanted her every bit as much as she wanted him. "Guy," she began, but he interrupted almost fiercely.

"I said we'd better get to work," he told her swiftly.

"Is that all you can think about in connection with me?" she asked him dolefully.

"No," he said honestly. "You are a very attractive young lady, Tracy. Stimulating, exciting. I'm sure you already know that; you must arouse most of the men you meet pretty easily. So, there are a great many things other than working on my book that I could think about in connection with you, but I don't want to. That's the difference."

It was a cutting thing to say, especially brutal because he spoke so incisively, without regret. She turned away feeling a little sick from pure letdown, and he said derisively, "What's the matter? Are you fed up with the job already?"

Anger came in the wake of the passion he had so carelessly discarded. She knew him well enough to be sure that he had been entirely aware of her feelings. Yes, he had realized very well that he had only to reach out and take her in his arms, and that if he so much as brushed her body with his it would start passion's molten lava flowing through her veins.

She said tensely, "Are *you* fed up with having me work with you?"

To her surprise, she saw his mouth tighten and the telltale muscle in his jaw began to twitch. Briefly he hesitated, then he said, "No. I appreciate what you've been doing for me more than I can say. I don't want you to feel you have to continue if it's becoming boring for you, that's all."

"It isn't."

"Then maybe we'd better get on with it," he suggested.

They went into the living room, Tracy ready with her

pencil and notebook. But a tension had arisen between them that couldn't be dispelled all that easily. Guy made several false starts before picking up the threads of his narrative, and even then he wasn't satisfied with what he was doing.

They took a midmorning break and had coffee, but Tracy found it impossible to relax. She thought of suggesting that she pack a lunch and they drive over to the Jetties for a change of scene, but she was sure Guy would only veto this idea. No doubt about it, she conceded dismally, he was in an odd mood.

They did better after the coffee break, and by lunchtime were fairly well in stride again. Lunch, by mutual consent, was a brief interval, and afterwards they progressed with the kind of swift ease that had characterized most of their work together.

It was nearly four when he suggested they take time out to walk to Sankaty Head Light together. This time, as he took her arm, his touch evoked sensations in her that she feared she couldn't camouflage. But when she shivered, he either didn't get the message or decided to be deliberately obtuse.

"You should have worn a warmer jacket," he told her abruptly.

She felt like telling him that it was her heart that was cold, and that there wasn't a jacket in the world that could do a thing for it. But she said only, "I'm fine."

He didn't comment. They spoke very little on the walk, and Tracy, disheartened, yearned for a recurrence of their earlier camaraderie. The rapport that had grown between them at first now seemed to be diminishing with each passing day. She could only wonder if this was because their time on the island was getting shorter.

Did Guy fear that she was going to try to see him after they both got back to Boston? Was this where

Gloria Denton really entered the picture? Was he so involved with Gloria that he wanted to be sure of leaving Nantucket without encumbrances?

Tracy didn't like to think of herself as an encumbrance. In fact the mere thought made her angry because it seemed to her that Guy should know her well enough to realize she would never want to be a millstone around his neck. Was *that* what he feared? True, he was wealthy, highly successful in his profession, and, beyond everything else, a disturbingly handsome and virile man. There was no doubt that many women must covet his attentions. There was little doubt, Tracy thought bitterly, that he had *ever* lacked for female attention.

That early marriage seemed to have burned him, though, burned him badly. Guy could become aroused as easily as any man—Tracy had proven that for herself. But he was possessed of an unusual amount of self-discipline. He would, she knew, let things progress only so far as he wanted them to, and it seemed that in her case he evidently didn't want them to progress very far at all!

Chapter Eleven

Tracy didn't think to tell Guy about her dinner engagement with Gerry until they were back at the cottage again after the walk to Sankaty Head, and she was mixing drinks for them.

She was surprised by his reaction. Obviously he was displeased. "Must you?" he asked coldly.

"Now, yes," she said, "because I've told him I'll go with him."

"And you never go back on your word?"

"Not if I can help it."

"I'd thought we might spend the evening doing a general runover of everything we've done so far," he said. "We haven't much more time, so I've got to think of wrapping the whole thing up. I realize we can't possibly finish it . . ."

"I was hoping we could," she admitted.

"No, I don't intend for you to burn the midnight oil over this," he said sternly. "I thought if I could get down the whole sweep of it then later I could fill in the details."

"I would be perfectly willing to burn the midnight oil, as you put it, tonight or any other night if you'd give me a bit of advance notice," she said. "When Gerry asked me to dinner, though, I saw no reason to refuse him. I didn't know you wanted to put in an especially long work stint, and since you've started to read the finished copy by yourself . . ."

He didn't answer this. Instead, he twirled the ice in his drink for a long moment, and then he said, "Tracy, I have no claim on you!"

"What does this have to do with having a claim on me?"

"Very well, then," he corrected testily. "I have no claim on your time. As it is, I intend to pay you fully for what you've done, even though we haven't discussed money. I've decided to give you a lump sum when we finish here."

She could feel her cheeks flame, and she stared at him in disbelief. "You're offering me *money?*" she demanded.

"You certainly didn't think I'd let you work like this for nothing, did you?" he countered.

"I hadn't considered payment at all. I knew you needed someone to help you out with the book. I thought I would qualify and that it would be an enjoyable project."

"But it hasn't been an enjoyable project?" He picked this up quickly.

"It's getting not to be!"

"I see," he said, and silence came between them.

Tracy felt as if she'd been charged with electricity. She quivered all over. She said, the words coming painfully, "I wasn't for hire, Dr. Medfield."

"Tracy . . ."

"No!" she said, every fibre of her flooded with resentment toward him. "You think you can buy anything you want, don't you, including people? Then, if you find you don't want to keep what you've gotten you just . . . throw it away. Well, I wasn't for sale in the first place, and I'm not about to become your castoff. I . . ."

She had gotten to her feet without even realizing it, and she faced him indignantly. But he said only, almost mildly, "You're taking this in entirely the wrong way."

"The hell I am!" she challenged. "What were you going to do? Write me a check? I guarantee I'll tear it in a thousand pieces if you do. If you offer me cash, I'll burn the bills up, right here in the fireplace. You can watch them sizzle . . ."

"Just as you are sizzling now?"

"All right," she said. "Yes, I'm angry. I'm furious!"

He was staring straight ahead at the leaping flames, and he said slowly, "I don't blame you for being angry. I . . . apologize, and I only hope you'll consider accepting my apology. I can't offer you any excuses for the way I've been acting because there aren't any. I've had quite a bit on my mind—there are so many decisions to be made once I get back to Boston. Maybe someday I can explain things better . . ."

Someday. It was the first time he'd ever indicated that there might be a place for her in his future. Someday. It wasn't much, but it was better than nothing.

The dinner with Gerry was not a success. Tracy had still been in an emotional turmoil when she had left Guy's cottage. In fact, he had in effect dismissed her, saying, "If you don't get along you're going to be late for your dinner date."

He had been sitting in front of the fire when she'd left him, and she had paused in the doorway to glance back at him. Again, he had seemed to read her mind. "Get along, Tracy," he had said, but not unkindly. His tone had been almost gentle.

She had chosen a gold wool dress to wear that was a deeper version of the color of her hair, and she used a little more makeup than usual. Tension had made her look tired, and she didn't want Gerry to start accusing her of working too hard with her next-door neighbor. She clipped on topaz earrings and fastened a gold chain around her neck, and was quite unaware of how lovely she looked.

Gerry drove up exactly at six, and she met him at the door. His eyes feasted on her, and he said huskily, "Between meetings, I keep forgetting how beautiful you are! I might add that our meetings are entirely too far apart, too. Your doctor seems to be a slave driver."

"Not really," she said lightly. Deftly, she switched the subject. "How is your aunt?"

"Fine, thanks, and she sent you her best wishes. She'd like to have you come to lunch again as soon as you can."

"I really can't take time off for a luncheon," she told him. "Guy was mentioning today that we've only a few days left, and we want to get down as much as possible?"

"What is this book?" Gerry demanded curiously.

"A very interesting blend of medical advice and philosophy, with a lot of compassion in it, humor, understanding."

"You sound quite taken with it."

"I am. Guy was asked to do it by a Boston publisher, and I have an idea it will be quite a success once he's finished."

"You plan to see it all the way through with him?"

"No. My part will end when I leave the island."

"You mean he hasn't asked you to come and work with him in Boston?"

"No," Tracy said, keeping a tight rein on the tone of her voice.

"Well," Gerry said, "that *is* a plus. I was afraid that now that he's got you in his clutches he would never let go."

"He hardly has me in his clutches, Gerry. This is a—working arrangement."

"I hadn't realized that," he said thoughtfully. "I thought it was a sort of mutual thing, I . . ."

"Can't we talk of something else?" she asked him.

They had come to the edge of Nantucket Town, and he glanced at her curiously. "Are you and your doctor at odds with each other by any chance?" he asked her.

"Not really. Why?"

"You seem edgy when you talk about him. Is he proving a hard taskmaster?"

"Guy is a perfectionist, to a point," she admitted. "I suppose most good surgeons are; they'd have to be, after all. He drives himself a lot harder than he does me, though. He's his own severest critic, and he won't let something go until he has it as he thinks it should be."

"I feel you've gotten yourself in over your head," Gerry said, and added. "I mean you must be spending an awful lot of hours on this, and that's not what you intended, is it?"

"At the time I said I'd work with Guy I didn't think that much about it," she conceded. "You pointed out yourself that there isn't all that much to do on Nantucket this time of year. I can rest only so much of the time, and although I enjoy trying to paint I can't spend hours on it, day after day after day."

"You could have opted to spend considerably more time with me," he suggested.

There was no satisfactory answer to this that she could think of.

At the Jared Coffin House they lingered over cocktails. Then Gerry ordered a succulent dish of fresh flounder rolled and stuffed with a mixture of shrimp and lobster. Tracy was sincere when she said that she had never tasted anything more delicious.

Even the edge of the excellent food was dulled, though, insofar as her real appreciation of it was concerned. She found it impossible to wrest her thoughts away from Guy.

This was the first time since they had been working together that she had not fixed dinner for him; simple meals, for the most part but far more nutritious, she suspected, than anything he would bother fixing for himself. She wondered what he might be eating tonight and told herself angrily that he was an adult, a doctor at that. He didn't need this kind of solicitude!

Over dessert, a warm, molasses-flavored Indian pudding topped with ice cream, Gerry said impatiently, "Where are you, Tracy? Not here with me, certainly."

"I'm sorry," she said, mentally shaking herself.

"Has he become all that important to you, Tracy? You're in love with him, aren't you?"

When she hesitated, he said gently, "I recognize the symptoms because I'm suffering from the same affliction myself!"

This gave her courage. "Yes," she said, voicing it aloud for the first time. "I am in love with him, Gerry. It wouldn't be fair to you to say otherwise. He is *not* in love with me, though. Oh, he has been attracted to me to a certain extent"—not to anyone would she ever admit how far that extent had carried the night she cut her arm—"but there is no room for me in his life. He has—other commitments."

"Are you talking about his career?"

"No. His career, too, of course, and he expects to resume it after he gets back to Boston, but there is definitely a woman. She visits Guy frequently. I've met her."

"Doesn't she object to his working with you in his cottage?"

"Evidently not. She knows what the book means to

him, I'm sure. She's probably anxious for him to get it down. You see, he's had a sort of mental block about it, but talking it out with me has helped."

"I can imagine," Gerry said wryly. He reached across the table, to grasp her left hand. Staring down at it, he said, "I'd like to put a ring on your finger, Tracy."

"Gerry, please . . ."

"No," he shook his head. "The time has come when you must hear me out. Once I leave here, it would be so easy to—to lose you completely and I want you in my life. I want you in my life more than I can possibly tell you, Tracy. You're so entirely right for me."

"I don't think so," she tried to tell him.

"I know so," he corrected her. "You're old enough to have gained a certain lovely maturity, yet you also seem so young, so untouched in many ways. There's a potential radiance about you, Tracy, still to come to the surface. I'd like to be the one to bring it out, and I think I could . . . given the chance by you. I know you don't love me, but you *like* me, don't you?"

"Of course I like you, Gerry."

"I think love could come later," he said, his tanned, handsome face earnest. "I think I could teach you to love me, Tracy, and we could have a glorious life together. You like to travel . . ."

"Yes," she admitted, "I love to travel, though I've done very little of it. There isn't a place in the world I don't want to see."

"You could see a great many of them with me," he promised. "I've traveled a lot myself, and there is so much I want to show you. Paris, for the first time. You've never been to Paris, have you?"

"No."

"I want to walk with you along the Seine," he said, "and take you down the river on a *bateau mouche*. I want you to see Notre Dame in the moonlight, and to go out to Versailles with me where you'll learn what opulence really means. While we're in Madrid, I want to take you down to the Costa del Sol. We'll go to a beach place I know on the way to Gibraltar . . ."

His words were tantalizing. He was, in effect, offering her the entire world on a sterling silver platter and she admitted to herself that it would be extremely easy to say yes to him.

Gerry was attractive, a good companion, he would make a wonderful husband and life with him would be fascinating. She didn't doubt that perhaps, in time, she really could come to love him. But it would be a love unrelated to the surging, consuming feeling she had for Guy Medfield. Gerry, she thought sadly, would be getting less than half a loaf if she were to marry him. It wouldn't be fair to him.

She said unsteadily, "I only wish I could say yes, Gerry, but I couldn't do that to you."

"What do you think you're going to be doing to me if you say no?" he demanded.

"You'll get over it," she told him and knew in her heart that this was true. "Right now, in Madrid, there is probably a beautiful señorita . . ."

"You must think I'm a very shallow sort of person, Tracy."

"No, I don't think that at all."

"What do you imagine, then? That some dark-eyed girl with a rose between her teeth could cause me to forget about you? How wrong you are!"

He had let go of her hand, now he finished the coffee he had been drinking and set the cup down firmly.

"I'm not willing to give up," he told her stubbornly. "Don't say *anything* tonight, not yes, not no, not maybe. Let's drive out to Surfside and watch the moonlight on the ocean. Don't look like that. I promise I won't even make a pass at you. After we've soaked up some moonlight, I'll take you home. Maybe Fate can weave a spell and make you dream about me!"

Gerry kept his word. They watched the moon ladle silver radiance over the dark, crested water. Then after a time he drove her home, leaving her at her door with only the briefest of kisses.

She didn't dream about him, although she did dream. Later she could remember only that her subconscious thoughts had been disturbing and she awoke before dawn was quite ready to lighten the eastern sky.

It was difficult to stay away from the cottage next door until nine o'clock when she and Guy usually started work. As she started out, she was surprised to see Tim Sousa's truck pulled up in front. Tim usually came to Guy's with supplies and such around their lunchtime, now, so that he would not interfere with their work.

Tim met her at the kitchen door, his usually merry face solemn. She asked swiftly, fear striking at her, "Is something wrong?"

"He's asleep," Tim said. "Matter of fact, I might as well tell you, since you're bound to find it out anyway, that he's going to wake up with a monstrous hangover. He really tied one on last night. I guess he drank everything in sight. He called me first thing this morning and asked me to bring him over some vodka and bloody mary mix. I guess he figures he needs some of the hair of the dog that bit him."

Tim added, worried, "This isn't like him. I've never seen him go off the deep end like this before. Did the two of you have a fight or something?"

"No," she said rather coolly, "we didn't. Tim, you can run along. I'll let Guy sleep for a while and then I'll take him in a bloody mary."

The boy hesitated. "I don't think he'd want you to

see him," he told her. "He's going to be kind of a mess. He was looking pretty seedy before he went to sleep."

"It doesn't matter," she said firmly.

Tim left reluctantly and Tracy cleaned up some glasses on the kitchen sink, recoiling from the stench of stale whiskey. She found the empty Scotch bottle in the trashbin and shook her head over it.

She checked the contents of the fridge, which were thoroughly familiar to her, and concluded that he had fixed himself nothing to eat since she'd left him the afternoon before.

"Idiot!" she said aloud. She didn't know what to make of his behavior. In retrospect, it seemed to her that he had been moodier than usual yesterday, although he had been so changeable lately that it was difficult to be sure about this. Guy, she decided, was like an unpredictable storm, like the hurricane, supposedly brewing to the south of Nantucket. Now she wondered, though, if someone had phoned him after she left last night or if, perhaps, he had received some upsetting mail? If it was the latter, he hadn't left any evidence of it around!

She tidied up the living room, straightening his stack of records among other things. Evidently he had been playing them last night, but he had concentrated on music, not the talking records. The César Franck symphony was still on the turntable, and she grimaced. Although it was a favorite of hers, it seemed gloomy fare to play when one was alone and already depressed.

There was a big leather armchair in the corner of the room. Now she noticed that the manuscript—the pages she had typed from her notes thus far—was heaped in a fairly neat pile on a table next to it. He had placed the same bright light he had used in the kitchen behind the chair, and on top of the manuscript pile there was a wide and powerful hand magnifying glass. The sight of it twisted something inside her. He had spoken so casually about reading the script himself. Now, she judged, reading was not all that easy for him. Even with the bright light and the magnifying glass he had not progressed very far at the task. She calculated that he couldn't have gotten through more than six or seven pages of the copy since the last time she had read the text aloud to him.

"Stubborn!" she said, and gritted her teeth. What could one do with a proud, obstinate man like Guy Medfield?

For the next hour Tracy glanced at the kitchen clock until she grew tired of looking at the face of it. The time crawled. She tried to busy herself with straightening some of the material, and she began to type up the dictation she had taken the previous day. She could as well catch up with this aspect of her work later on, though. From what Tim Sousa had told her, it didn't seem as if Guy would be putting in much work today himself.

Finally, she couldn't stand it any longer. She crept to the door of his bedroom to see that the window curtains had been drawn and the light was dim. Even so, his long length was revealed to her and she drew in her breath sharply at the sight of him. Her eyes lingered on his face and she thought with a rueful smile that Tim had been right about one thing. Guy did look a mess. He badly needed a shave, and the dark hair was tousled as if he had run impatient fingers through it again and again and again.

She spoke his name softly and when he did not respond she went to sit down alongside of him. Tentatively, she reached out a finger and touched his cheek. To her astonishment his hand crept up to find hers and in another instant she was being drawn down on the bed next to him, his arms encircling her while, with definite urgency, he pushed his body against hers so that they were contoured together. His masculinity was blatant, and she felt suffocated by the sharp rush of desire that swept over her.

He was holding her tightly, mumbling things she couldn't entirely make out, but then she was not really listening, she was *feeling*. Each fibre of her being was brought to total life as he ran his hands along the length of her body, impatiently thrusting his palms up under the sweater she was wearing, seeking her swelling breasts.

He reached the back of her bra, and he said thickly, "For God's sake, take your clothes off."

Tracy, drunk in a way that she never had been on alcohol, was more than willing to comply. But even as she reached to draw her sweater over her head he pushed her away violently with a kind of pure, instinctive recoil.

His face was grim and his eyes raked her. "What in hell do you think you're doing?" he demanded. "Are you so desperate you're willing to have me take you when I don't even know what I'm doing?"

Her passion ebbed, leaving an ivory stillness in its wake. She couldn't possibly have answered him; she had no voice. She sat on the edge of his bed staring at her hands which she had clasped before her like a young girl going to church. She felt herself washed by shame, hot and searing, cascading over her and leaving no part of her untouched.

After a moment, she rallied enough to stand and started walking toward the door on legs that seemed to have turned to wooden stilts. At once, he called angrily, "Where do you think you're going?"

"Does it matter?" she asked him dully.

"Tracy!"

"I'm going home, Guy," she told him, "and as soon as I get in the cottage I'm going to find out what time the next boat leaves. I'll plan to be on it."

He groaned, and she couldn't refrain from looking back at him. He lay stretched out fully on the bed, his body taut as steel, and she saw that his hands were clenched tightly at his sides.

"I thought I was dreaming," he said huskily. "Then all at once, I knew you were really in my arms. I came to, as if someone had shot me. My God, Tracy, do you think I would . . ."

"I don't know what you'd do," she admitted. "But you've made yourself plain. You have said what you think of me . . ."

"I have never said what I think of you," he contradicted.

"If there's much more to it, I don't think I ever want to hear it."

He struggled to a sitting position, and she saw him press a hand to his head. She stared down at him unsympathetically, "You deserve a headache," she said.

"Thanks."

"Why did you do such a ridiculous thing?"

He glared at her. "I'm not aware I owe you any sort of accounting," he said stiffly.

"No," she agreed, "that's for sure. You don't owe me anything and I don't owe you anything. The score is even. Let's keep it that way."

"If that's the way you want it." It was his pride speaking, and she knew it. But this time, she warned herself, she was not going to let sympathy win out over common sense.

She hesitated. "I told Tim Sousa I'd make you a bloody mary," she said. "Do you want one?"

"Yes, I do."

"Very well, then, I'll get it before I go. I'm going to take the typewriter across with me."

"Don't be ridiculous," he said shortly. "It's a standard model, and it weighs a ton."

"It doesn't matter. I'm stronger than I look."

He winced. "You can't stand the thought of even typing in the same house with me?"

"Frankly, no. I feel I should do up my notes though, because it would be impossible for anyone else to read them, and we covered quite a bit yesterday."

"I'm touched by such dedication to duty."

"It's the way I do things, that's all."

"No personal favor."

"No!"

"I don't know whether I believe that or not," he said slowly. "Maybe it's because I don't want to believe it."

"Please, Guy," she cut him off. "I'll fix your bloody mary. After you've had it, you may want to get some more sleep."

She didn't wait for his answer. Once in the kitchen, she found that her fingers were trembling as she opened the bottles of vodka and bloody mary mix. Before she could fix a drink and take it to him, though, she heard his voice from the doorway.

"Tracy."

She froze.

"Tracy, what can I say to you?" He sank down into one of the chairs at the kitchen table, burying his dark head between his hands. "Oh Christ!" he said simply.

She fought the impulse to go to him. She couldn't brush aside the things he had said to her so lightly. Guy hadn't tried in the least to curb a more than slightly acid tongue with her; she couldn't believe that he was so blatantly rude to other people.

She put the bloody mary in front of him and said, "Here's your drink."

He looked up at her and she was startled by the misery in his eyes. Then, in a convulsive movement, he reached out for the glass, but he sideswiped it as he did so and it crashed to the floor.

He cursed under his breath, then said abjectly, "What more can I do to turn you off?"

"It was an accident," she told him brusquely. "Sit where you are! There are glass fragments all over the place!"

"You're the one who should be careful!" he said, as if to remind her that she already had proven she was accident-prone. "Don't cut yourself again!"

"I have no intention of doing so," she told him icily. She found a broom, and carefully swept the glass shards into a dust pan. When she was convinced that there were no fragments left on the floor, she finished mopping up and then made a second drink for him. This time, she placed the glass directly in his hand.

"Thanks," he said. "Tracy, I'm sorry. I was still groggy . . ."

"I don't wonder," she told him.

"You needn't act so damned disapproving!" he said, stung.

"I think I do disapprove of you, Guy."

"Tracy, do you really plan to go home on the afternoon boat?"

"No," she said decisively. "For one thing, I told Gerry I'd have dinner with him and his aunt tomorrow evening, and I see no reason to change that. It would involve too many explanations that I don't want to make."

"I see."

"I don't think you do, but it doesn't really matter

very much. Anyway, I intend to type up my notes as I told you. We did quite a bit yesterday. It will take awhile."

"Would you type them here, please?"

"What's the matter?" she demanded, surprised at her own cynicism. "Do you need company?"

"No, it isn't that. I don't want you lugging that heavy machine by yourself, that's all, and I admit I'm not in shape to carry it for you just now." He added, bitterly, "Okay, I acted like an adolescent fool last night. I admit it. I was jealous as hell . . ."

"You were *what?*"

"You heard me. Doesn't it occur to you that I might like to take you out to dinner somewhere myself? It will be awhile before I'm up to it, though. Maybe this winter, in Boston . . ."

She said tersely, "Don't make promises you don't intend to keep."

He jerked his head up, startled. "What do you mean by that?"

"You have no intention of seeing me once you get back to Boston and you know it," she told him flatly. "No, never mind . . . don't deny it. I don't *need* hollow protests, Guy."

"You don't have much faith in me, do you, Tracy?"

"No," she said coldly.

He winced visibly, but he said only, "I suppose I have that coming. But would it do any good at all to ask you—to please reconsider. I know I have a nerve to even suggest it, but it would mean a great deal to me if you'd go on working with me for just these few more days."

She bit her lip. Even when he was asking a favor of her, there was an assurance to Guy's manner; his confidence in himself, she decided, was inviolable. He would never grovel to anyone, that was for sure, most especially to a woman.

Yet, it would be childish to refuse him. She wanted to see the book through as much as he did.

"Very well," she said stonily.

"Thank you, Tracy," he said, his voice grave. He finished the bloody mary and stood up. "Shall we get to work?" he asked.

She couldn't conceal her surprise. "Do you feel you're up to it?"

"Yes, if you are," he said easily. "You might give me a few more minutes to shave so I won't look like such a villain. Maybe you wouldn't mind making a pot of coffee in the meantime?"

He smiled at her as he spoke, and she was captivated all over again. She turned away from him, busying herself with filling the coffeepot, but her treacherous pulse was pounding.

He was impossible, she told herself. Utterly impossible!

Chapter Twelve

Guy behaved very well the next day. He was extremely polite to her, like a courteous stranger, and she almost wished for a return of the tantalizing man who could be so annoying, so disturbing, but also so irresistible. Now she began to feel at moments as if she were his patient rather than a temporary secretary, and as if he were giving her the best possible example of his professional manner.

The following morning, though, she saw Tim Sousa's pickup truck out in front again, and she was tempted to turn back. She promised herself that if she found Guy in the throes of a hangover once again she would fulfill her earlier resolution and take the afternoon boat back to the mainland!

He was at the kitchen table, however, making a list while Tim watched him.

"Tracy," he greeted her. "Sit down, will you? Would you like some coffee? Tim just brewed a fresh pot."

"Thank you, yes," she said, regarding him curiously.

The silver gray eyes swept her face. "I don't want to frighten you," he said, "but the hurricane I've been telling you about is heading this way. It looks as if it may go out to sea somewhat to the south of us, but we're certainly going to get a fair brush from it. Tim's going to bring in some supplies for us, candles and some of the other things we mentioned the other day.

You might add a jug of bourbon, Tim, for inner fortification, and a couple of chocolate bars for sugar energy."

"Sugar energy?" she questioned. "I thought that theory had been dispelled."

He grinned. "Let's just say I like to eat candy in a crisis," he said agreeably. He turned back to Tim. "I think we have a Coleman lantern, don't we?" he asked.

"Yes, out back in the shed," the boy agreed. "There's one over at Mrs. Thorndyke's place, too."

"Good. That should do it," Guy said. "You'd better pick up some extra cans of fuel for the lanterns, though, to be sure we have enough." He handed the list to Tim, then added, "Check around outside, both at the Thorndyke place and here, will you? If there's anything loose, either batten it down or, if it's portable, put it inside." He turned back to Tracy. "Trash cans, lawn furniture, barbecues, anything movable, can become airborne in a big wind and do considerable damage to other things—to say nothing of people. Tim, you might close up the shutters in the Thorndyke cottage. I think you should leave a window open on either side, though, just a slit." Again he turned to Tracy. "That's to equalize pressure so the glass doesn't shatter," he explained.

"What about your own windows?"

"We'll be here, we can do it when the time comes," he told her.

Tim said, "I'll get going, Mr. Medfield." She had noted that Tim never did call him "Doctor," and this rather amused her. "After I finish here, there's going to be a fair bit to do around my own place."

"Right," Guy nodded.

Glancing out the kitchen window, Tracy said, "It doesn't seem possible there's a major storm coming this way. It's still beautiful out."

"The weather will worsen as the morning gets on,"

Guy promised her. "Right now, if you went up to Sankaty Head you'd see that there's an odd, oily look to the ocean. I always notice that sort of slickness first before a storm. Later it makes the sea like gray satin. Sometimes there's a stillness, too, as if Nature is getting ready for a big show. Then, long before the wind rises, it begins to rain. Hurricane rain is quite fine, at first, like a dense drizzle. Later, it really pours."

"You sound as if you've had quite a bit of experience with hurricanes," Tracy said.

"Enough," he agreed. "We haven't had a head-on one here on the island for a number of years, but now and then you do get the edge and it can be pretty fierce. There are still old timers around who remember the great New England hurricane back in 1938 . . ."

"Do you mean to say that was before your time?" she demanded wickedly, remembering the way he tended to lay such emphasis on his age.

"Yes, witch, it was," he said, with no change of expression at all. But for the moment, something warmer seemed to come between them, and it left in its wake a twinge of physical pain for Tracy.

It would be as well when October came, she told herself. She couldn't go on much longer being so close to Guy while at the same time so far away from him.

"I should have mentioned it sooner," she said now, "but did you ask Tim to get enough candles for me, too? I meant to check over at Aunt Sally's to see if there were any, but I forgot about it."

He said smoothly, "No need. You'll be staying here."

She was rinsing out her empty coffee cup and she turned to confront him, not quite believing what she had heard. "I beg your pardon?" she asked.

"Well," he said, "it's a question of either my going to your place or your staying here, and it seemed to me that this was the better choice, unless you have a real objection to it."

"Is there any reason why we can't ride out the storm under our own roofs?" she demanded.

"Is there any reason why we should?" he countered.

"Yes, I think so."

"For God's sake, Tracy!" The old irascibility was surfacing and, perversely, she welcomed it. "I'm not going to attack you!"

"I'd rather be alone, if you don't mind," she insisted steadily.

"Very well, then, I do mind."

"What's the matter?" she taunted. "Are you afraid of the dark? You said the power might go out."

He drew a long breath, and she shrank from the expression on his face. It combined anger and bleakness in a frightening way. "Perhaps I *am* afraid of the dark," he said tonelessly. "Many people are, it's nothing to be ashamed of. But I wasn't thinking of the dark. I was thinking of the fact you might be frightened if we really get hit by this. Even the edge of a hurricane can bring a certain amount of terror with it. I wouldn't want you running out to try to get over here in the middle of the whole thing. The wind takes large tree branches and snaps them off as if they were twigs, then thrusts them through the air like giant javelins."

"Thank you," she said, "but you don't scare me. I can assure you I'd have no intention of running over here during the middle of anything."

He stared at her moodily. "You're a long way from forgiving me, aren't you, even though you agreed to stay on and see the book through?"

"There is nothing to forgive you *for*," she said wearily. "Let's not get personal, Guy."

"All right, Tracy, we won't get personal but we will be sensible. It would be ridiculous for you to be there and me to be here when we would be more comfortable sharing the same space. We can conserve our resources and make better use of them. That could be important if the storm is a big one, and the island gets cut off from the mainland as far as supplies are concerned. Nantucket, remember, is thirty miles out to sea. The island depends on getting supplies primarily by boat. To a lesser degree, of course, planes can bring things in. However, the boats get through when the planes can't fly, so water is still the big communication link for Nantucket and the rest of the world. Sometimes in winter Nantucket Sound freezes over and the island has to live on its own resources for days at a time. The same thing could happen in a major storm. I'm not being capricious when I say there's no point in using two candles, two lanterns, two stoves, when one would do."

He was making sense, of course. Tracy was forced to acknowledge this even though she wished she could refute what he was saying. The thought of being with him on a round-the-clock basis until the storm was over was almost more than she could contemplate.

He said now, "There's no reason not to work today, unless you don't want to. Hurricanes don't suddenly descend, they give fair warning if you know how to recognize it. In any event once Tim has us battened down there's nothing we can do but sit it out. Do you want to take dictation or do you want to type up yesterday's notes?"

"It's entirely up to you."

"Very well. Suppose you take dictation for an hour or so and then type for an hour or so. It might be easier for you to alternate back and forth today." He smiled at her. "Variety tends to take one's mind off things," he told her.

"All right."

They went into the living room, Guy settling down in

his usual chair. Tracy picked up her note pad to discover that her fingers were trembling again. This, though, had nothing to do with apprehension about the hurricane. Rather, it was because the thought of being here with Guy was overwhelming.

How long did a hurricane last? She had no idea, nor did she want to ask him. He would read her thoughts much too accurately.

"Ready?" he asked.

"Yes."

"You sound nervous, Tracy."

"I'm not nervous," she said, trying not to look at him. He was wearing a pair of snug-fitting jeans today that left little to the imagination, and a cream-colored Irish knit sweater that was devastatingly becoming. Since they had been taking the daily walks together, a healthy glow had come into his face. He had lost the pallor that had been so noticeable when they first had met. It seemed to her that he had never been more attractive, and she had to force her thoughts to the work at hand with all the inner strength she could muster.

Before he began to dictate, he said, "I think we've come to the point where I'm going to generalize. I'm going to sketch things out rather broadly, and then I may indicate where I want to elaborate. That's something I'll do later. If we work in this way, I estimate we should be able to finish what we're doing over the next two days unless the storm really puts a crimp in our style. That will give you your last slot of time on the island free."

She couldn't answer. Two days! She wanted to stop time, to grasp the clock and turn it back.

"Tracy?" he asked. "Is something the matter?"

"I've broken my pencil," she said. "Excuse me, I'll be right back."

The pencil sharpener was in the kitchen. She sharpened not one but three pencils while she was at it, nearly destroying the first one so that with a muffled, impatient exclamation she threw it away. Her mind was whirling and she knew she had to get a grip on herself. Otherwise Guy would soon diagnose, accurately, what was really the matter with her: him. She was obsessed by him, and this was an illness for which, she knew very well, he was not about to offer a prescription with any lasting, curative powers.

Back in the living room, she said, "I'm sorry I took so long."

"That's all right. Now, if we can pick up where we left off yesterday . . ."

They worked assiduously for the next hour, after which she went out to the kitchen again to take her place before the typewriter and transcribe her notes of the previous day. As always, she became absorbed in the task. It disappointed her to think that she wouldn't be seeing the book through to its entirety.

But again, as she worked, she wished that Guy would be more personal in his writing. This was the only thing the book lacked, but it was an important ingredient. There was a detachment to his work which she felt sure was because he was so determined not to reveal anything of himself. The contents still carried the book, yet she knew it would be much better if he showed glimpses of his own fears—certainly he must have them—and his own humanity.

He came, finally, to interrupt her typing. She was going at quite a pace when he appeared in the doorway to say, "It's a wonder those keys don't clatter right off the machine. You're a speed demon."

"I wanted to get this done so I could read it back to you later," she explained.

She had resumed reading copy to him at the end of

each working day, usually after a quick supper which she prepared for them. He had not again mentioned leaving the manuscript for him to read himself once she had left, and she didn't like to think of his having to cope with a magnifying glass as he tried to make out his own words.

Stacking up the paper she said absently, "Do you want lunch?"

"Tracy, you're not punching a time clock," he told her reprovingly. "Do you suppose we could sit down and have a glass of wine together first?"

"Wine?"

"Yes. I have some soave, or perhaps you'd rather have sherry. Both are in the liquor cabinet."

"It doesn't matter to me. Which do you want?"

"Soave, please. You might make it on the rocks. I should have put it in the fridge to chill."

Again, her hands were trembling as she poured the wine and she wondered if he noticed this. Could he see that well yet?

Evidently he could, for after a moment he said, "Why are you so jittery?"

"I don't know," she hedged. "I guess it's because it's a rather odd feeling knowing you're going to get struck by a storm before the day is through."

"Not struck by it, exactly," he corrected her. "At least I hope not. But these cottages over here in Sconset have been around a long time, Tracy. They've weathered many a storm. They're snug, well built. I doubt we have anything to worry about. Unless, that is, you suddenly become incensed by something I say or do and rush out into the thick of it."

"Guy!"

"I do seem to have that effect on you . . . more often than I would wish." He lifted the wineglass she had handed him. "May the roads rise with you and the wind be always to your back, and may God hold you in the hollow of his hand," he toasted her.

He spoke with a gravity that brought a lump to her throat, and she said shakily, "That's quite beautiful."

"I didn't make it up," he admitted. "Despite the rather nautical sound of it, it's actually an old Irish prayer. I may not have quoted it verbatim, but the thought is the same. I—I do only wish everything that is good for you, Tracy." He laughed, but it was a forced laugh. "Hey," he said, "we'll be getting maudlin if I go on this way. Have you noticed, incidentally, that the weather is changing? The sun has gone into hiding."

He was right. Glancing through the kitchen window she saw that the sky was gray and it seemed to have gotten warmer. There was a stickiness to the air.

She mentioned this and he said, "You always do get warmer weather with a hurricane. It's a tropical storm, remember? I guess you could say it brings its own environment with it. Look, come sit down, will you?"

"I thought I'd make some sandwich filling," she told him, because she was still shaky and she didn't want to evoke any more comments from him.

"The sandwiches can wait."

"We should get back to work, Guy," she reminded him. "We don't have that much longer."

She tried to read the fleeting expression that passed over his face. Pain? Anguish? Why should it be either? Anyway, it was gone so swiftly that it was as if it never had happened and he said evenly, "That's true. Well then, go ahead and make your sandwich filling, Tracy. I suppose the sooner we get back to our private salt mine, the better."

The rain started toward the middle of the afternoon. As Guy had suggested, Tracy had alternated between typing and taking dictation during the day. She was finishing the typing when she became aware of the steady, gentle downpour outside the windows.

When she went back to the living room she found Guy listening to a weather report on his small portable radio.

"The storm hit land in the Carolinas and did quite a bit of damage around Hatteras," he told her. "Now it has veered to sea again, and it's heading in our direction. But it's that first hard hit that's usually the most devastating. We've lucked out, in that sense, which doesn't mean to say that we're not going to get a good measure of it."

"When?"

He shrugged. "It's started to rain," he said, "but rain like this can go on for quite a while before the wind really rises. A storm like this is huge, remember. It has giant tentacles. The outer edge can extend for a couple of hundred miles. People will be feeling some of the effects of it, rain and some wind, far to the west of us unless it alters its course radically over the next couple of hours."

"Is there really an eye—when the sun comes out so that it seems like a perfect day, yet actually it's right in the middle of the storm?"

"Yes, but unless you get a direct hit from a hurricane you're not apt to experience the eye. The eye is the core of the storm. Let's say the hurricane itself is a doughnut, but it is constantly swirling in a counterclockwise motion. This means that when you are right in its path, and the eye—which is like the hole in the doughnut—finally goes over you, the balance of the storm will have the wind blowing in the opposite direction to the first part of it. That's why it's wise to open a window on each side of the house. Otherwise, you'd get the drop in pressure from the far side of the storm, and when a hurricane is severe enough that can be very significant."

"I see."

"As to how long it lasts," he continued, "Well, that depends on the magnitude of the storm and on the part of it which touches us. If we get the broad edge, we'll have quite a blow for a number of hours. The wind hasn't really started to pick up yet, but I would say we'll know we're in for something more than a sea breeze later tonight. From the storm position they just gave on the weather report it would seem that we'll feel the full effect around midnight or early in the morning . . . unless it changes course, that is. Look, am I making you jittery again with all of these details?"

"Of course not."

"Teacher, would you say the cocktail hour is at hand?"

She surveyed him narrowly. "Why do you call me teacher?"

"Because lately you've been treating me like a naughty pupil," he said promptly, a teasing note in his voice. "You make me feel like a disobedient kid who's being kept after school."

"Guy, if you don't *want* to work on your book you have only to say so," she said, miffed by this. "It's . . ."

"Have you no sense of humor at all, Tracy?" he interrupted.

"What does my sense of humor have to do with it?"

"A great deal, potentially. It seems to me you take many things too seriously . . ."

Gerry had made the same accusation, and she was chagrined at the thought of this.

"It would seem," he said drily when she didn't answer him, "that I've touched a sore spot."

"Perhaps you have."

"Sometimes you have to hurt first in order to effect a cure, Tracy."

"You should know."

"I was not speaking as a doctor. I was speaking as someone who—cares a great deal for you. You're much too young, too lovely, to let life get you down the way it seems to have done. Are you still in love with Ben Devlin?"

She was startled by this, and surprised that he had remembered Ben's name, but there was no need to hesitate in her answer, no need at all!

"No," she said. "Very definitely not!"

"I wondered," he admitted. "I thought maybe this business with Gerry might be on the rebound, and that's never good."

"I suppose you should know about that, too."

"Whew!" he said. "You *are* touchy, aren't you? As a matter of fact, I've never fallen in love on the rebound, so I *don't* know very much about it. But that's beside the point. The subject just now is you, and for once I'm not going to let you wriggle out of discussing it."

"Why must we talk about me?" she asked him, then felt a real sense of reprieve when the telephone out in the kitchen rang before he could reply.

"I'll answer it," she offered, at once getting to her feet. It wasn't until she was about to lift the receiver that it occurred to her that it might be Gloria Denton at the other end of the wire. She had no wish to speak to the other woman.

It was Gerry, though, who asked anxiously, "Tracy?"

"Yes."

"My God, I've been trying to get you at your cottage for hours. Then I finally decided to ring Medfield," he said. "If this storm hits us, the phone lines may go down. Tracy, Aunt Sally wants you to come over here until this blows over."

"Thank her for me, please," she said, "but I can't do that."

"I don't expect you to drive across," Gerry told her. "Just throw some things into a suitcase and I'll pick you up in half an hour."

"No, Gerry, really."

"I insist, Tracy," he said firmly. "Either that or I'm going to come out and stay there in your cottage with you."

"That won't be possible. I'm not going to be in my cottage."

She could hear the sharp intake of his breath, then he said, "Are you telling me you're planning to spend the night with Medfield?"

"You make it sound absolutely illicit, Gerry!"

"What the hell else could it be?"

"Purely practical," she told him. "Guy pointed out to me that it's the sensible thing to do."

"Tracy," he reminded her, "you've told me how you feel about your doctor. Don't you think you're asking for trouble for yourself?"

It was a good question and she was glad she was spared making an immediate answer to it when he added, "To say nothing about how *I* feel about your being there."

"You are making something out of nothing," she said, trying to speak with a firmness she was far from feeling.

"Am I?"

"Yes. With Guy and myself, it's entirely business."

"I wish I could believe that."

"You can."

"Between thinking about you and the storm, I'm not

going to get much sleep tonight," he complained. "I can imagine what Aunt Emily is going to say about this!"

"If you explain it to her in the right way, I'm sure she'll be very understanding," Tracy suggested.

"That's putting the burden on me, isn't it?"

"I didn't intend it to, Gerry."

"Darling," he said, "change your mind, will you? Let me come and get you."

It took a few minutes to refuse him and end the conversation gently, but firmly. When she hung up the receiver and turned around she wasn't surprised to see Guy lounging in the kitchen doorway, an expression of decided amusement etched on his face.

"What's so funny?" she asked, close to anger.

"The whole situation," he said. "I feel sorry for Stanhope, but not too sorry for him. If it were me, I'd be out here to whisk you away from your evil captor, no matter what you said to me."

"The bold, macho approach?" she asked sarcastically.

"Call it what you will. If I felt about you the way Stanhope does, I certainly wouldn't put up with your spending a night in another man's house."

If. Surely, she thought dismally, it must be the biggest "if" in the entire world!

"On the other hand," he said, with an infuriating smile, "you and I know, of course, that this is a strictly platonic situation. What was it you told Stanhope? That with you and myself it is all entirely business?"

"Yes," she said. "It is, isn't it?"

"Do you really expect me to give you an affirmative to that?" he demanded. "Can you tell me you believe it yourself?"

"Well," she said, "there *is* nothing else for us, don't you agree?"

Watching him, she felt as if he were putting on his dark glasses. His face became a mask. He said slowly, weighing each word, "I suppose you're right. I suppose there isn't anything else for us. But don't try me too hard, Tracy. I do have my limits when it comes to endurance . . ."

Again, there was an interruption and this time Tracy couldn't be sure whether she was glad or sorry. It was Tim at the kitchen door with a blueberry pie his mother had baked and two loaves of homemade bread. She also had sent over a quart of clam chowder plus a crock of baked beans.

Guy and Tracy decided to have the clam chowder for their supper with some of the bread and blueberry pie for dessert. It was ambrosial fare. They ate in front of the fireplace and it seemed to Tracy that the wonderful camaraderie she had experienced earlier with Guy now came back as a bridge between them again. She was determined to do nothing to destroy it this time, and she blessed Mrs. Sousa. Her gift had changed their mood.

When Tracy had forked up the last succulent bit of blueberry juice, she sighed blissfully and said, "That was good beyond belief."

"Yes," Guy said quietly, "sometimes things are." He had put on a Tchaikovsky record, and now as the last strains of the Andante Cantabile died away, Tracy said, "Shall I read copy to you?"

"I'd rather just talk. We might both have a liqueur, don't you think? I believe there is both Amaretto and Lochan Ora."

She chose the Lochan Ora, filling small crystal cordial glasses for both of them. She had become accustomed to placing the glass directly in his hand. As his fingers closed around the slender stem they inevitably brushed her skin, and looking down at his dark head she felt herself fused by her sense of closeness to him.

He had put another log on the fire, and sparks sputtered from it until it settled down to burn with even, gold-orange flames. Maybe, Tracy thought, love was like that. Maybe, at first there were sparks; then the flame gained in confidence, steadied, and burned clearly.

She sat down in her usual chair, the small table between them, and she knew that no matter how old she might become the sight of a log burning always would evoke his memory in her. There were many things for that matter that would eternally remind her of him.

He said softly, "Tracy, there's something I've been wanting to ask you."

"Yes?"

He laughed. "I'm almost afraid to," he confessed. "I'd like to know what you really think of the book. You told me back in the beginning, but you haven't said much about it lately."

"I still like it very much, Guy."

"I detect a certain reservation, right?"

"I think you know what my reservation is. As I've already said, I'd like to see you put more of yourself and your own experiences in the book."

"I can't bring myself to be more personal," he said flatly.

"Then I have no other criticism, and no other suggestions," she told him. "The book is excellent. I think it should do very well."

"But not as well as it might, is that it?"

"I'd be dishonest if I didn't admit that's the way I feel about it."

"And you don't tell lies, even white lies, do you, Tracy?" he asked softly. "Perhaps you've never felt the need to tell a lie."

"No, I suppose I never have."

"We should all be so fortunate," he said ruefully. He hesitated. "I don't like to think you're disappointed in the book," he said then. "I guess I've come up against an emotional hurdle when it comes to writing about myself that I didn't realize I'd have to face, and I suppose I should try to get over it. I'll try, but I still can't imagine being able to—well, to lay it all out on paper for other people to read."

"No one else can do it for you," she pointed out.

"No," he agreed. "There's a great deal in life that no one else can handle for you."

In the silence that fell between them they could hear the moan of the rising wind, and Guy said, "I'll try to get another weather report on the radio before long."

"Perhaps I'd better do up the dishes while we still have power," she suggested.

"Not a bad idea. Tim brought over some jugs of drinking water, but it might be wise to have a surplus. We'll need water for the bathroom. If the power goes out so does our plumbing! You might fill the tub in case we get into that kind of an emergency."

"You make me feel woefully ignorant," she complained. "I guess I don't know much about coping when it comes to natural disasters."

"You're a city girl," he teased her. "A suburban girl, anyway. I'm city bred myself, but summers I was either over here or off at camp, so there were times when I had to learn to make do."

"A good thing," she said with a smile.

"I hope so."

Tonight he didn't suggest that he help her with the dishes. She left him twirling the dials on the radio and washed things quickly, conscious that the rain was pelting down hard while the wind had begun to howl outside the kitchen windows.

Through all of this, though, Tracy felt totally secure, and she knew this was because of Guy. Turbulent though he could be, she had complete confidence in him. She knew that whatever the crisis, he would be calm in it; in that sense, she could forever depend upon him.

When she went back into the living room he was listening to a weather report. Then, switching the radio off, he said to her, "We won't be facing the full brunt of the hurricane, but we're going to get a pretty good storm. In the wee small hours you may think this cottage is going to shake apart. Look, about sleeping arrangements . . ."

"Yes."

"I'll take the couch out here," he told her, "and you can have the bedroom. Maybe, a bit later, you could ferret a pillow out of the bedroom closet. I think there are a couple of pillows on one of the back shelves. I could do with a blanket, I suppose, though it's not apt to be cold."

"I can perfectly well sleep on the couch, Guy," she said.

"Is this an equal rights demonstration?"

"No, but there's no reason why you should give up your bed for me."

"Would you rather share it with me?" he demanded wickedly, then added hastily, "All right, all right. I promised you I'd behave, and I intend to keep the promise. It's too early to go to bed, though. Maybe we should catch up on the manuscript reading unless the sound of the wind bothers you too much?"

"No, I'd be glad to read."

She read to him for well over an hour until they had

reached the point of his latest dictation, which she had not yet had time to transcribe.

When she had finished, he said reluctantly, "I do see what you mean. There's a certain sterility to it, isn't there? Probably the best thing to do after I get back to Boston would be to put it aside for a while. Then when I go back to it, maybe I can whip myself into getting more involved in the narrative."

"I think so."

"I like the confident way you say that, Tracy."

"Well, I feel confident about it."

"So," he mused, "it would seem that I have my winter's work cut out for me. What about you?"

"What about me?"

"You mentioned that Florence Anders wants to make you a partner in her business. I hope you plan to take her up on that."

"I haven't decided," she admitted. "When I went to work for Florence we both considered it a temporary arrangement. I had no idea that I would find the work so interesting. I'm still not sure I want to make it my life's work, though."

"I predict that you'll become an authority on antiques," he said, smiling.

Tracy didn't echo the smile. She had a vision of Florence and herself years from now in the Charles Street shop, and it was not a heartening one. She could picture Florence as a fragile little old lady, and by then she herself would be past middle age—a tight-lipped spinster who had loved and lost . . .

As Guy had predicted it would, the storm mounted to a full crescendo in the middle of the night.

They had gone to bed shortly before eleven, Tracy fixing a bed of sorts for Guy on the living room couch. It had given her an odd feeling to undress in his room, slipping into an old-fashioned nightgown that was white, sprigged with blue flowers, and made her look like a girl on a Victorian valentine. It had been even more odd to slip down under the blue and white candlewick spread and put her head on his pillow. She had drifted off into sleep with a strange sensation of loneliness. It was as if a part of her had been severed and placed somewhere else.

As she slept, she seemed aware of the storm that really had begun to rage. Rain, whipped by the wind, lashed across the windowpanes. Then as the strength of the hurricane intensified and the cottage literally seemed to be shuddering under the brunt of it, she came awake suddenly, feeling as if she had been plunged into the vortex of a nightmare and an involuntary cry of fear was forced from her lips.

It took a moment to realize where she was and what was happening. A long moment, because by the time she was fully back to reality, Guy called from the doorway, "Tracy, what is it?"

"Nothing," she said. "I woke up suddenly and I was startled, that's all. I'm sorry I disturbed you."

"You didn't disturb me," he crossed to the bed and sat on the side of it, a dark silhouette she found very comforting just now. "It's hard to sleep with this thing pounding all around you," he said wryly. "God, what a blow!"

A violent gust of wind rattled the window as he spoke, and in the distance Tracy heard something crash.

"Sounds like there were some loose trash cans around down the lane," Guy observed. "Flick on the lamp and see if the power is still with us, will you?"

She obeyed, but light failed to come at her command and he said, "It would seem we've lost it. Did you bring a candle in here with you?"

"Yes."

He shifted, and she could feel his thigh edging her leg. Even though there was a sheet and a blanket between them an intense awareness of him came over her.

He said, "You're frightened, aren't you?"

Yes, she was frightened. But was it because of the storm, or because of him?

"Look," he said, "you're safe, darling. By morning, we'll have been through the worst of this. By afternoon, the sun may be out again."

He reached for her hand and found it, and the touch of his flesh made her tremble. He leaned toward her, his other hand smoothing the hair back from her forehead. Then he bent to anoint her face with his lips, moving them slowly, lingeringly, from place to place, passing lightly over her mouth to kiss the hollow of her throat. Softly, he said, "Your pulse is pounding."

She knew this only too well, and it was telltale evidence. One couldn't control one's pulse rate, at least she couldn't.

"Tracy," he murmured huskily, "Oh, my darling!" He thrust away the sheet and blanket that covered her, his fingers finding the buttons at the neck of her nightgown. Involuntarily her arms reached toward him to discover that she was encountering bare, firm skin. He wasn't wearing a pajama top.

There was no haste to his movements. Outside, the storm waged its own war around them. But here in the cottage they were encased in their own time capsule and strangely the hurricane seemed to protect it, to isol them, setting them apart from the rest of the e two people marooned on a desert island.

 ved to lie alongside her. Slowly his hands
 lore her body as if preparing the way for
 hich left a trail of descending kisses,

lingering upon first one breast and then the other, while her nipples tautened and she became aflame with her need of him.

She was beyond protest when he drew the nightgown over her head, and she knew that he was slipping off his own pajama bottoms. But she made no move to stop him. It seemed to her that she had wanted him in this way forever, wanted the totality of his nearness with their bodies curved together as their passions mounted to match the swirling hurricane. The storm was an orchestration of her emotions. Even as she moaned the wind moaned, plunging her into a rapturous turmoil completely unlike anything she had ever experienced. Together, she and Guy became two travelers, seeking, exploring, and finding ecstasy in its deepest sense, only to emerge, finally, somewhere on the other side of love's rainbow.

Chapter Thirteen

Sometime during the early morning hours, Tracy fell asleep with Guy at her side, his arm around her, his head close to hers. When she awakened, though, gray light was streaming through the window and she was alone.

There was a profound sense of loss and a moment in which she wondered if it had all been a dream. But, almost immediately, she knew better. This had been no dream! She stretched and sighed blissfully. Last night had been a milestone. She would never be the same again, nor did she want to be.

It was still raining, but the rain seemed lighter and the wind had diminished. She looked at the bedside clock and saw that it was nearly nine. It was only as she started to get up that she realized she was naked.

Guy had tossed her nightgown onto a nearby chair. Now she put it on and went in search of him. She found him in the living room listening to the radio again, and he said, "We're through the worst of it. By afternoon, you can take a ride out to Surfside. The sea should be spectacular."

She saw that he was fully dressed, wearing jeans and a dark red turtleneck pullover. Although her nightgown was entirely modest, she suddenly felt uncomfortable coming before him like this. But he seemed unaware of her attire. In fact there was a seriousness about him this morning that puzzled her in the light of what had happened between them just a few hours earlier.

"I'd better go get dressed," she said.

"Yes," he agreed absently. "The power's still out, incidentally, so there's no hot water. I made coffee earlier if you want some."

"What about you? Would you like another cup."

"Not right now, thanks. I've already had two."

They were speaking to each other like polite strangers, and he had set the tone for this. Stung, Tracy could only wonder if he regretted what had gone between them at the height of the storm.

He said, "Do you want to work today?"

Work. The book. The fact that he could think about their project just now was a blow, bringing her quickly back to reality. The night, it would seem, had been only an episode to him. But whether he regretted it or not was not so important as the fact that he seemed able to put it behind him as if it had never happened at all.

She faced him coolly. "Yes," she said, "we might as well work. As you've said, we can finish up in a couple of days if we keep at it. Would you rather dictate this morning, or do you want me to type yesterday's notes?"

Was it her imagination, or did he seem relieved by her apparent willingness to get back to their former footing? He said, "Let's start with some dictation. Then this afternoon I'll try to block the rest out mentally so I can give you a fairly comprehensive outline of what I want to do with the balance of the book tomorrow. That should take care of it."

She nodded. "I'll go change and be right back." But as she slipped on dark purple slacks and a matching sweater, then fastened her hair back into a pony tail, Tracy was seething. She knew it was going to take all the self-control she could muster to get through this day with him.

The suspicion that to Guy she was just another in a series of female conquests was a searing one, yet she could think of no other explanation for his behavior. This was perhaps a conquest he would as soon not have made, fearing that afterwards she might cling to him.

She stiffened. That, she promised herself, was something he need have no worry about!

She was the perfect secretary during the balance of the morning and they got a great deal done. At noon, she was fixing sandwiches when Gerry called and she agreed that he could pick her up at six o'clock and then she would go back to his aunt's house with him for dinner.

When she washed up the lunch dishes she took time to pack up the few things she had brought across with her and to take them back to the Thorndyke cottage. A brief tour of exploration convinced her that everything at the cottage was intact. The rain had stopped now and she closed the two windows Tim had left open and removed the towels he had put on the sills to sop up moisture.

She spent the afternoon typing up her notes while Guy worked alone in the living room. Guy didn't again mention going over to Surfside, nor did she suggest to him that they take a break. She worked steadily, making an extra effort to get as much done as possible before leaving for the day. It was with an actual sense of relief that she said good night to him and went back to her own place.

This time, he surely hadn't seemed to mind the fact that she was going to have dinner with Gerry. In fact she sensed that it was something of a relief to him. Even Ben's defection had never left her with the sense of bitterness that this did now.

Dinner at Emily Stanhope's was pleasant, but not without tension. Gerry had received a call from Washington during the afternoon asking him to report for a briefing even sooner than he had expected. This meant, he told Tracy glumly as they drove across the island, that he would have to leave Nantucket the day after tomorrow.

Mrs. Stanhope was charming as always, but she said that now that Gerry was leaving she thought she would soon close up her house and go back to New York. Gerry, she said, had invited her to come to Madrid for Christmas and she added archly, "It would be fabulous if you could come with me, Tracy. We'd have a fantastic time. You and I could spend hours together in the Prado, to say nothing of the other museums and galleries."

Tracy managed to sidestep this by asking about the Goya collection in the Prado. But hearing Gerry and his aunt discuss their own plans seemed to bring the moment when she would be leaving Nantucket herself that much closer, and this was depressing.

Common sense told her that the sooner her departure time came the better. But her heart, she decided wryly, was not always in tune with common sense!

She said good-bye to Emily Stanhope fondly and promised to keep in touch. On the drive back across the island, both she and Gerry were silent. But as he pulled up in front of the Thorndyke cottage he asked, "Will I see you tomorrow?"

"I don't see how," she said with honest regret. "I promised Guy to work all day. I think it will be our last time and I'm anxious to get through."

"Oh?" he asked, surprised.

"I want to be back in Boston and at work by Monday morning," she told him.

"Has there been a change of plan?"

"Not really. I never planned to stay beyond the beginning of October."

"I know that's what you intended originally. But I thought you might have changed your mind. Or, I suppose I thought your doctor might have changed it for you."

"He is not 'my doctor,' Gerry," she said impatiently. "I've tried to tell you all along that as far as he is concerned ours is just a business relationship."

"Even after last night?" he asked.

She stiffened. "What do you mean by that?"

"I find it difficult to think the two of you could spend the night under the same roof and he could still remain indifferent to you," Gerry said slowly. "I don't know him, true, but you make him seem like a pretty macho individual. And you are a very alluring woman, Tracy. A guy would have to be inhuman to resist you."

She laughed shakily. "Gerry, my dear," she said, "you have an exaggerated opinion of me!"

"No," he insisted stubbornly, "I don't. It's the other way around, Tracy. You tend to downplay yourself. Anyway, I didn't get much sleep last night thinking about you out here alone with him."

"I don't think anyone got much sleep, with that storm raging the way it was," she evaded.

"Tracy," he said, "you must realize I simply can't go off and *leave* you here. Let me come in tonight."

She shook her head. "We'd both be sorry," she said gently. "And I'm tired, Gerry. I'm bone tired. I worked very hard today when I should have taken time off for some rest. I . . ."

"You don't have to make excuses to me," he said. "I'd like to think I'm one person in the world you can level with." He sighed. "I have to see you before I go, though. If it can't be tomorrow, will you have breakfast with me the morning I leave? I'll ask Aunt Emily to drop me off at the ferry dock, if you'll meet me there. There's a restaurant nearby that opens for breakfast."

She nodded. She and Guy should be through with the book by then, she told herself. There was no reason why she couldn't come and go as she pleased thereafter.

As Tracy walked into her living room, the phone was ringing. She glanced at the old banjo clock on the wall, saw it was nearly eleven and couldn't repress a feeling of alarm. Could Florence be ill again?

It was Guy at the other end of the wire, however. "Sorry to call you so late," he said coolly, "but I heard the car door slam so I knew you'd still be up."

"Yes, I just got in."

"We won't be able to work tomorrow," he said. "I'm going to have a visitor so I won't be free till the following morning."

"I have a breakfast date with Gerry that morning," she said, her own voice touched with frost.

"Oh? Could you postpone it?" he asked.

"No, I couldn't."

"Then we'll have to do the best we can," he said. "If it wouldn't be too much for you, maybe we could work on straight through the evening the day after tomorrow. Then, I think we can finish off."

"Very well." Tracy spoke calmly enough, thoroughly provoked with him as she hung up the phone.

So, he was going to have a "visitor"! Who would it be this time? she wondered. Gloria Denton, or yet another beautiful woman? She told herself it didn't matter, she mustn't *let* it matter. She must accept the fact instead that Guy was being painted in his true colors, and it was just as well that she was being shown him as he really was.

His arrogance was infuriating! That casual air of

command, of taking it for granted that people were going to do whatever he wished, was more than a little galling! She was glad she had made the breakfast date with Gerry so that she'd been able to tell him flatly that she couldn't—wouldn't—leap to his bidding!

Guy's telephone call had thoroughly awakened her. Finally she went and poured herself a glass of sherry and forced herself to settle down with a rather dull book, channeling her concentration toward the printed page. Eventually it worked. She grew sleepy and went to bed, only to toss restlessly so that she wasn't in the least refreshed when, a bit later in the morning than usual, she climbed out of bed.

She ate breakfast and then drove across to Surfside, hoping that a walk along the beach would whisk the tired cobwebs from her brain. The sea had not yet subsided, having been whipped into a fury all of its own far offshore by the effect of the hurricane. It was magnificent. Towering teal blue waves crested and crashed, trailing spumes of spray that Guy had told her one day were called "white horses."

Tracy was enraptured by the spectacle, and she was not alone on the beach today. Many of the islanders had driven down to see the ocean and some were picking up pieces of silver gray driftwood and other flotsam and jetsam left in the wake of the high tide.

The storm had tossed shells up on the sand, and though most of them were broken Tracy found one perfect whelk. She ran a tentative finger over the smooth gloss of its inner surface which fused from a lovely deep rose shade to pure ivory. As a child she had been told that you could hear the sound of the sea if you put a shell to your ear. She tested this, blocking off her other ear with her palm and it seemed to her that from somewhere within the whelk there came a simulated sound of the surf she was watching.

She resolved that the whelk shell would be her own personal memento of Nantucket.

When Tracy got home the red car was parked in front of the cottage next door. Even though she had conjectured about Gloria Denton being the visitor Guy had mentioned, the impact of the truth was shattering.

She felt sick as she let herself into the house. Sick, and cheapened, and she despised herself for letting desire trap her as it had, for yielding to Guy in what she could now regard only as blind weakness.

It was a bad day. She thought of calling Gerry and telling him she could see him after all, but she knew this would be another kind of folly. It would be entirely too easy to turn toward Gerry for comfort. Such a move could only bring eventual unhappiness to both of them.

Still, it proved to be very difficult to say good-bye to him when the time came. Neither of them could eat much breakfast. They were solemn as they left the restaurant, strolling hand in hand toward the ferry dock. Cars were lining up to go aboard, and Tracy saw the red sports car among them with Gloria Denton at the wheel.

So, the "visit" was over!

She stayed with Gerry at dockside until the last boarding call was sounded over a loudspeaker system. She didn't resist when he swept her into his arms, moved partly by pity to return his kisses, pity because she knew only too well what unrequited love could be.

She stood on the wharf watching the boat pull out, and glancing toward the upper deck, she saw Gerry standing at the rail. Briefly she yearned to be with him. It would solve so many problems!

She waved until the yellow shirt he was wearing was a dot in the distance. Then she stayed to watch the big white boat round Brant Point.

She was in no mood to go to work at Guy's once she got back to Siasconset. How could she possibly face him casually? How could he face *her?* It seemed to her that he must be a person utterly without conscience.

Also, she found he obviously was capable of taking charge of any situation. He was making a fresh pot of coffee as she walked into the kitchen and promptly suggested that she pour cups for both of them and bring them into the living room.

"I think I can finish dictation in a couple of hours," he told her. "Then, once you've typed your notes we can read them over and that will do it!"

He seemed relieved that their work together was almost over and she resented the fact that he was so blatant about it. Damn him, she thought fiercely, he didn't have to be afraid that she would linger once they were through!

He was especially efficient today. He had his material thoroughly organized and dictated to her with seemingly effortless precision, his words coming so quickly and smoothly that it taxed her shorthand talents to keep up with him.

She made sandwiches for lunch, and as they ate he asked if she had managed to get over to Surfside.

When she told him she had, they spoke of the fantastic spectacle made by an ocean churned to fury and this led to a discussion of the sea and the tides. Guy told her he had gone to a boys' camp in Nova Scotia one summer when he was in his early teens, and he described the amazing tidal bore near Digby, Nova Scotia, on the Bay of Fundy, where there was a change in the water level of some forty feet.

"It's incredible when the tide comes rushing in," he said.

Tracy was interested, despite herself. She had to give Guy points for being an excellent conversationalist.

Talking with him was never dull. Nothing about him was dull, for that matter. Living with him would never be dull . . .

She shut a mental door firmly on that line of thought and told him she had better get on with her typing.

As the afternoon progressed she found that there was considerably more to do than she had realized there would be. She had taken quite a volume of notes and it began to seem to her that she had been sitting at the typewriter forever.

She paused to rub a tired hand across the back of her neck. Guy, standing just behind her, said, "Don't you think you should knock it off?"

She'd had no idea that he was near, and she was startled.

"I can't knock it off," she told him irritably, rallying. "I still have a lot to do."

"There's always tomorrow," he suggested mildly.

"I thought the idea was to finish today," she reminded him.

"Well," he said, "there were interruptions."

She couldn't keep the acid out of her voice. "Yes, weren't there!" she agreed caustically.

"I gather you saw Gloria's car," he suggested.

"Yes."

"Tracy . . ."

"Guy, please. Leave your invention to your book."

She glanced up quickly as she said this, and was surprised by a strange expression on his face. He was looking at her longingly, and there was a cloud of pain in his light gray eyes. But, as he became aware of her gaze, it was as if he had whisked an eraser over a chalkboard.

"Why don't I fix you a drink?" he suggested blandly.

"If you like."

"What would *you* like? Scotch or bourbon?"

"Scotch and soda, please."

She went back to her typing as he set about mixing the drinks. But it was impossible to be unconscious of his presence. She found to her chagrin that her fingers were striking the wrong keys.

When he said, "Come on in the other room and take a break for a few minutes," she was willing to agree, but she didn't tarry there. Just now she didn't want to talk to Guy, and evidently he shared her feeling for he put on a Beethoven record and sat back to listen to it, closing his eyes.

Again, that lock of dark hair had fallen over his forehead and it gave him a look of defenselessness which Tracy reminded herself sharply was purely an illusion.

There was security in getting back to the typing. She had hoped she might finish before it was time to think about dinner, but this proved to be impossible and he came back into the kitchen again to ask, "Shall I turn chef?"

"No," she said, wishing that he would not try to be quite so agreeable. "I'll fix us some omelettes, if that's all right with you."

"Since you make the best omelettes I've ever eaten, how could I possibly veto such a suggestion?" he asked smoothly.

He insisted that they open a bottle of chablis to have with their dinner and the wine made her sleepy. She began to realize how tired she was and the thought of going back to work again was daunting.

Guy seemed to sense this and said, "Why not stop for today, Tracy? Would it cut into your time too much if we finished up tomorrow?"

"No," she said, then added, "but we *will* have to get through with it then. I'm taking the boat back the following morning."

"You are?"

"Yes."

"That soon," he said, adding regretfully, "I've really usurped your vacation, haven't I? If I had known you were going to cut your time short . . ."

"Actually, I'm not cutting it short," she said testily. "Not by enough to matter. I'd like to be back at the store on Monday, though."

"To start a fresh week?"

To start a fresh life, she thought, without relishing the idea at all. But she said only, "Yes, I suppose that's part of it."

"Well, you certainly should have your last day on the island free," he said. "Have you been to the Whaling Museum yet?"

"No. It's one of those things I've been intending to do."

"You shouldn't miss it. They have a fascinating collection. Some really beautiful scrimshaw, incidentally."

"I may come back to Nantucket again," she told him. "Aunt Sally is always inviting me to come out here. Maybe next summer . . ."

But she knew she would not be coming back to the island once she left it, once she lift *him*. Not, in any event, for a long, long time. It would hurt too much.

Guy was lounging back in his favorite chair, his long legs thrust up on a hassock in front of him. There was a brooding expression on his face and he said suddenly, "I will miss you very much."

She had no intention of allowing herself to become emotional in front of him. She had learned her lesson; now she told herself she had better remember it! So, she retorted lightly, "I haven't left yet."

"Tracy . . ."

"There is nothing in particular I want to do tomorrow," she said. "I don't have that much to pack. I'll come over in the morning if you don't mind. I think I can finish typing the notes in a couple of hours."

"As you like," he said indifferently.

She left shortly afterwards. Guy had slipped into one of his odd moods and she only hoped he wouldn't take refuge in the Scotch bottle.

He didn't. He had already shaved by the time she arrived at the cottage the following morning and was disturbingly handsome in a yellow sweater that emphasized his dark good looks.

He left her to her own devices, burying himself with something in the living room while she typed in the kitchen. She typed steadily without taking a break and he didn't interrupt her. Even though she worked at a good pace it took her nearly three hours to transcribe the notes. Once she had stacked the pages together, she sought him out to ask if he wanted her to read them to him.

"Thanks, but it won't be necessary," he told her politely. "Gloria Denton is coming over on the afternoon boat and I'll ask her to skim through them with me." He hesitated. "I had intended to ask Tim's mother to help me stage a festive little farewell dinner for you," he said, "but I couldn't put Gloria off. Will I see you tomorrow before you leave?"

"Yes, of course," she said and was relieved when Tim arrived just then with an order of groceries.

She hadn't intended to go to the Whaling Museum, but she spent the better part of the afternoon in it, and it was as fascinating as Guy had said it would be. The museum exhibits were beautifully done, bringing the whaling days into a focus that transcended time. Tracy could have lingered for days, rather than hours, in the old brick building that once had been a sperm candle factory. The jawbones of an enormous sperm whale gave a vivid idea of the size of these huge sea creatures and it became easier to understand why a whaleboat and its crew, put out from the whaling ship to harpoon their prey, could be staved in and capsized by a mammoth whale fighting for its life. At that, whaleboats—and there was an original one on display—were still considered the most seaworthy craft of their kind ever built by man.

A complete "try works" had been set up, an exact replica of the try works that had been installed on the deck of every whaling ship in which great slabs of whale blubber were placed in cauldrons over a roaring fire to be rendered into oil, then cooled and stored in barrels.

Stern-faced whaling captains, captured forever by artists of the day, stared down at Tracy, their gold-framed portraits adorning the walls. In the reading room she found original log books, some so old that they were bound in ship's canvas instead of leather. As Guy had said, the scrimshaw collection was fascinating, the carefully tooled work exquisite in its detail. To Tracy it underscored the vast number of lonely hours the men had spent aboard ship, time they had turned to profit by evolving a unique art form.

Leaving the museum, she thought of going to the nearby Jared Coffin House for dinner, but opted instead for a small restaurant near Steamship Wharf that was still open. She chose clam chowder, fresh blueberry muffins and Indian pudding topped with whipped cream for her supper.

There was no pleasure in eating alone, though, and there was even less in the thought of going back to Siasconset tonight.

Although Tracy had seen the movie that was playing and hadn't particularly cared for it, she decided to go see it again anyway. It would delay pulling up at her cottage and facing the galling sight of the red sports car parked next door.

There were still lights on in Guy's cottage when she got back and it was misery of the purest sort to know that Gloria was there with him tonight. Tracy couldn't wait for morning to come.

She had called Mike's Taxi Service in advance, and Mike had promised to be on hand in plenty of time to get her to the ferry. Now she ate a scanty breakfast, finished her packing, then stared irresolutely across the way. The car was gone, which made it likely that Gloria Denton would be taking the same boat back to the mainland she was taking. She hoped not.

Despite everything, though, it was impossible to leave without saying good-bye to Guy.

She walked across the space that separated the two cottages slowly, feeling the finality of every step she was taking. During their working days she had used the kitchen door, and Guy had once said laughingly that this was an old Nantucket custom. Now, she instinctively reverted to formality and went to the front of the house.

She stood on the high stoop and let the brass knocker sound once, then when there was no answer, she raised it again and finally raised it a third time. Puzzled because Guy almost never went out in the morning, she finally tested the door knob and it turned under her touch.

The living room was empty. In his bedroom, the bed had been made, the blue and white candlewick spread pulled neatly into place. In the kitchen the typewriter had been removed; Tim, she supposed, already had returned it to whomever he had borrowed it from. But there was a small box in the middle of the table wrapped in bright paper and the name "Tracy" was printed clearly on a white envelope lying next to it.

For a terrible moment she wondered if there were a check for her services in the envelope. If so, she vowed, she would tear it into shreds and leave the remnants for him to find! But there was only a single sheet of paper. On it he had written, "You will never know how much I thank you, Tracy. The memento is something for you to keep and wear. Think of me sometimes, will you?"

Tears brimmed as she opened the box to find a beautifully fashioned scrimshaw pendant. There was a squat white lighthouse etched in black in the center of it, a single gull soaring overhead.

Brant Point, she thought, and the tears fell as she remembered the Jetties and sharing the beauty of a September day with him.

She was waiting at the door when Mike pulled up in his taxi. He was as exuberant as ever, putting her suitcases in the trunk then climbing into the driver's seat to begin a patter of conversation that lasted all the way to Steamship Wharf.

Chapter Fourteen

October brought a zenith of beauty to New England. Often during lunchtime, Tracy took a walk across the Boston Common, returning to Charles Street via the Public Gardens. The trees and bushes were an artistic study in autumn colors, painted from a lavish palette of burnished tones that ranged from the palest gold to the most vibrant crimson. The swan boats that had been such a part of the Boston scene for so long had finished sailing the frog pond for this season, but Tracy walked across the arched bridge that spanned the pond, pausing midway to appreciate this oasis set into the middle of a constantly changing city. Boston to her was a fascinating blend architecturally and in every other way—older than yesterday, yet newer than tomorrow.

The Boston Common and its adjacent Public Gardens represented the foresight of the country's founders. Tracy remembered how amused she had been as a schoolchild when she learned that in 1634 the fifty-acre tract had been set aside for use as a cow pasture and military training field. By law it actually was still available for those purposes; this was land that belonged to the people.

Her eyes lingered on the golden dome of the state house. She had liked history in school, and she remembered that the state house had been designed by Charles Bulfinch, America's first professional architect, and had been built in 1795, not all that long after the end of the American Revolution. For a long time she had meant to take a tour of it, especially to visit its famous Hall of Flags. But like so many other things this was something one somehow didn't get around to when one lived in a place.

Well, she told herself, there would be time for all sorts of enterprises from now on and she would need them to fill in potentially lonely hours. She promised herself that she would fully explore Quincy Market and its neighboring Faneuil Hall, and she would plan to take an entire Saturday afternoon to "do" the magnificent Isabella Stewart Gardner Museum out on Huntington Avenue. Mrs. Gardner had been a Boston beauty and a patron of the arts and the museum was housed in her former mansion.

She sighed as she walked down Charles Street on her way back to the shop. She wanted to do all of these things and more, of course, it wasn't that. Rather, it was the thought of doing them alone.

I shall have to get used to it, she told herself firmly.

There were customers in the shop when she got back and it proved to be a busy afternoon. Tracy was pleased during the course of it to sell a lovely antique Chinese snuff bottle to a collector from Westwood who was delighted to find it. When they closed the shop shortly after five o'clock Florence reported trimphantly that she finally had gotten rid of the Victorian hair bracelet she had begun to believe would never go. It was fashioned of a braid made with strands of human hair, woven together and then lacquered and centered by a gold locket with the initals Z.B.

"Would you believe it," Florence said happily, "this man's wife has the same initials and so he's going to give it to her for their anniversary! I just hope she doesn't mind wearing somebody else's hair!"

Florence had made tea and Tracy had bought jam tarts earlier in the day at a bakery up the street. They were in the little patio area back of the shop. It was still warm enough to linger there till dusk if they wore sweaters.

As she stirred sugar into her tea, Florence said, "We won't be able to do this much longer. Daylight savings will be ending in a couple of weeks and it will be getting dark sooner. Winter," Florence said. "I admit I don't look forward to it."

Winter. It seemed to Tracy that she could hear Guy saying, that afternoon at the Jetties, "When winter comes we can look back to today," and she shivered.

She felt as if a dark cloud were flitting across the window of her mind. All at once she was stabbed with the sharp certainty that something was very wrong.

Memories came flooding over her and there was a new clarity to their recall. She remembered, for instance, the day Guy had tripped over the bag of groceries she had left on the high stoop. A vision of his long, prone figure flashed before her and she thought with growing horror of how he had struck his head. Later he had sutured her arm, using the brightest of lights, even though he had told her that for the sake of his eyes he must avoid bright light. Again, he had used extremely bright light in removing the stitches and it seemed to her now that toward the end of their working time together he had bothered less and less to wear his dark glasses, even when they went out for a walk together while the sun was still shining.

Why? Was it because it no longer mattered? Had the fall, or the bright lights, or a combination of both, caused a setback? Had his vision been failing, rather than improving, over the days they had worked together?

There had been times on the island when she had wondered about this, then inevitably he would say something that made her think his eyesight was getting better. Yet, when he had told her he would read his manuscript by himself she had discovered that he had to use a powerful magnifying glass to read at all, and evidently it had been heavy going even so.

Tracy stared bleakly at the brick wall of the building next door. There had been so *much* between Guy and herself. They had shared passion, but they also had shared a rare depth of emotion, something precious and wonderful. She had come to love him—oh, God, how she loved him! And there had been times when his touch, the way he looked at her with a certain indescribable tenderness had made her certain he was experiencing the same miracle in his feeling for her.

Dear God, she thought now, *did Guy know he was going blind?* Was *that* why he practically forced me away from him?

Florence asked anxiously, "What is it, Tracy?"

"Oh," Tracy said, startled, and for a moment couldn't dismiss the ghastly, overwhelming premonition that she was right about this. Then she recovered and said hastily, "It's nothing, Florence."

"Ah, but it is something," Florence said wisely. She reached for another jam tart, then added, "He's still very much in your mind, isn't he, Tracy?"

"Gerry?" Tracy hedged, for she had told Florence quite a bit about Gerry but very little about Guy. Gerry, for that matter, was still in Washington and telephoning her regularly, still hoping against hope that she would at the least come to Madrid with his aunt for Christmas.

"No," Florence said, with just a touch of impatience, "not Gerry. Your doctor, darling."

She started to say, *He is not my doctor,* then stopped. He *was* her doctor, her beloved doctor; he would always be her doctor, even if she never saw him again.

Never saw him again. As she silently phrased the words she knew that this was totally impossible. She *had* to see him again, she had to see him one more time to either confirm or deny her dark suspicion. If she were right, if her terrible fears were verified, she would not leave him, no matter what he might say. She would stay with him.

But if she were only imagining things? Tracy faced this and prayed that she *was* only letting her imagination roam, even though she knew it would mean that Guy would forever be out of her life. Otherwise, by now she would have heard from him.

She said helplessly, "I love him, Florence. But I'm afraid I'll have to get over it. I *will* get over it. But there's something I have to do first. Do you suppose I could take some time off tomorrow afternoon?"

"Definitely," Florence said. "You came back from Nantucket looking almost more peaked than you did when you went out there. I'd like to send you off on a cruise somewhere, but I've the feeling it wouldn't do much good until you resolve this problem."

She didn't add that she only hoped it could be resolved. A long time ago she had been in love in the same way she suspected Tracy was in love now. There had been a problem then, too, but life had handled it brutally. He had been killed in a plane crash. Though years had passed, though there had been other men, she had never gotten over it. Now she lived with a shadow.

She didn't want the same thing to happen to Tracy.

Tracy only knew that Guy's family home was in Chestnut Hill, and she picked up the phone book with the sinking feeling that he probably had an unlisted number.

Fortunately, he didn't. The black letters forming his name stared up at her from the printed page looking oddly unfamiliar: Guy Huntington Medfield, M.D.

Temptation to dial his number gripped her. Just the thought of hearing the sound of his voice at the other end of the wire was enough to make her giddy. Dear God, how would she behave if she were to confront him face to face?

I must not make a fool of myself, she told herself sternly as she sat in front of the mirror brushing her hair. She was wearing a suit of vivid royal blue wool that made her eyes look like sapphires. As a final touch, she clasped the silvery chain around her neck that held the scrimshaw pendant he had given her. She spent much more time than she usually did over her makeup, then told herself tightly that she was being a fool. Chances are she would not see him at all. In fact, she had come to the conclusion that it would be better not to, not today. She would go to Chestnut Hill and walk by his house. She could judge from exterior physical evidence whether or not he was practicing again. If he were, there *should* be cars around, patients coming or going, activity.

For the moment, seeing this much would be enough. On another occasion, she might garner courage to come back and call on him, briefly, during the course of his office hours just to be sure he was all right!

It was a perfect October afternoon. The sky was cloudless, the Chestnut Hill reservoir reflecting a deeper shade of the same wonderful blue.

Guy's house sat atop a rise overlooking the reservoir, and although Tracy had known that Chestnut Hill was an especially lovely residential area, she had not expected his home to be quite so magnificent. It was a brick mansion with a three-car garage attached to one side of it and a low ell on the other. The wide expanse of lawn in front of it was still vivid green, studded by shade maples that blazed in tones of orange and scarlet. A curving driveway swept up from the street and Tracy imagined there must be a parking lot behind the house for patients' use since there were no cars parked in the driveway. On the other hand, it occurred to her that perhaps Guy was not practicing here at all. Possibly his eyes had strenghtened to the point where he had been able to go back to surgery. In that event, he might be doing most of his work at Commonwealth Medical Center, where he was on the staff.

She had intended to walk right past his place, but now her footsteps betrayed her. As if propelled by a force she couldn't control she started up the narrow sidewalk that bordered the driveway and knew that with every step she took she was going past the point of no return.

She came first to the ell and saw a doctor's sign hung from a slim, wrought iron bracket at the side of the door. A small brass plate over the doorbell read "Ring and Enter," and Tracy placed one slightly shaky finger on the bell and pushed.

Then she opened the door and stepped into a reception area beyond which there was a waiting room, decorated in soft shades of blue and green with nautical prints lining the walls.

She had hoped there might be patients in the waiting room, but to her distress she found it was empty. Thoughts of making a quick retreat came to her, but she was forestalled when a plump, gray-haired woman appeared in a doorway at the end of the room to glance across at her, plainly perplexed.

"May I help you?" the woman asked politely.

"I . . . I wondered if I might see Dr. Medfield for just a minute," Tracy said hesitantly. "I don't have an appointment, but it wouldn't take long . . ."

The woman said gently, "Dr. Medfield isn't having office hours today. In fact . . ."

"Sara? Who is it?" It was a woman's voice calling, and, a moment later, Tracy was confronted by Gloria Denton.

Gloria, Tracy had to concede, was stunning today. She was wearing a dress in a deep orange shade that was a perfect foil for her brunette coloring. She managed a taut smile, and Tracy realized that they were equally startled.

"Miss Graham, isn't it?" she asked.

"Yes."

"Perhaps I can help you?"

"It isn't important," Tracy said, her tongue stumbling over the words so that she gave the effect of stammering. "I was in this area, and it occurred to me to stop by and see Dr. Medfield. I . . . I wondered how he was doing."

Gloria Denton surveyed her curiously. "Why," she said, "he's doing very well. You live in Boston, Miss Graham?"

"Yes. I work in an antique shop on Beacon Hill," she added superfluously.

"Gloria?" The voice, coming from an inner room was overwhelmingly familiar, and as she identified it Tracy knew that she couldn't bear to face him.

She started to tell Gloria Denton that she didn't want to interrupt anything further and would be on her way, but the other woman spoke first. "It's your little friend from Nantucket, Guy," she said, and Tracy held her breath.

The ensuing silence was brief, but traumatic. Then Guy Medfield said, "Ask her to come in, will you?"

Tracy's legs were shaking as she followed Gloria down a narrow corridor and into an office at the end of it. She had a swift impression of dark woods, beige and orange drapes at the windows, bookshelves lining the wall, and then her eyes were drawn to the huge desk at one end of the room and the man seated behind it.

He was wearing a masterfully tailored gray suit with a snugly buttoned vest. His white shirt was crisp and his striped maroon and gray tie conservative, yet giving just the right touch of color. He'd had a haircut since the last time she had seen him. The dark hair was contoured, molding his perfectly shaped head and emphasizing his clearcut features.

He had never been more handsome. As he stood to greet her, Tracy realized anew how tall he was, how magnificently proportioned, and she could feel her throat constrict.

He smiled as he stretched out his hand, his silver gray eyes friendly and, she thought, faintly amused. "Tracy," he said. "How great to see you! You're looking lovelier than ever! That shade of blue you're wearing is terrific!"

She flushed, feeling like an awkward schoolgirl as she shook his hand, especially since she was intensely aware that her fingers had turned icy.

She took the chair he indicated near the desk and he sat down again, contemplating her in a casual, almost lazy fashion that she found extremely disconcerting. Gloria Denton said, "I want to go over a few things with Sara, Guy, so I'll leave the two of you alone. Would you like some coffee, Miss Graham, or a glass of sherry?"

"Thank you, no," Tracy managed.

"You, Guy?"

"Nothing, thanks, Gloria."

"We have to leave here in fifteen minutes," the brunette reminded him.

"Yes," he said, and turned his attention back to Tracy. "Well," he said, "what are you doing with yourself these days?"

It was trite, a total cliché. But, she asked herself dully, what had she expected? She had invaded his house without invitation, and at least he was being courteous enough to see her. He needn't even have done that.

But it hurt, it hurt terribly to think that Guy was merely being polite to her.

She said lamely, "Well, I'm back at work again. I've decided to accept Florence's offer, and to become her partner in the business."

"Good," he nodded approvingly. "I'm glad to hear that."

It seemed to Tracy that he had established a patient-doctor relationship between them in the space of just a few minutes; he was kindly, he was interested, but it was difficult to believe that there had ever been anything personal between them, impossible to think that on the night of the hurricane they had been swept together into an ecstasy she never expected to approach again.

She wrenched her thoughts back to the present and asked, hesitantly, "What about you?"

"Everything's going very well," he said. "I'm sorry I have to go off with Gloria shortly. It's an appointment that must be kept. Otherwise I would suggest you stay and have a drink with us."

Us. Togetherness, completely connoted in a word only two letters long. A dull ache came to nag Tracy. Us. He and Gloria. A pair.

She wondered if they were going to get married, or if they had already gotten married? Gloria certainly had an assurance about her. She was supremely self-possessed, thoroughly at home here in his office and undoubtedly even more so in his house.

Tracy tried to veer away from visions she didn't want to encourage and found herself fingering the scrimshaw pendant at her throat. She said, haltingly, "I've never really thanked you for this."

"There was no need for you to thank me, Tracy," he told her smoothly.

"You chose Brant Point," she reminded him. "It—it means Nantucket to me."

"I'm glad it does. And the pendant is very becoming." Briefly, she thought she saw something flicker in his eyes. Nostalgia? Regret? She couldn't define it. In an instant it was gone and he was as urbane as ever.

"One of these days," he said, "I shall have to drop around to your antique shop."

It was in the nature of a dismissal. "Do that," she suggested, and then added, "I'd better be going," and he didn't attempt to deter her.

Even as she stood up, Gloria came back, and walked to the door with her. She smiled in parting and it seemed to Tracy that there was sympathy in the other woman's eyes.

"I'm sure Guy would have looked you up before now," she said, almost kindly, "but he's been terribly busy with other things ever since he got back to Boston."

By other things, Tracy thought grimly, Gloria Denton almost surely meant herself!

Florence was closing the shop when she got back to Charles Street. Tracy hoped almost desperately that the older woman wouldn't ask questions, and Florence was wise enough not to.

She said, "I think it's a bit cool for the patio this

afternoon. How about skipping tea today anyway and having a drink instead?"

She couldn't have made a more welcome suggestion!

Friends dropped in during the evening and the conversation was lively. Tracy and Florence knew an interesting group of people with diverse backgrounds and opinions that ranged from ultraconservative to utterly radical. Usually discussions in the apartment over the Beacon Hill store were stimulating and Tracy participated fully in them. She was quiet tonight, though, and fortunately the others were in the frame of mind to discuss Boston politics, a forever controversial subject, and so the ebb and flow of voices covered her own silence.

It was when she finally went to bed that the tears came, flowing freely until her pillowcase was damp.

For all of her own personal sense of grief, though—for she knew now that Guy was definitely lost to her—she was profoundly grateful.

He could see again. He was healthy, vitally alert, and there surely had been nothing wrong with his eyesight. He had commented on her appearance, he had been able to see the scrimshaw pendant from quite a distance, and there had been an easy confidence in his manner and in the way those arresting light gray eyes had swept her face.

Yes, he could see again. Nothing, she told herself, was as important as that.

Nothing.

Chapter Fifteen

November was a very busy month, which was fortunate for Tracy. She had little time to think about her own problems until she was alone late at night, and then she was too tired to dwell on them.

Florence had the chance to go down to Cape Cod and buy the contents of a house which belonged to a ninety-year-old woman who had decided herself that the time had come for her to go into a nursing home.

"I understand the place is loaded with antiques and there will be all sorts of collectibles, too, I'm sure," Florence told Tracy eagerly. "I suspect this is going to be my biggest single purchase, and it may take a few days to go over everything; I'll have to make an inventory to arrive at a price." She hesitated, "It would mean leaving you in charge again."

"Well," Tracy said, "that should prove whether or not I'm really cut out to be your partner, don't you think?"

"You're still too tired and wan to get trapped into a lot of work, even if it's for me," Florence said frankly. "Don't bite me for this, but I think you should go to Spain with Emily Stanhope for Christmas."

"No," Tracy said abruptly, and then softened. "I don't deny the idea is tempting," she admitted, "but I'd be crazy to yield to it."

As it was, it had been difficult to persuade Gerry not

to make a quick trip to Boston before taking off for Madrid. He already had phoned her from Spain the previous weekend, to her consternation. Although she knew money wasn't a matter that worried Gerry, she hated to envision the tariff he would run up if he persisted in making transatlantic phone calls. In any event, she would have preferred to have made a cleaner break, for the time being.

She wanted Gerry's friendship, true. But she had learned that it was close to impossible to be "friends" with someone with whom you were in love, or conversely, who was in love with you.

Florence said, "I'm not trying to influence you, Tracy. I just don't like to think of your sitting here hibernating. Actually, when I suggest you go to Madrid I'll have you know I'm being highly unselfish! There would be a definite danger that you'd decide to stay."

"I doubt that," Tracy said firmly.

"Well, then," Florence shrugged, "I'll take the cue and change the subject. I'll plan to drive down to the Cape Thursday, and I should think I'd be back by Monday."

As it happened, she wasn't. She phoned Sunday evening to say that the process of taking inventory at the old house was going to be far more time-consuming than she had thought it might be.

"It's a veritable treasure trove," she reported happily. "Mrs. Benton is a dear old lady, too, and I'm glad it's I she called in; I hate to say it, but a lot of dealers would take advantage of her. She inherited most of the things she has. She has always taken them more or less for granted and she has no idea of their real value on today's market. I want to be sure to give her a fair price, even though it's going to take a chunk out of our current assets, Tracy."

"I can help," Tracy said quickly. "I can't think of a

better way to put some of the money my mother left me to use, Florence."

"I wouldn't hear of it!"

"Florence . . . it would really make me feel like a partner in your business," Tracy suggested.

"All right," Florence said, "we'll see when I come up with a final tally. Look, my dear, I want you to close the shop an hour or so earlier each day while I'm away. There's no need for you to work yourself to death."

"Florence, business is excellent just now," Tracy protested. "People actually are beginning to think about Christmas shopping, difficult though that is for me to believe! I'm a last-minute present buyer myself. But I think we're going to do a good gift business. I think people are realizing that even trifles are so expensive they might as well put their money into an object that can offer a worthwhile investment."

"Beautiful reasoning," Florence commended. "I've told you all along, my dear, that you're a natural for the antique business. Look," she went on, "Sue Denmore told me a couple of weeks ago that she's available to work afternoons if we need help. She lives right across the Public Gardens in Bay Village and she's very knowledgeable. I think the two of you would get on well. Her number is in the card box on my desk."

"Perhaps I'll call her," Tracy conceded. "Ann Phelps is coming in from eleven to three each day, though, and that's our heaviest time except for the after-four period. I wouldn't *think* of closing then, Florence!"

"All right, all right," Florence agreed hastily. "Use your own judgment—as long as you don't get too tired doing it. I'll call you in a couple of days."

It was the end of the week before Florence came back from the Cape, tired but exuberant at the results of her trip. When the antiques she had purchased arrived in the shop, Tracy shared her elation. There were boxes of beautiful Sandwich glass, some of it the lacy variety, some in the famous Daisy-and-Button pattern, but individual examples too in the glowing cranberry, cobalt and vaseline colors for which the Sandwich factory had been famous.

There was exquisite Celadon, brought from the Orient years before, the soft, milk-green finish a visual delight. There was an entire collection of heirloom dolls with real hair and charming, painted china faces. Setting them out and arranging the flounce of a full beige satin skirt trimmed with black lace, Florence said wryly, "Those huge, innocent blue eyes on this one remind me of you, Tracy."

There were heavy old brass candlesticks, a spinning wheel that still worked, Victorian music boxes, and one of the first Edison "Morning Glory" phonographs which operated with cylinders instead of records. Hatpins, some of them jewel-tipped, elaborate beaded bags, and a series of beautifully executed hand-painted miniatures were some of the other treasures.

"What a bonanza!" Tracy exclaimed as they unpacked. "Honestly, Florence, it's going to be hard to part with some of these things."

Florence had agreed to let Tracy invest in a part of this purchase, and her enthusiasm ran high. Fortunately her interest in what she was doing was usually enough to sustain her during working hours, but inevitably night came. As the days grew colder, night seemed an especially bleak and dark time.

A week or so before Thanksgiving she received an invitation from her father and his new wife to join them over the holiday, and there was a sincerity about it that was heartwarming. She declined, but wrote a note in doing so that was almost affectionate. Maybe, she thought, someday she and Elise could learn to be friends and then at least some of the old rapport with her father might be reestablished.

Also, late in November, she read of Ben Devlin's marriage in the society pages of the Boston paper and saw a photo of his bride. She seemed very young and had a happy, expectant look. Tracy found herself feeling sorry for the girl who had married Ben and only hoped that she wouldn't become too disillusioned. Maybe Ben had changed? Maybe, she thought ruefully, there really was a pot of gold at the end of the rainbow!

Tracy and Florence had been invited for Thanksgiving dinner at the home of friends of Florence's who lived in Arlington, people who also had known her mother. They welcomed Tracy warmly, but even in the midst of feasting she was intensely lonely.

Thanksgiving. She remembered Guy telling her about his accident. It was just a year ago today that it had happened. Wherever he was, she thought, he must be thinking about it too.

By Thanksgiving, Boston's store windows had been decorated for Christmas. Animated, bigger-than-life toys and talking Santa Clauses enticed wide-eyed children, and everywhere one went there were the bittersweet refrains of the old, familiar Christmas carols.

In early December, colored lights were strung through the trees on the Boston Common, and the atmosphere was laced with a mixture of holly and mistletoe. The festive Christmas spirit, tied with red ribbon bows, was everywhere. Tracy only wished that she could snatch just a wisp of it and implant it in her own heart. It was very hard to be happy.

Her work at the shop was her salvation. Florence had built up an excellent clientele, and right now they were very busy. Sometimes it became a question of finding a particular item someone wanted to get as a gift for a friend who was a collector. This could involve considerable detective work. There was an information exchange of sorts among the good dealers, and Tracy found that usually one could buy from another dealer at a discount and still sell at a profit. The profit margin, to be sure, was not as great as it might have been had the object in question been gathered from another source. Still, it paid to satisfy good customers.

She was pleased when she tracked down an old black iron "George Washington" trivet for a customer who wanted to give it to his aunt. This was only a week or so before Christmas. Just a couple of days later a regular customer who collected Flow Blue china came in to ask if they had an old Irish Belleek demitasse cup and saucer or could get one for her as she wanted it for her daughter who had started a demitasse collection.

They had sold a lovely one, not long before, pale cream in color and seemingly so fragile that Tracy marveled it could have endured for decades. Now she wondered if it would be possible to find another Belleek that even approached it with so little time left.

She spent an hour on the phone one afternoon and was successful. A dealer on Newbury Street agreed to part with a Belleek that sounded exactly like what she wanted and she determined to walk across the Public Gardens and pick it up.

It was a gray day with a hint of rawness to it. Florence, having gone out for a while to do some Christmas shopping, returned to say, "It smells like snow."

Tracy smiled, "Are you serious?"

"Of course," Florence said promptly. "I always can smell snow, the first snow of the season anyway. It's a clean smell, but it has something extra to it. You'll have to go out and sniff for yourself, then you'll know what I mean."

Tracy laughed, but later as she cut across the Public Gardens she sniffed and there did seem to be something different about the tingling air. A special kind of freshness.

A courtly, elderly man was the owner of the antique shop on Newbury Street and one of his assistants took Tracy to him directly. The Belleek demitasse cup was all she had hoped it would be and they quickly came to terms on it. The purchase concluded, Logan Eldredge insisted that she stay and have a cup of tea with him, and for the better part of an hour they talked together. It was a conversation Tracy found delightful; Mr. Eldredge was an authority on old glass, among other things, and he deplored the "fakes" often passed off as genuine on unsuspecting clients.

"Lacy Sandwich can be especially hard to detect," he told her. "Sometimes, so can Daisy-and-Button. But there's a roughness to the edges of the old stuff . . ."

Tracy could have lingered for the whole afternoon, listening to her fascinating colleague talk, and it was with regret that she took her leave. On her way out of the shop, though, she paused when her attention was captivated by a small inlaid mosaic box in a glass showcase. Florence collected boxes and it would make the perfect gift for her. But it was a gem of a piece and Tracy feared the cost would be well beyond her budget.

Before she could ask the price, Mr. Eldredge, at her shoulder, said, "If Miss Graham sees anything she wishes, she is to receive our special discount."

The clerk smiled, and quoted a figure for the box that was half what Tracy had expected it would be.

"I'll take it, of course," she said, then turned to Mr.

Eldredge, still standing by her, and said reprovingly, "You shouldn't have done that!"

"Then I shall impose a surcharge," he said, and smiled. "You owe me another teatime visit!"

Tracy was warmed by the whole encounter and left the shop after tucking the little box into her handbag. As she crossed Arlington Street and entered the Public Gardens the first snowflakes fell, and she smiled to herself. Florence had been right in her prognosis.

The flakes came faster as she walked, and with them magic touched the city streets. The light bulbs on the tall lamps that marked the bridge across the frog pond glowed in the snowy dusk like giant pearls, and when the myriad colored tree lights were switched on the world became suffused with winter enchantment. Tracy felt like a figure caught in the midst of an old-fashioned paperweight as the snow swirled around her.

Soon, she thought, the frog pond would freeze over completely and then there would be skaters on it, youngsters wearing bright knit wool caps, flashes of color against silver gray ice.

It was a bad analogy. Silver gray, even silver gray ice, would forever remind her only of Guy's eyes.

As she came out of the Public Gardens onto Beacon Street then turned at the corner of Charles, she was afraid that she'd lingered so long that Florence would be closing up by now. The shop, however, was still open. Both Sue Denmore and Ann Phelps were working full time in this immediate pre-Christmas period, and they were busy with customers.

Ann paused to beckon Tracy, and when Tracy approached said hastily, "Florence wants to see you in her office."

It was not an unusual request. Probably, Tracy thought, someone wanted something they couldn't find and Florence was going to ask her to try to track it down. She was becoming quite an antiques detective!

Before she reached the office, though, Florence appeared in the doorway and she was frowning.

Tracy said hastily, "I didn't mean to take so long but," and she thrust out the package she was carrying, "here's the Belleek. It's even nicer than the one we had before."

"Great," Florence said and took the box, but obviously she had something else on her mind.

Her next words confirmed this. "I think we've a real problem on our hands this time," she said. "We've acquired a client, it seems, who wants to start a collection of paintings with Nantucket Island as the theme. He is especially anxious to find something showing Sankaty Head Light. I've been trying to tell him that this isn't precisely in our line, but perhaps you might talk to him and see if there is anything we can do for him."

Tracy could feel her pulse leap, and then it began to throb. Easy, she warned herself. Easy! There are lots of people interested in Nantucket. There is no reason, no reason at all, to let the mere mention of Sankaty Head Light do this to you!

But, as if drawn by a magnet, her eyes swept past Florence into the interior of the office. When she saw the tall man standing by the desk she literally rocked back on her heels and was afraid for a moment that she was going to faint.

He was wearing a superbly tailored camel's hair coat, cinched in by a belt at the waist, and it made him look even more powerful than usual. But his head was bare, and there was still that heart tugging hint of unruliness to his thick, dark hair.

Then, as he turned toward her, Tracy saw the heavy

framed glasses he was wearing and something caught in her throat, making her speechless.

He, on the other hand, seemed incapable of movement. But he said, "Tracy!" and there was a whole gamut of emotion encompassed just in the sound of her name.

At her elbow, Florence said, "Tracy, I've some telephoning to do. Take Dr. Medfield up to the apartment, will you? I'll join you both as soon as I can."

Still speechless, Tracy led the way, suffocatingly conscious of Guy coming up the stairs behind her and of his overwhelming nearness as she opened the living room door. She went in, switching on lamps so that Florence's tastefully decorated room was suffused in a soft, creamy glow.

Then he said huskily, "Turn around, will you?"

Slowly she complied, but she still couldn't speak, nor could she bring herself to look up at him.

There was a note of awe in his voice as he said wonderingly, "I can see you. I mean . . . *really* see you. Both Gloria and your friend Mrs. Anders told me you were beautiful, and of course I had my own ideas, derived from those times when I practically pushed my face into yours. But I still wasn't prepared for the total reality."

Now his words were so soft she could hardly hear them. "Can't you bear to look at me?" he asked her.

Instinctively, her eyes flew upward, and she saw him touch the frame of his glasses. He said ruefully, "As you can see, something new has been added. Do—do you find them so abhorrent, Tracy?"

Her eyes became riveted to his beloved face. She stared at him, noting that the heavy lenses were tinted slightly, and they tended to obscure those clear gray eyes. Still, the glasses in no way distracted from his attractiveness. Nothing, Tracy thought, could ever possibly distract from his attractiveness!

To her horror, tears she couldn't suppress crept into her eyes, and in that instant before his face started to swim before her she saw his jaw tighten, saw the familiar telltale muscle begin to throb.

She knew only too well how sensitive he could be. She wanted to assure him that her reaction had nothing to do with his glasses, that she was breaking down right in front of him because the miracle of having him near her once again was almost more than she could bear. But, though she tried, she still couldn't manage to speak, and through a misty veil she saw him take a handkerchief out of his pocket.

He said, his voice wry, "I wonder how many times before I've made you cry without knowing it, because I couldn't see your tears." To her surprise, his steady surgeon's hand was shaking as he daubed carefully at her eyes. "Dearest Tracy, I . . ."

Dearest Tracy.

She swallowed hard and used all the force she could muster to pull herself together, taking the handkerchief away from him, then wiping her eyes quickly, angry at her own weakness.

She said in a polite, funny little voice, "Would you like a drink?"

That quizzical eyebrow shot upwards. "You've always suspected I was on the verge of alcoholism, haven't you?" he demanded, the asperity of his tone sounding considerably more like the Guy she had known.

"No," she returned. "Right now, I'd like a drink myself! Wouldn't you?"

Unexpectedly he grinned, a total smile that was so disarming she caught her breath. "Since you put it that way," he said, "yes, I would!"

"Scotch and soda?"

"Please."

As she busied herself with ice and glasses out in the kitchenette, Tracy was painfully conscious of his presence in the very next room. It seemed unbelievable. She went back into the living room with their drinks, almost afraid that he might have vanished. But he was standing at the window looking down at the little patio which was bathed, now, in the lavender of a winter twilight.

He said, "The snow's getting thicker. It looks like we'll have a white Christmas."

"Yes," she said, "it does."

He took a long sip of Scotch, and then he laughed shakily. "We're acting like two strangers," he observed. "Tracy . . ."

"Yes?"

"There is . . . so much to explain to you," he said slowly. "I couldn't come any sooner. I've had these glasses less than a week, and this is the first time I've ventured outdoors with them on. I have quite an adjustment period ahead before I'll be really comfortable with them. They warned me that's the way it would be, but it's rather hard to take. I'm still awkward as hell with them, and there's always a good chance I'll go off the edge of a curb and wind up flat on my face in the street."

He set his drink on an end table, then took her glass from her unresisting hands and placed it beside his. He said gently, "Talking's no good, is it? But how can I possibly hope to make you understand?"

It was the note of hopelessness in his voice that reached her. It didn't seem possible that Guy, who always so supremely self-confident, so sure of h could sound so doubtful.

The glasses gave him a certain inscru

yearned to see behind them, to read his expression. Then, in a moment of pure revelation, she knew it wasn't necessary. Eyes, perhaps, were windows of the soul. But so were hearts.

He held out his arms in mute appeal and in an instant she was in them, and now it didn't matter whether she understood anything or not. Her world was suspended entirely within the circle of his embrace, and as she clung to him, as their lips met and fused, she felt herself drowning in the depth of his kiss.

Finally he grasped her shoulders, holding her away from him as he said, unsteadily, "We have to talk first, darling. This time . . ."

He didn't finish the sentence, but those two words, "This time," resounded between them, and Tracy flinched from them.

What about "this time"? Was he warning her that he was going to cut short passion until . . . until what?

Again, he seemed to have an uncanny knack of reading her mind. "Don't jump to conclusions," he warned her. He picked up their drinks and passed her glass to her.

"Let's sit down," he suggested, and actually laughed. "You'd better take one end of the couch and I'll take the other!" he said, "I'll never be able to say what I have to say to you if you're too close to me."

Once they were settled down, though, he fell silent. His face was stern in repose, and dressed as he was today in a dark suit with a charcoal and white striped shirt and a discreet gray tie, he began to seem very remote, very professional, very much the doctor.

She fought down a growing sense of defeat and forced herself to take the initiative.

"Guy," she said slowly, "you don't owe me any explanation . . . about anything. I . . . I'm just terribly glad about the way everything has worked out for you, that's all."

"I don't think you know how everything has worked out for me, Tracy," he chided her gently. "Also, aren't you at all curious about my erratic behavior on Nantucket? Or"—and a sad little smile came to quirk the corner of his mouth—"did you really think I was such a monster?"

"I seldom knew *what* to think," she confessed. "You were so changeable."

"Yes," he agreed, "I was. I was fighting an inner war, though I admit that's a poor excuse for the way I behaved toward you. But, you see, I was torn between logic and emotion, and from the beginning I wasn't honest with you."

"Oh?"

"Such a small little 'oh,'" he said, "but it's got a lot behind it, hasn't it, Tracy?" He sighed. "I've never been much for deceit," he said. "I suppose that as a doctor I long ago learned it's folly to dissemble with one's patients, to say nothing of oneself. But I was . . . very touchy about my eyesight. I went out to the island to get over the shock of knowing my vision was always going to be . . . limited."

"You mean," she said, "you knew from the beginning you wouldn't be able to go back to surgery?"

"Yes," he said grimly. "I knew it, but I couldn't accept it. Also, it's true that it was thought initially that my vision would improve. The idea was that a few weeks on the island without using my eyes much should do a considerable amount of good.

"After a time, though, I knew things weren't working as planned. It seemed to me my sight was getting worse instead of better and I became pretty depressed. Then you came. And the first thing you asked me to do was peer under the hood of your damned automobile."

"I know," she remembered. "You explained about that later."

"Yes," he said wryly, "that was the first hurdle. I had to tell you I couldn't see very well, and it wasn't easy. I felt as if I were confessing to some terrible weakness I was personally responsible for. Now I know how ridiculous that was. Being a doctor, I, of all people, should know that *real* strength goes beyond the physical. Over these past few weeks I've given a lot of thought to what you said about my book, Tracy. You're right. It needs what I've learned from my personal experience as a patient, not as a physician, in order to make it complete. And I'm going to revise it along those lines."

He took a sip of his drink. "To get back to Nantucket," he said, "there became no doubt after a while that my eyes were getting worse."

She could hardly bear to ask the question, but she had to know. "Guy," she ventured, "was it because of the fall over the bag of groceries? Or using that bright light when you fixed my arm?"

He shook his head. "Neither," he said firmly. "I thought at first maybe the fall had done some damage, but I called Gloria and she came out the next day and looked me over. She kept coming to check at regular intervals and finally one day she came out with it. She told me she thought there was very little hope that permanent, total blindness could be staved off."

Even now there was a bleak tone to his voice and he stared straight ahead of him. He said, "By then I had fallen in love with you. So very much in love that I . . . I didn't think I could take it when she said that. The thought of tying you to a blind man was an impossible one, though I admit at moments I weakened. I didn't see how I could possibly go through the rest of my life without you, and I came very close to telling you the way it was, and asking you if you could even consider . . ."

She yearned to move close to him, to take his hand in hers. He had never seemed to vulnerable to her. She said softly, "You should have . . ."

"No," he told her firmly, "I shouldn't have. I knew, by then, that you had a heart bigger than the universe. I could imagine what your capacity for pity would be. I could imagine all the moments through our future when you'd be looking at me with pity in your eyes, and I wouldn't be able to see it. I wouldn't realize that you were only feeling sorry for me."

"Guy!"

"All right, Tracy," he said, "maybe at first it was just stupid pride, but then there was Gerry . . ."

"Gerry?" she demanded incredulously.

"Yes."

"Are you telling me you really were jealous of him?"

"Jealous as hell!" he told her glumly.

"I can't believe it!"

"Every time you went out with him, those dinners at the Jared Coffin House and all, well, I'd wait till I heard your car door close and knew you were home again. Then I'd wonder if he was there in the cottage with you. It was only when I heard his car drive away that I had any sense of peace. I used to count the time intervals."

"I don't believe it!"

"It's entirely true."

"Let me tell *you*," she assured him, "that I was considerably more than jealous of Gloria Denton. When she came back after . . . after the hurricane . . ."

"I realized that," he said soberly. "Several times I nearly told you the truth about Gloria. Then it occurred to me that if you thought I was having an affair with Gloria, eventually it would infuriate you to the point where you could leave the island . . . and me."

"And that's what you wanted?"

"It seemed to me I had no choice," he said simply. "The world seemed a very dark place just then, Tracy . . . in every way."

"But," she said, "the day I went out to your office in Chestnut Hill you could see. And you weren't even wearing glasses."

"No," he shook his head. "By then my vision had deteriorated to the point where about all I could recognize were shadows."

"But you told me the color I was wearing was becoming," she reminded him.

"You were a haze of beautiful blue," he said, "and it was a color I knew became you."

"You commented on my wearing the pendant you had given me."

"No," he said, "I didn't. You said you had something to thank me for and I didn't know what you were talking about. Then you mentioned Brant Point, and it connected. I knew you were talking about the pendant, so I took a chance on it."

"Still," she said, "you also told me I looked—lovelier than ever."

"And so you did," he said. "But I was seeing you with my heart, not with my eyes. Gloria told me later that she nearly told you the truth about me as you were leaving. She said you looked like a stricken child, and when she came back into the office she gave me hell. She said I was being unfair to you. Sara Besse, who worked for my father before me, totally agreed."

"But you didn't, of course?"

"No," he said. "Certainly not at the time." He

hesitated. "The appointment Gloria and I were keeping that afternoon was a hospital date," he confessed.

The question had to be asked. "What is Gloria to you?" she demanded courageously. "Are you going to marry her, Guy?"

He smiled, "That would be difficult," he said, "because she's already married to my best friend. He's the anaesthesiologist who phoned one afternoon while you were at the cottage to see if Gloria was still there. Gloria's like a second sister to me, actually. But she also is one of the best ophthalmological surgeons in Boston, and she has been my physician ever since the accident. It was she who has operated on me both times."

"Both times?"

"Yes. Shortly before I left the island, she told me she thought my only chance was to submit to a procedure which is still considered highly experimental. She said she wouldn't have considered trying it if she thought I would be able to see at all without it. That's what she had hoped after the first surgery; that I would have limited vision, at least. Now she was convinced that within another six months I would be totally blind, and at that point there would be no chance of ever doing anything about it. As you know, Gloria came over to Nantucket frequently to check me out, and those last times we talked into the wee small hours about all of this . . . and about you.

"She told me if the operation succeeded, and she was the first to admit the chance was slim, I should be able to lead a near normal life by wearing these specially ground glasses that are, in their own way, optical innovations. It was," he continued slowly, "a very big 'if.' Much too big a one to share with you, my darling."

"You had so little faith in me?"

"No. On the contrary, I had so much faith in you that I knew very well you'd never let me down. I knew no matter how the surgery came out you would stay with me, no matter how much of a burden I might become. And I couldn't face putting you through a lifetime with a blind man. I knew I . . . had to go it alone.

"I left the island only a day after you did. Gloria put me into the hospital for tests, and I was at home only a couple of days to take care of some necessary business details before going back to the hospital, this time for the operation. You happened to pick one of those afternoons to come along . . . and the hardest thing I've ever had to do in my life was to let you leave.

"These past few weeks have been strictly convalescent," he told her. "I was very much restricted, and then finally they let me try out the glasses. Gloria is pleased with my progress, she says the prognosis is better than she ever believed it might be. But, there will still be limitations, Tracy, and my days as a surgeon, of course, are over."

"Do you plan to go back into practice?"

"Yes. I think I told you once I might go into family practice, and that's what I've decided to do. You treat people of all ages. I think it could be a challenging and absorbing experience. I might be even better at it if, one day, I have a family of my own . . ."

He looked at her directly and she held her breath. He said carefully, "That, of course, depends upon whether or not I can get up the courage to ask the girl I love to share my life with me."

"Guy . . ."

"I know only too well," he continued, "that no one who lives with me is going to find it easy. I've never had what you'd call an even disposition, I guess. And I can't deny, now, that there will be moments when I'll want so much to be back in the operating room I'll probably get morose as hell. There will be times, too, when I'll wish to God I could drive a car again, or when I try to do something as simple as hammering a nail into place and flub, and out of sheer frustration I'll be irritable and difficult, but . . ."

"But?" she questioned.

"I suppose," he said, as if the words were being torn out of him, "the 'but' is I love you so damn much I can't avoid being selfish."

He had looked away from her again as he spoke, and Tracy's eyes misted as she gazed at the profile that was so indelibly etched in her memory that she resolved one day to try to paint it. Love! Oh, dear God, how she loved him. She knew now that she was going to spend the rest of her life convincing him just how much, and in easing his frustrations, in trying to make difficult things easier for him.

She would have to be careful in the way she handled him, though. His pride was as intense as ever, and he would be quick to suspect pity and to resent it.

She saw that he was forcing himself to smile, and he said, "We've been talking entirely about me. How about telling me about you and your new career? Florence Anders says you're such a jewel she never plans to let you go."

"I love the work," she said. "I'm getting better at it, too, I'm learning more all the time. It's a lifetime study, really."

"And do you—plan to spend your lifetime at it?"

There was a catch to his voice. Again she found it difficult to believe her aloof, confident Guy could be so uncertain . . . especially when it was *her* he was so uncertain about.

"Well," she said, deliberately teasing him, "I would like to continue with Florence, but only on a part-time basis."

"I see."

"Do you, Guy?" She laughed. "You know," she confided, "it's as well you've decided to go into family practice. It would be a disaster if you opted to become a cardiologist."

The telltale eyebrow shot upward as he turned to her. "Why?" he demanded.

"Because you'd fail so dismally in your diagnoses," she told him. "That is, if I can base what you might do on my own experience. Don't you realize, my dearest darling, that my heart became so severely damaged the first time I ever met you there's no chance of it ever belonging to me again?"

This time she moved toward him without invitation and in an instant she was in his arms. Now, as he brought her close to him and as their lips met, she knew that this love was forever, which was exactly the way she wanted it to be.

Florence Anders, having finally closed the shop, came softly up the stairs, suspecting that this might be an occasion when three made a crowd. She opened the apartment door, looked affectionately at the dark head and the blonde head so close together on the couch that they seemed to have become one, and she concluded that there really were times when everything ended happily after all.

A smile curved her lips as she went back downstairs. This Christmas romance, she decided with satisfaction, had not even needed mistletoe!

If you enjoyed this book...

...you will enjoy a Special Edition Book Club membership even more.

It will bring you each new title, as soon as it is published every month, delivered right to your door.

15-Day Free Trial Offer

We will send you 6 new Silhouette Special Editions to keep for 15 days absolutely free! If you decide not to keep them, send them back to us, you pay nothing. But if you enjoy them as much as we think you will, keep them and pay the invoice enclosed with your trial shipment. You will then automatically become a member of the Special Edition Book Club and receive 6 more romances every month. There is no minimum number of books to buy and you can cancel at any time.

--- **FREE CHARTER MEMBERSHIP COUPON** ---

Silhouette Special Editions, Dept. SESE-1D
120 Brighton Road, Clifton, NJ 07012

Please send me 6 Silhouette Special Editions to keep for 15 days, absolutely free. I understand I am not obligated to join the Silhouette Special Editions Book Club unless I decide to keep them.

Name _____

Address _____

City _____

State _____ Zip _____

This offer expires October 31, 1982

Coming Next Month

Tears And Red Roses by Laura Hardy

Carly Newton had made her choice in life: she wanted a career, not a man, and her position as editor-in-chief satisfied her in every way. Then she met Adam Blake, and the storm he unleashed in her swept away all her resolution. Could she live without the lightning in his eyes, the passion in his kiss and the winds that blew through her at his every touch?

Rough Diamond by Brooke Hastings

Dani Ronsard and Ty Morgan, the spoiled heiress and the star of the baseball diamond. What match could be more unlikely? Yet his muscled body awoke in her sensations that more cultured men had never aroused and the passion that lay beneath her veneer of sophistication drove him to the edge of control—and beyond. Under the hot summer sun they played a game without rules, for the greatest prize of all.

A Man With Doubts by Linda Wisdom

Actress Tracey White was tired of playing the *other woman*. When she met Scott Kingsly he seemed all too convinced that the roles she played reflected the real Tracey. But slowly they learned to trust, to share a passion and an intimacy she had dreamed of, though never found. Together they created a blaze strong enough to melt the Colorado snows and keep out the winter's chill.

Coming Next Month

The Flaming Tree by Margaret Ripy

Blair St. James was the aspiring songstress who would give anything in exchange for a chance to make music. Dirk Brandon was the famous composer whose fee for collaboration was marriage. He taught her the melody of love, the changing rhythm of desire, the forté of true passion. Her zest for life and his masterful skill, harmonized in a melody as sweet as love itself.

Yearning Of Angels by Fran Bergen

Violet eyed Nina St. Clair was determined to make her own dreams come true—and when she sold her first screenplay, she thought she had found the gold at the end of the rainbow. But the success of one goal led her to a tall, dark prize she'd never expected. In Hollywood mogul Robert Whitney, she found the one man who could hold her heart like a captive bird and teach her body the ways of love.

Bride In Barbados by Jeanne Stephens

Lost in love, Susan married Travis Sennett and followed him to Barbados, land of searing heat and sunsets of fire. But Travis married Susan for a very different reason—a selfish reason—and suddenly time was running out for them. There in that honeyed land, on an island lush and made for love, could they carve out their future and build a dynasty that would survive forever beneath the flaming sun?

Silhouette Special Edition

MORE ROMANCE FOR
A SPECIAL WAY TO RELAX

$1.95 each

- __# 1 TERMS OF SURRENDER Dailey
- __# 2 INTIMATE STRANGERS Hastings
- __# 3 MEXICAN RHAPSODY Dixon
- __# 4 VALAQUEZ BRIDE Vitek
- __# 5 PARADISE POSTPONED Converse
- __# 6 SEARCH FOR A NEW DAWN Douglass
- __# 7 SILVER MIST Stanford
- __# 8 KEYS TO DANIEL'S HOUSE Halston
- __# 9 ALL OUR TOMORROWS Baxter
- __#10 TEXAS ROSE Thiels
- __#11 LOVE IS SURRENDER Thornton
- __#12 NEVER GIVE YOUR HEART Sinclair
- __#13 BITTER VICTORY Beckman
- __#14 EYE OF THE HURRICANE Keene
- __#15 DANGEROUS MAGIC James
- __#16 MAYAN MOON Carr
- __#17 SO MANY TOMORROWS John
- __#18 A WOMAN'S PLACE Hamilton
- __#19 DECEMBER'S WINE Shaw
- __#20 NORTHERN LIGHTS Musgrave
- __#21 ROUGH DIAMOND Hastings
- __#22 ALL THAT GLITTERS Howard
- __#23 LOVE'S GOLDEN SHADOW Charles
- __#24 GAMBLE OF DESIRE Dixon

SILHOUETTE SPECIAL EDITION, Department SE/2
1230 Avenue of the Americas
New York, NY 10020

Please send me the books I have checked above. I am enclosing $_____
(please add 50¢ to cover postage and handling. NYS and NYC residents please add appropriate sales tax). Send check or money order—no cash or C.O.D.'s please. Allow six weeks for delivery.

NAME _____

ADDRESS _____

CITY _____ STATE/ZIP _____

Silhouette Desire 15-Day Trial Offer

A new romance series that explores contemporary relationships in exciting detail

Four Silhouette Desire romances, free for 15 days! We'll send you four new Silhouette Desire romances to look over for 15 days, absolutely free! If you decide not to keep the books, return them and owe nothing.

Four books a month, free home delivery. If you like Silhouette Desire romances as much as we think you will, keep them and return your payment with the invoice. Then we will send you four new books every month to preview, just as soon as they are published. You pay only for the books you decide to keep, and you never pay postage and handling.

---- MAIL TODAY ----

**Silhouette Desire, Dept. SDSE 7E
120 Brighton Road, Clifton, NJ 07012**

Please send me 4 Silhouette Desire romances to keep for 15 days, absolutely free. I understand I am not obligated to join the Silhouette Desire Book Club unless I decide to keep them.

Name_____

Address_____

City_____

State_____ Zip_____

READERS' COMMENTS ON SILHOUETTE SPECIAL EDITIONS:

"I just finished reading the first six Silhouette Special Edition Books and I had to take the opportunity to write you and tell you how much I enjoyed them. I enjoyed all the authors in this series. Best wishes on your Silhouette Special Editions line and many thanks."

—B.H.*, Jackson, OH

"The Special Editions are really special and I enjoyed them very much! I am looking forward to next month's books."

—R.M.W.*, Melbourne, FL

"I've just finished reading four of your first six Special Editions and I enjoyed them very much. I like the more sensual detail and longer stories. I will look forward each month to your new Special Editions."

—L.S.*, Visalia, CA

"Silhouette Special Editions are — 1.) Superb! 2.) Great! 3.) Delicious! 4.) Fantastic! . . . Did I leave anything out? These are books that an adult woman can read . . . I love them!"

—H.C.*, Montery Park, CA

* names available on request